Praise for the Romaine Wilder Mystery Series

"The amusing narrative zips along, providing a multilayered plot with loads of plausible suspects and possible motives. Cozy fans will look forward to Romaine's future exploits."

– *Publishers Weekly*

"Fiery, fun, and fast. You have everything that Texas provides, from scenery to Stetsons, and that French Creole Auntie who you will absolutely adore."

– *Suspense Magazine*

"Vandiver's debut, which launches a character-driven series, has plenty of local color and interesting tidbits on Creole history."

– *Kirkus Reviews*

"With a dash of humor, a dollop of Southern charm, and a peek at current social issues in the mix, it's a fun romp around East Texas to solve a murder mystery of the cozy kind."

– *Any Good Book*

"If I could choose my relatives, I would certainly choose 82-year-old Auntie Zanne...Follow along with Romaine and her family and friends as they struggle to identify the victim, find the killer, and restore order to their tiny Texas town...Can't wait for the next book in the Romaine Wilder series."

– *Criminal Element*

"A fun new cozy series...I loved the Southern culture, the characters and the small-town location."

– *Cozy Cat Reviews*

Potions, Tells, & Deadly Spells

**The Romaine Wilder Mystery Series
by Abby L. Vandiver**

SECRETS, LIES, & CRAWFISH PIES (#1)
LOVE, HOPES, & MARRIAGE TROPES (#2)
POTIONS, TELLS, & DEADLY SPELLS (#3)

Potions, Tells, & Deadly Spells

A Romaine Wilder Mystery

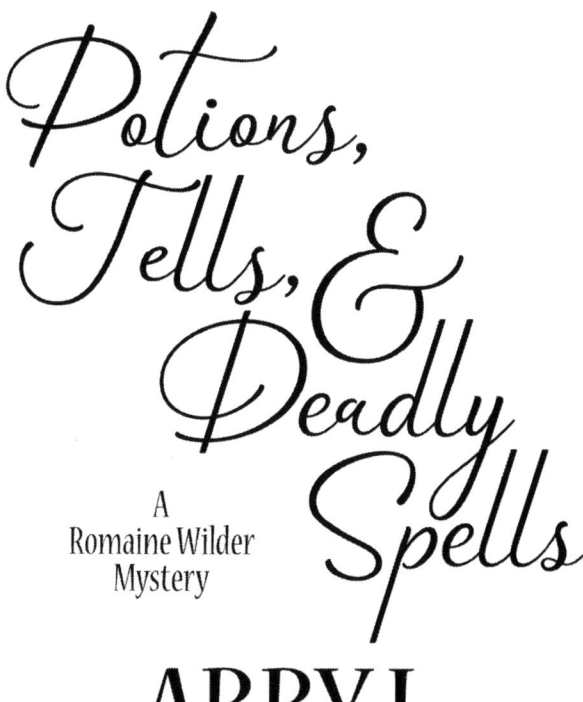

ABBY L. VANDIVER

HENERY PRESS

Copyright

POTIONS, TELLS, & DEADLY SPELLS
A Romaine Wilder Mystery
Part of the Henery Press Mystery Collection

First Edition | June 2019

Henery Press, LLC
www.henerypress.com

All rights reserved. No part of this book may be used or reproduced in any manner whatsoever, including internet usage, without written permission from Henery Press, LLC, except in the case of brief quotations embodied in critical articles and reviews.

Copyright © 2019 by Abby L. Vandiver

This is a work of fiction. Any references to historical events, real people, or real locales are used fictitiously. Other names, characters, places, and incidents are the product of the author's imagination, and any resemblance to actual events or locales or persons, living or dead, is entirely coincidental.

Trade Paperback ISBN-13: 978-1-63511-503-1
Digital epub ISBN-13: 978-1-63511-504-8
Kindle ISBN-13: 978-1-63511-505-5
Hardcover ISBN-13: 978-1-63511-506-2

Printed in the United States of America

My mother, who always gave me the best advice

ACKNOWLEDGMENTS

I always want to thank God first, my keeper and my friend. My mother who keeps Him company, as do my sisters. I miss you much.

And a thank you to my publisher, Henery Press.

As always, I want to thank my writing group, #amwriting, at South Euclid Lyndhurst Public Library—Rose, Molly, Carla, Melissa, Zach and Nicole—you guys are the best, thank you. And of course, to Laurie and Kathryn, thank you my friends.

Chapter One

The Green Fairy had arrived.

She was intoxicating. Hypnotic. Iridescent. And tonight, she was being served as a frappe.

It was the opening ceremony for the 100th Boule of the Distinguished Ladies' Society of Voodoo Herbalist. The menu was casted with liquor-infused foods—pheasant under glass, drunken mushroom soup, and my auntie's favorite, Bananas Foster. But the green, sparkling absinthe frappe was the star at center stage.

The once prohibited, hallucination-inducing, clouded liquor referred to fondly as The Green Fairy was a mostly pure botanical drink. Made up of anise, fennel and wormwood and known to represent an unrestricted lifestyle and all things unconventional it was, for the women at this occasion, apropos. Chilled, the tall cocktail sling footed glass brimmed with crushed ice, the condensation glistening as it beaded and slid down the sides of the clear goblets.

The hundred or so older Society woman that were in attendance bristled over the high-proof spirit as white-gloved gentleman servers brought it in held overhead on silver trays. Eyes lit up, hands clapped in delight, glee imbued the essence of the Voodoo herbalists seemingly more than any potion they could devise.

"*La fee verte,*" I heard more than one exclaim among others oos and ahhs.

I stood with my back against the wall and surveyed the tables and their occupants. I didn't know why my presence had been required. I was never one to get involved in my Auntie Zanne's "side business." But she had insisted.

Suzanne Babet Derbinay, my distinguished auntie, called Auntie Zanne by me, she answered to Babet for everyone else. She brewed up teas and concoctions to help her clients find true love, used her mortar and pestle to grind dried plants to cure what licensed practitioners deemed incurable, and bottled up nasty smelling swills that she claimed could dispense of any cheating spouse out of the back of our house. Out of the front of it, she ran a funeral home. People came from all over East Texas for her services.

Tonight, it was her back-door antics that held her in high esteem. Although, Auntie Zanne was usually the one in charge of the many auxiliaries and clubs she proclaimed membership to, whether officially or not, here it was true. Revered and respected, she was the Most High Mambo. The highest honor bestowed on a member of the Distinguished Ladies' Society of Voodoo Herbalists and one which only a few had held.

The banquet room of the Grandview Motor Lodge Motel, owned by one Rayanne Chambers, my auntie's friend and fellow Red Hats Society member, had magnificent mammoth crystal chandeliers hanging from its ceiling with matching sconces along the gold-leaf papered walls.

The hall was crammed with round tables covered in white table cloths, purple table runners and orange rosebud folded napkins. They were surrounded by gold Chiavari chairs and in the middle centerpieces of soaring sprays of white dendrobium orchids and long curly sprigs of willow branches stuffed into fluted vases. Sitting around—some clad in capes, others in long opera gloves, or feathery hats—were an array of invitation-only herbal healers.

Auntie Zanne tapped a butter knife on the side of her water glass turning the ladies' attention onto her.

"Ladies! Ladies!" she chirped. "Welcome!" She swung out her arms, spreading them like an eagle with such force I thought she was going to topple over.

She stood dead center at the fourteen-foot long dais table, dressed in an all-black sheath dress and matching dress coat. Her head, however, was another story. It was a plume of colors—literally. Her five-foot-three body was topped with a two-foot-high headdress that had to weigh at least seven pounds. Red roses adorned the band of the cap that went around the crown of her head and down in front of her ears. Sequins and lilies were stuck in the midst of a mass of rooster, peacock and pheasant feathers. They were sticking out everywhere. I had to wonder whether the pheasant feathers and the night's entrée had ever been acquainted.

And that headdress may just as well have been a crown. She had been floating among her adoring subjects all evening. In return, they appeared to be enamored and enthralled by whatever attention she bestowed as she passed their way.

I zoned out listening to the rest of her welcoming address, she had everyone else's rapt attention, she didn't need mine. I moved along the wall to the back of the room and stilled myself in a corner near the swinging, black vinyl padded kitchen doors. Servers regularly going in and out, I had to duck out of the way a few times.

I kept getting dragged further and further into my Auntie Zanne's big time life in the small town I'd grown up in. Something I had been running from since the day I moved in with her at the age of twelve, but, as of late, was learning to appreciate. But even with the growing positive acceptance of being back home, I still tried to steer clear of being drawn into her world of hocus pocus, magic, potions and spells.

I cringed at the thought of the American Medical Association finding me at the fore of a Voodoo event. I was sure they'd summarily revoke my license to practice.

Auntie Zanne waltzed over after her speech ended. In trying to stay incognito, I hadn't noticed she'd headed my way. Her one arm loaded with bangles and bobbles, she held on to her headdress with her other hand as she floated down the aisle toward me.

"Great turnout, huh, Romaine?" she said, sidling up next to me and looping her arm through mine. She smelled airy and floral.

"Did you expect anything less?" I asked.

"Not for a minute, kiddo. Not for a minute." She poked her elbow in my side. "We've got quite a few young herbalists in the Society. Did you see?" she said, a proud look on her face.

"The old corrupting the young, huh?"

"They're easy to corrupt," she said giving me a wink. "Oh!" She stuck her arm up in the air and started waving at two women entering on the other side of the room. They were dressed in goddess-styled sheer, empire waist gowns. One carried a black box in her hands. "Time to take the vote," Auntie Zanne turned back to me and whispered. "I'll be right back." She patted my arm. She went a couple of feet, turned and walked back to me. "They're serving the salads now, but we'll get the main course soon." She nodded. "Good thing, huh? You look hungry."

I looked "ready," I thought. As in ready to go.

"I was just going to head into the kitchen to find me something to eat. A quick bite," I said. "Hang out back there."

"Nonsense, Sugarplum," she said and kissed my hand. "I have a place for you at the table with me. So, hurry and come take your seat."

She floated away just as the bile rose from my stomach into my throat. Just the thought of being in the midst of her dais was enough to make me ill.

But before she could catch up with the goddesses, there was a clamor from a table that sat in the center of the room.

"Oh for Pete's sake!" I heard a woman shout. She pushed her chair back from the table. I couldn't see who she was, her face hidden underneath the angled, wide-brimmed canary yellow cartwheel hat she sported, but her irritation was clear as day.

One of the servers, probably having sampled too much of the alcohol laced food in the kitchen, spilled something in her lap. From where I stood, it didn't seem like it was a large amount. All the ladies around the table wide-eyed, mouths covered, watched without lending a hand.

The woman, trying to soak up the liquid from her pantsuit that was the same hue as her hat, grabbed one of the orange napkins from the table. It, in turn, snagged a glass full of absinthe, causing it to tumble over and splash into her lap making even more of a mess.

"Ahhh!" she squealed and stomped her foot, hitting the table and making all the glasses atop, quiver. With that, the women on either side of her hopped up, decidedly not wanting to be included in the slosh fest.

That frustrated Ms. Canary Yellow even more. And she turned her anger on the server. "Now look what you've done!"

"I'm so sorry," the server said, stepping back from the woman, her face not showing one bit of remorse. The plastic cup still laying on its side atop her tray.

"Sorry doesn't cut it," the woman said.

I saw Auntie stop, her eyes searching the scene then finding and locking in on mine. It seemed she was beseeching me to go and help.

I shook my head gesturing I didn't need to get involved. Auntie tilted her head, catching the mountainous headdress before it went sliding off with one hand, and slapping the other hand on her hip. I guessed that was her way of telling me to do what she'd asked.

I scanned the table to assess the damage. It seemed to me nothing more than a harmless interruption and an unfortunate destruction of what had been a beautiful table setting. I sighed as I glanced back at Auntie Zanne, she was now narrowing her eyes at me. Perhaps that was why I was there. To keep the ladies calm and clean. I decided to heed my calling and take a closer look at the kerfuffle.

Once tableside, I realized I knew a few of the women around it, including the spillee under the brim. It was Eugenia Elder, an herbalist that had visited our house many times while I was growing up.

Miss Eugenia, a usually pleasant woman, was tiny in stature with a big personality. I'd never seen her without makeup or a fresh perm. Time had given her a few wrinkles, but like my Auntie Zanne, she wore her age—somewhere near seventy—well. She looked exactly the same as the first time I'd seen her.

Mrs. Eugenia Elder, I'd always been told, had lots of money and a scoundrel husband who spent as much of it as he could. None of that seemed to interfere much with her demeanor, though. Each time I'd seen her she'd been humble and always had a smile to share.

Except for at that moment.

Out the corner of my eye, I could see Auntie trying inconspicuously to get my attention. I turned, looked at her and hunched my shoulders. What was I supposed to do? Eventually, I was sure, Miss Eugenia would dry off.

Then I saw a woman from the other side of the table turn and give Auntie a nod, signaling, I assumed, she'd handle it. She popped open a bottle of hand sanitizer sitting on the table in front of her, dumped a blob in her hand, and as she rubbed it in, she rose from her seat to head around the table.

Good, I thought, I can go back to my place against the wall. But just as I was set to leave, I heard Miss Eugenia moan and saw her put a hand up to her head like she was going to faint.

"Miss Eugenia," I said. "Are you okay?"

"Oh wow," the server said, her eyes wide, as she put her gloved hand up to her face. "It wasn't supposed to hurt."

"I don't think she's hurt," I said. I looked down at Eugenia. "Are you hurt?"

"Of course she is," the herbalist who had nodded to Auntie she would help said. She came floating around the table. Petite she looked like a 1950s Hollywood star. She reminded me of Rita Hayworth. A black Rita Hayworth. Her hair, falling into her face, was blondish, thick and wavy, too blonde and too thick for a woman of her age or color. She had on teal green cigarette pants that had ball skirt attached to it. She wore a matching green sheath top that was sheer along the neckline and down the arms. Her entry into the foray was gracious but commanding.

"She's a mess!" Miss Rita Hayworth said, she looked at me and pointed a finger at Miss Eugenia. "Can't you see?"

"Here," the server said, picking up another napkin off the table and offering it. "I'm sorry."

"Don't touch her! You've done enough," Herbalist Helper said, scoffing, her penciled-in eyebrows rising to meet her furrowed brow. "Shoo!" And with that, Miss Helper Herbalist grabbed ahold of the petite waitress's shoulder, turned her around and placing her hands on the server's back, pushed her on her way. But I could see out the corner of my eye, the server didn't go far. She turned around and watched. She'd only gone a far enough distance away not to have to suffer any more of the herbalist's scoffing.

Eugenia grabbed my arm and looked up at me, distress in her eyes.

"Are you alright?" I said.

She drew in a breath and hastily blew it out. She was shivering from the ice that clung to her and was melting in her lap. "Yes. I'm fine," she said. "But that absinthe kind of stings and..." she looked down at herself. "Oh dear, I'm a mess." Miss Eugenia's voice got shaky. "My pants are ruined."

"Of course they are," the helper herbalist answered in my stead. "That incompetent girl has made a mess!" Sympathy rising in her voice, Helpful Healer leaned in close to Miss Eugenia. "And you can't sit through the entire dinner and ceremony like that."

"Let me help you," I said, reaching for the cloth napkin she was holding. "We can go to the restroom and see if we can't get cleaned up."

"Don't talk nonsense, Dr. Wilder," Herbalist Helper said, looking at me with disdain, she swatted my hand away. She evidently knew me, but I still didn't know who she was. "Eugenia can't take care of this mess here. She has to change out of that." She looked down at Eugenia in the chair. "Don't worry, Dear. I'll have my driver take you home. You'll feel better once you get out of those clothes."

"I'm sure I will," Eugenia said. "But I hate to miss..." her voice trailed off as she looked around the room.

"Not for you to fret," the woman leaned down and spoke into Miss Eugenia's ear. "I'll tell you everything that happens tomorrow."

Chapter Two

The rest of the night went off without a hitch. Herbalist Helper orchestrated a move for the occupants of the entire table where Miss Eugenia had had her mishap to a new, unadulterated table. Then had the fledgling server, still donning her gloves, clear the table. She watched over her like a cobra studies its prey before it strikes. The waitress wasn't too pleased.

Fortunately, the server's dour demeanor was the last vestige of the little debacle. Once she disappeared into the kitchen, everyone else forgot about the little *faux pas*, making the all-seeing Most High Mambo (my Auntie Zanne) happy.

We got home late, Auntie's white hair, tapered in the back and usually puffed high in the top, was deflated. I carried her seven pounds of feathers into the house for her then went straight to bed. I needed to sleep, my duties as chaperone hadn't come to an end. As of yet. I needed all my strength. There were still two more days left of the Boule and I had a part to play in it all. The next morning, I was a designated chauffeur for the Sunrise Breakfast.

The spread, per the brochure, was going to be a feast, and, as the name indicated, was set for the crack of dawn. It was, in my opinion, planned with the elderly in mind—who else is up and set to eat at six a.m. on Saturday morning?

At least I wasn't going to be the only youngish sidekick on duty. One of Auntie Zanne's "oldest and dearest" friends, as she always said, had come to the Boule to vote. Not wanting to vote by proxy, Vivienne Pennywell (although, I'd heard she recently married so I wasn't sure what her last name was anymore), Miss Vivee for short, was to only stay for the dinner and breakfast, after that she was on her way to Turkey for an archaeological dig.

That, of course, surprised me. Miss Vivee was as old, if not older, than Auntie Zanne. Surely, I thought, she couldn't be traveling to roast in the hot sun and sift through buckets of dirt. But as Auntie explained to me, Miss Vivee's soon to be granddaughter-in-law, Dr. Logan Dickerson (she was my youngish cohort), was an archaeologist from Ohio with a pretty famous archaeologist mother, and Miss Vivee was tagging along with Logan on a dig. Something I could easily picture my auntie doing.

Old age, from where I stood living with Auntie Zanne, didn't seem like much of a hindrance to anything anymore.

Most would agree, the offspring should take up the mantle in caring for an elderly parent. Auntie Zanne was the closest thing I had to a parent and was already into her early eighties. As she aged, I would have loved seeing to her just as she had done for me. I had even thought about and planned for it, thinking I'd get her into a senior residence up by me in Chicago. Make sure my auntie's twilight years were calm and comfortable—her life had always been busy and hectic. But all I could think about as I slugged down the stairs from my bedroom the morning after the Boule dinner was that that little Energizer bunny had more get up in her than I did at forty-ish—even on her bad days.

Evidently, so did Miss Vivee.

"Morning, Sugarplum," Auntie said when I stumbled into the kitchen. Still droopy eyed dragging my feet, she was busy as a bee. Bouncing from the sink to the stove with her teapot. Opening and shutting cabinets, washing dishes and sweeping under the kitchen table it seemed all at the same time. I got dizzy watching her with the one eye I could get open.

"Morning," I managed to mumble.

"You nearly ready?"

"Mmm-hmmm," I said and headed over to the counter to feel my way through making a cup of coffee.

"Because you know Eugenia is on your list to be picked up." She dragged her kitchen step stool over, climbed up on it and tried reaching for something in the cabinet above my head. "I'm anxious to see how she's doing today," she grunted, standing on her toes to make herself taller. "The sooner we leave the better."

I lifted a hand to wave her away from the top of my head. "Better for who?" I mumbled. I popped a pod into my Keurig, got a cup out of the cabinet and sat down at the kitchen table to get out of Auntie's way. Nursing the empty mug between my hands, I struggled to get my other eye opened.

"Hey," Auntie said and snapped her finger at me. Twice. "You woke over there? I need you bright eyed and bushy tailed this morning. I can make you some tea. A little brew that'll wake you right up."

"No thanks," I said. "That's what the coffee is for." I held up my cup, pointing it toward the coffee maker. "I'm just staying out of your way until it's done."

I resisted in every way I could drinking anything my "Voodoo herbalist" auntie pushed under my nose to drink. She had it in her that she was going to convince me to stay in our hometown of Roble, kiss Chicago goodbye for good. That had never been my plan, and even though my mind was rethinking what I wanted to do, I wasn't taking any chances of her getting one of her "staying" brews in me.

Not that I believed they actually worked.

"Phooey," she said. She grabbed a spice jar off the shelf, turned and shook it at me before she climbed back down. "Coffee won't do a thing for you. I've got something better," she said. "You can't go driving us around with one eye propped open." She came over and tried to take my cup.

"Oh no you don't," I said and stuffed my coffee mug in the bend of my elbow and covered the top of it with my hand.

But I knew that wouldn't stop her, she'd be on my tail with every step I took trying to wrestle my mug from me. At such an early hour, I didn't have the strength needed to wear her down. So,

I gave up. I went back upstairs to the bathroom and threw cold water on my face. I came back down and glanced toward the kitchen. I knew Miss Holly Homemaker had already dumped the coffee and scrubbed the pot clean. She couldn't "abide by" (her words) dishes left in the sink, or the kitchen being unkempt. I grabbed the keys, went out to the van, and waited in it for Auntie to come out.

Auntie owned a fleet of white Cadillacs. Used mostly for funerals, it included an Escalade and a hearse. She sometimes used the sedans for personal use, but for my weekend services she'd rented a huge black van. All I needed was a chauffer's hat.

Our first stop: Picking up Miss Vivee.

Auntie informed me as we pulled out the drive that in addition to her soon-to-be granddaughter-in-law accompanying her here, she'd brought her new husband, too. Macomber Whitson.

Ah, so that's her new last name.

I arrived at their hotel and without a honk of the horn or a summons by the bellhop, the three of them filed out and loaded into the van. Amidst introductions and comments, Auntie Zanne held the door open, giving up her front seat to Miss Vivee. The rest of them piled in the back.

"Mac," as Miss Vivee introduced him, was short, walked with a cane due to, I assumed, the pronounced limp he had. He took off his straw Panama hat and gave me a small bow when he was introduced. He had a shock of white hair sitting up from a wrinkled brow that he kept trying to slick down with the palm of his hand. It didn't work.

A quiet demeanor, he didn't say much, and was very mindful of whatever Miss Vivee wanted him to do.

"He's a doctor, too," Miss Vivee informed me with a proud nod.

"Retired," he said and smiled. He patted me on my shoulder as he slid across the backseat and put his hat back on his head. I felt an instant connection.

The archaeologist was young, and pretty. Her skin was the

color of mocha, and she had shoulder-length black hair with the same frizz problem I complained of. She appeared nonplussed about it, having it pulled back in a ponytail which stuck out the back of a baseball style cap that read: I Dig Dead People. Auntie pointed at it and mouthed, "I want one of those."

Logan wore khaki colored cargo shorts and a t-shirt. Ready, it seemed, to hit the grid and start her work.

And Miss Vivee, like Eugenia Elder, the next person on my list to pick up, didn't seem any different from my memories of her as a child. Pocketbook over arm, her long, mostly white braid swung over one shoulder, and even in the sweltering heat, she still donned her thin, blue, round collared coat that I remembered so well.

Miss Vivee dug into her purse and took out a glasses case. She stuck on a pair of prescription glasses then dug out a pair of sunglasses and placed them on top of the first pair. After securing the cases back in her purse, she gave it a pat and looked at me.

"Let's roll!" she instructed.

All loaded and locked in, we headed over to get Miss Eugenia. I hoped she was the last on my list. Even though we'd rented a seven-seater van, we were filling up fast.

Plus, I needed to find a cup of coffee.

When we pulled up to Miss Eugenia's house there wasn't one light on. I didn't understand how she wouldn't be ready knowing we were on our way. I was sure that she knew that sunrise only came around once and they needed to be at the Grandview eating when that happened.

Auntie Zanne, Miss Vivee, and Mac, at his wife's request, all had to go in to get Miss Eugenia. I'm guessing they were her entourage.

Logan was so attentive to Miss Vivee. After I parked, she hopped out, came around the van and unbuckled Miss Vivee's seat belt and held the door for her. Then she trotted back around the car and took her place in the back seat. I think Auntie Zanne would've hit me if I tried to do any of that for her.

"So you've known Miss Vivee a long time?" Logan asked me

after we watched the three go inside the house. She'd wedged herself between the two seats to speak to me.

"Yeah—" I started.

"Hold on," she said, "let me come up there. I'll get a crick in my neck trying to talk to you like this."

She opened the door, climbed out of the backseat and came around the car to sit in the front with me.

I waited until she'd gotten settled before I answered. "Yes. I have known her for a long time," I said. "For as long as I can remember. Her and my auntie are old friends."

"That's what Miss Vivee told me," she nodded and swallowed. "Do you know how old Miss Vivee is?" she asked, a question that came from out of the blue. "I have been trying to figure it out ever since I met her."

I chuckled. "Oh." I looked at her and tilted my head. "Doesn't *she* know how old she is?"

"She says she's a hundred."

"A hundred?" I laughed. "Really? Is she?" I thought about Miss Vivee, just as spry as my Auntie Zanne who is, and I used quotation marks around the word, "only" eighty-two.

"Yeah. I don't know if she is," Logan said, her brows furrowed. "I don't think so. I've been trying to find out."

"She couldn't be," I said. "I mean, if she is, she is in really good shape."

"Yes," she said and closed her eyes taking a breath. "I can hardly keep up with her."

I knew that feeling. "Well, what do her daughters say?" I asked. "What are their names?" I gazed off trying to picture them. "I haven't seen them in so long. They're older than me, but they used to come with Miss Vivee when she'd come to visit."

"Renmar and Brie."

"Right!" I said. "Renmar and Brie. Yep. That's it. And Renmar married..."

I thought about it only a moment before I remembered that Renmar had married a black man from Louisiana, something that was unheard in the south at that time.

"She married Louis and he played the blues saxophone," I said, smiling at the memory. His visits were the few times there was music in Auntie's house that reminded me of my father. He even used to tell me stories about hearing my father play his Les Gibson guitar.

"Yes, that's right," she said. "I never met Renmar's husband."

"You're marrying Bay!" I said, working through the rest of that memory. "I remember when he was born."

She blushed. "Yes, I am." She held up her hand showing the ring.

"How beautiful," I said taking her hand and turning it to watch the large center diamond shimmer. "Well, Bay should know how hold Miss Vivee is," I said letting her hand go. "I remember he was her heart. He should know everything about her. Just ask him."

"He's still her heart. But, here's the thing—he doesn't know. And neither his mother nor his aunt knows how old she is."

I chuckled. "How could they not know?"

"That's exactly what I said," Logan quipped. "How do you not know how old your own mother is? Then Renmar told me that it wasn't polite in the south to ask women their age."

"That's true," I said and nodded. "Some people don't get it. The respect we're taught to show our elders in the south. Not inquire into certain things, not to call them just by their first name. Some people, especially northerners, no offensive," I said. "Don't get it when we allow those older than us to tell us what do."

"I'm from up north," Logan said.

"I know," I said. "Didn't mean anything by that, I saw how you treated Miss Vivee."

"Right. And I know my mother's age."

I laughed. "I've heard about your mother. She's a famous archaeologist?"

"Yeah, but I try not to talk about that too much."

"Why? Because of her Mars theory?"

"Oh my goodness," Logan said. "How did you hear about

that?"

"Small towns are notorious when it comes to gossip. You haven't figured that out yet?"

"I have. But my family is from Cleveland." She held up her hand. "We're still taught to respect our elders, but we at least get to ask questions."

Chapter Three

I liked Logan. She was smart and reminded me of myself. It was easy to see that she was happy. She had a glow about her that outshined that two-carat diamond engagement ring she was wearing.

That's the way I wanted to be.

Happy and in love.

I'd left my man in Chicago with him giving me the promise that he'd come for me. That we'd be together. Once he straightened out things in his life.

Those things that needed straightening out had included a divorce.

Dr. Alex Hale, Chief-of-Staff at Memorial Lutheran, where I'd been employed, was tall, good looking, and had an in with the powers that be, giving him the ability to help me get my job back. Or at least one in the morgue of a hospital.

Being a county medical examiner had been a job I coveted. The one that afforded me the life I'd dreamt about. But with the economy slow on the upswing, downsizing had taken that away from me. It hadn't only been my lack of a job and living arrangements, though that had sent me back to Roble with my tail between my legs, it had also been Alex.

I found out that I had fallen in love with a married man. It wasn't as bad as it sounded, although I had a hard time convincing my Auntie Zanne of that when she'd first learned about it.

I worked in a basement morgue, albeit a semi-modern one, it was the last place that gossip came to rest. And when it did make its rounds, I readily passed it up—it was too reminiscent of my small hometown and the life I wanted to leave behind. So, I hadn't known. I had completely missed that the man I was dating was married—separated for more than four months—but still married.

I couldn't count on Alex to help me out of my bind. Oh sure, he gently and sweetly wiped my tears away when I had to leave, but he couldn't offer me a place to stay or security in our relationship. No, all he could offer was hope. And that now seemed fleeting. True, he had just visited with news the divorce was final and he was working on getting me a job, but deep down I felt like it might not be what I wanted any more.

I glanced over at Logan, smiling down at her ring.

That *was* what I wanted—the promise of forever love—I just wasn't sure Alex was the person I wanted it from. Lately, it seemed, there was another man I'd been thinking about.

"You like living in the south?" I asked Logan, thoughts of me doing the same and leaving Alex. "You said you were from Cleveland, but I take it that'll change after you get married? You'll move to Georgia?"

"I've sort of made Yasamee my home already." I saw a smile cross her face. "It's different, but I think it's growing on me. And what about you?" She asked. "Miss Vivee was surprised you were here. She said you lived in Chicago."

"Yeah," I said turning and gazing out of the window. "I was in between jobs, had a love life that wasn't going as smoothly as yours, so I came home."

"Home is always a good place to regroup," she said. "You plan on staying?"

I let out something between a chuckle and a groan. "When I first got back home all I did was plan on going back," I said. "I had planned my life," I turned and looked at her, "meticulously. I mean down to the letter. I didn't want to ever have to come back here."

"There's a 'but' in there, though, huh?"

This time it was me that showed a hint of a smile. "This may be bad to say..." I shifted in my seat and turned to face her, "but—you know that I'm a medical examiner, right?"

"I knew you were a doctor," she said.

"I deal with death a lot," I said. "I mean, I grew up in a funeral home."

Logan chuckled. "Now that's interesting."

"It was. And you're an archaeologist." I pointed to her cap. "So you understand this working with dead people thingy."

"I do."

"I work as a medical examiner, I live in a funeral home and lately..." I bit my bottom lip, I was sure I was sounding morbid enough already without adding what I was going to say. "There have been a couple of deaths—murders here. Recently. And I've been kind of...You know...involved in solving them." I blew out a breath. "And to be honest, that has made me want to stay here." I shook my head. "I know that sounds bad. It should be because my family and friends are here. Or some sentimental reason like that. But the autonomy I have as the medical examiner and the..." I paused. "The feeling I get when I solve a murder. It makes me feel...I don't know...purposeful."

Logan broke out into a hearty laugh. I let a grin spread across my face, joining in her merriment, but I wasn't sure what she was laughing about.

She wiped tears from her eyes, shook her head and started laughing again.

"Is it that bad?" I asked, scrunching up my nose.

"No," she said, not being able to say much more through her laughter. She held up one finger, I guessed she had to work through whatever had tickled her funny bone.

"Let me get this straight," she said. "You've been solving murders here and that's why you are reconsidering how you feel about staying?"

"Yeah. I know. It sounds crazy right?"

"No. Actually it doesn't." She drew in a breath and let out another chuckle. "I have been doing the same thing."

"Really?"

"Miss Vivee says it's my destiny."

"Your destiny?"

"Her destiny, too, but yes. She said that she was told by a seer or something a long time ago that she would solve murders. And that she'd have...I don't know... a sidekick."

"And that's you? You're the sidekick?"

She nodded her head, a look of sheer amusement on her face.

"And the two of you are solving murders in Yasamee?"

There was a little tidbit Auntie left out when she updated me on happenings with Miss Vivee.

"Yes." She gave a single nod. "Well really, the three of us. Mac, too. And we've been solving them all over. Even one in Fiji."

"Wow," I said. "And how is that working out?"

"Miss Vivee and Mac have this—I don't know, sixth sense when it comes to murder."

"How so?"

"They can just look at a dead body and almost instantly know what the cause of death was."

"Before the autopsy?" I was skeptical that anyone could do that. It took an examination and many tests for me to make such a determination.

"Yes," she said, her eyes opened wide. "She calls it before the medical examiner even has a chance to open up the body." She seemed to be reading my mind. "It's true. Once a girl walked into their family B&B, coughing, a little dirt on her jogging suit. Not fifteen minutes later she keeled over into her bowl of bouillabaisse dead."

"Heart attack?" I asked.

"No. Dry drowning."

"Really?" I asked.

"Really," she said matter-of-factly. "And Miss Vivee had told me before the autopsy came back that that was what had killed her."

"Before the autopsy?" I chuckled to hide my disbelief.

She nodded. "Once they figured out a man had died of water

intoxication."

"Just by looking at him?"

"Practically."

"I'm amazed." I looked at her out of the side of my eye. "And a little skeptical," I said aloud what I'd been thinking.

"So was I. I developed a close and personal relationship with Google," Logan said. "I had to whip out my cellphone," she pulled it from her pants pocket, "and look up everything they said to see if it were even possible. I still do. I mean whoever heard of dry drowning and water intoxication?"

"I've heard of it," I said. "But I'd never be able to identify it as a cause of death without an examination first. I can guess a lot of the times what it may be from a decedent's history, but I usually wait until the toxicology report comes back to make my final determination."

"Well, the two of them don't need a toxicology report." Logan waved a hand toward the house where they'd disappeared. "I know it's hard to believe without seeing them in action, but they are good."

"And so that's how they solve the murders?"

"They figure out the cause of death that way, but for the actual whodunit? Those two are master liars. They should win an award. Miss Vivee comes up with her suspect list and we go out to 'interrogate,'" Logan made air quotations. "They come up with these stories," she chuckled and shook her head, "I mean at the drop of a hat, and with that they get people to tell them stuff. They could sell tennis shoes to Nike."

I chuckled. That reminded me of Auntie Zanne. She could get people do what she wanted, too. But for the two murders I had solved, what Auntie contributed may have helped in some way, but mostly she was just in the way.

"I don't suppose they'll be any more murders," I said, "they were the first ones we'd had in God knows when. Roble is not Chicago. But," I shrugged, "I think it helped me make my decision."

"You've made your decision to stay here?" Logan asked.

Good question, I thought. Had I? My eyes drifted off, thinking that maybe I had decided to stay in Roble, only I'd never said it aloud. But before I could, I saw my three passengers as they exited the house *sans* Miss Eugenia.

Dr. Mac Whitcomb came out of the house first. Behind him was Auntie Zanne then Miss Vivee. They stopped long enough to line up and walk next to each other, arms looped together, heads straight ahead, but no words were shared between them.

Why was Eugenia Elder MIA?

Looked like the sun might rise before I could get them to their buffet.

Auntie pulled open the door to the back and climbed back into the van. Logan had gotten out when she saw Miss Vivee and Mac and did her usual—she got out and opened the door for them, giving Miss Vivee a push into her seat.

"I hate these vans," Miss Vivee said.

"Where's Eugenia?" I said.

"She's dead," Miss Vivee said.

"She's not coming?" I said.

"You got cotton in your ears?" Auntie Zanne said from the back seat.

I sat quiet for a second, registering what happened in relation to this conversation. The three of them had walked out of the house, looking no different than when they got out of the car and walked in. Nothing as catastrophic as a death could have happened in that short of time and no reaction to something so devastating registered on their faces or in their demeanor.

"I was thinking dead means she didn't want to come," I said as explanation.

"Dead means dead," Auntie Zanne said.

"It's not she didn't want to come," Mac said his voice soft, understanding, as if I needed help grasping the concept. "It's that she *couldn't* come."

"Because she's dead," Miss Vivee said, no tolerance in her voice for my slow uptake.

Chapter Four

I glanced through my rearview mirror at Logan to see if she was having as much of a problem with what was being said as I was. She raised an eyebrow, shrugged, and pursed her lips as if to say, "I don't know, either." So I shifted in my seat and turned to look at their expressions.

First, I searched Auntie's face, then our two elderly riders'. Maybe I could get some insight on the meaning of this conversation, because right now I was confused. But just as I was about to speak, sirens attacked my eardrums, and the red glow from the emergency truck's light flashed across the faces of the van's occupants assaulting my eyes.

There did seem to be an emergency somewhere...

The driver of the ambulance laid on his horn and blared it at me.

"Alright. I'm moving," I muttered. I started up the car, jerked it into gear and slammed on the gas pedal. The car lurched forward.

"No need you trying to kill us to get out of their way," Auntie Zanne said. "Nothing they can do for her."

"What in the world happened in there?" I asked, putting the car in park but leaving it idling. "You weren't in there ten minutes."

"She died," Miss Vivee said, exasperation in her voice.

"While you were in there?" I asked. I was finally wrapping my head around it, but it just seemed so crazy.

"Is she really a doctor, Babet?" Miss Vivee asked, jerking her thumb toward me.

"Sugarplum," Auntie Zanne said, turning to me and adopting Mac's tone. "She was already dead when we got there. She died in her sleep."

"Her husband said she'd had a heart attack," Mac said. I turned to him. It was the first I heard his voice take on the mocking tone of the two women's.

"Was it a heart attack?" I asked.

The three of them looked at each other, then at me, but no one said a word.

"So?" I said, trying to goad someone into answering me. Logan had just filled me in on Miss Vivee and Mac's power, I was sure, if what she'd shared with me was true, they had the answer.

"I think it was the absinthe," Auntie Zanne said sheepishly. "It probably wasn't a good idea to serve it to a room full of septua- and octogenarians."

"It was the kind that's legal in the U.S., right?" I asked, worried about my auntie and her tendency to do things her way even if it were not within the bounds of the law.

"Of course it was," she said. "Just maybe too strong." She raked her teeth over her bottom lip. "I'm guessing."

"So what now?" I asked.

"So, no breakfast with Eugenia," Auntie Zanne said.

"I was looking forward to that," Miss Vivee said. "Always enjoyed her company."

"Should I go in?" I asked aloud, even though I was more or less speaking to myself. I watched as the paramedics took the gurney from the back of the van. "I am sort of the coroner around here."

"Go in for what?" Miss Vivee asked.

"I can pronounce her dead."

"I already did that," Auntie Zanne said. "Did you forget that I'm the justice of the peace?"

"Did you forget that you're not a doctor?" I asked. "You can't declare someone dead." I had made sure to keep abreast of all Texas' laws pertaining to her justice of the peace job. Auntie thought that that little title gave her the power to do just about anything.

"Well, you can go and do it again," she said waving her hand at me and emphasizing the word "again." "Won't make her any deader."

I shook my head. "Then what are we going to do?" I asked.

"Take us to the Grandview," Auntie Zanne said.

"I'm not hungry anymore," Miss Vivee said.

"I'm not either," Auntie said. "But we've got to tell everyone the news. And we're going to have to vote on another Lesser Mambo since Eugenia can no longer take the position."

I glanced over at Miss Vivee as I put the gear in drive. She was shaking her head slowly from side to side. "That position is coveted, any member would probably kill for it. But I declare, the position must be jinxed," she mumbled. "I don't know how anyone would want it."

The Mambo positions in the Distinguished Ladies Society I had learned, were coveted and given as lifetime positions. Only death could separate a Mambo from her title. And it took years of membership for one to even be considered for the position. After the vote at the dinner the night before, Eugenia Elder had been elected unanimously and would have been installed as the Lesser High Mambo on Sunday, the last day of the Boule.

"Was picking Miss Eugenia for the position being contested?" I asked wondering why Miss Vivee didn't seem too excited about a new vote. She had been chosen by everyone and I heard no one grumble about it the night before. All seemed sad that she wasn't there to accept her nomination.

"Oh no," Auntie Zanne said. "Although several people may run for it, everyone is always on board with the new Mambo. That is what is expected, and that is always what happens."

"I was just trying to figure out what Miss Vivee was saying."

"You're having a tough time with that today, aren't you?" Miss Vivee said and raised a wrinkled eyebrow. But before I could answer, she told me what she'd meant. "The last Lesser Mambo was only in office six months. The one before her about eighteen months."

I nodded a few times. That I understood. Auntie Zanne had been the Most High Mambo for the last ten years at least. I guess a lifetime appointment wasn't a good thing if you didn't live long.

"It's beginning to seem as if being installed in that position may be the cause of your life being shortened," Miss Vivee said.

"If people believe that," Logan chimed in for the first time since their return to the car, "how are you going to be able to fill the position?"

"They'll step up," Auntie Zanne said with a firm nod. "It's their duty and they know that I don't abide by people not doing what they're called to do."

I pulled off and for a long while the van was quiet. I noticed that Miss Vivee kept trying to glance back at Mac. He sat in the middle, but with her being only about five feet tall, it didn't seem easy for her to turn and catch his eye.

I wondered what she was thinking. I glanced in the mirror at Logan, but she wasn't sending me any signals.

"Is there a diner close by?" Miss Vivee said making me not have to wonder anymore. She *was* thinking about food.

"I thought you weren't hungry," I said.

"I'm not," she said. "Mac and I need to talk to Babet."

"Diners are where they do their thing," Logan said, finally giving me something to help me understand.

I glanced in the mirror at her. She grinned and nodded her head.

"Oh," I said. Now I understood. Logan was telling me that Miss Vivee was on to something. I thought back over the conversation Logan and I had just had.

Was she saying that perhaps Miss Vivee thought that Miss Eugenia had been murdered?

Oh no. Couldn't be...

Chapter Five

Nothing else was said until I pulled into the parking lot at the Grandview.

The Grandview Motor Lodge Motel, reminiscent of the Econo Lodge-style motels, was a u-shaped three-story building. Room doors were all outside along a concrete walkway where planters of rose trees stood sentinel. The safety railings where painted white, and in the center of the yard, there was a yellow tiled swimming pool. The motel, as I remembered, was frequented by hikers, bicycle enthusiasts and the like, so no one would ever guess of the hints of glamour inside.

Auntie Zanne was the first to speak. She seemed to have a sixth sense with Miss Vivee.

"You wait here," she instructed me. "Vivienne and I will go in and tell Nola the news. I'm going to have her make the announcement after everyone has eaten. No need spoiling everyone's breakfast."

"Nola?" I said. The name sounded familiar, but I didn't know why.

"Nola Landry," Auntie said. "She's the one that helped Eugenia last night."

"Oh," I said, thinking Rita Hayworth. I hadn't heard anyone say her name the night before, so I still couldn't place why I knew her.

"She's the Sergeant-at-Arms," Miss Vivee added.

"Right," Auntie Zanne said. "Then we'll go over to Momma

Della's." She looked at Miss Vivee. "You remember the little diner, don't you? Momma Della's Place."

Miss Vivee nodded. "I do. That will do just fine." She peeked in the back. "Mac, I'll be back in two shakes of a lamb's tail. You keep the girls company."

"It'd be my pleasure," he said and tipped the brim on his Panama hat.

It wasn't fifteen minutes later before the two of them were back, looking sadder than they had when they'd found Miss Eugenia, and we were on our way to Momma Della's Place. I was on pins and needles the entire time. If it were true and Eugenia had been murdered and Miss Vivee and her husband had figured that out...

Oh my goodness. I was going to be sick. Why hadn't I pulled that van over and gone in to take a look at Miss Eugenia? Maybe I could've figured out the manner of death just as they had.

If they had.

Was it possible?

Ugh!

I was definitely jumping the gun. It hadn't been determined conclusively by anyone that Eugenia Elder had been murdered. And, I resolved, I, as the acting medical examiner would be the one to conclude that.

That made me sit up a littler straighter in my seat. Yep, in the end, whether they called it or not, the cause and manner of death was up to me to decide.

I pulled up to the diner. I didn't want to seem too anxious, but I was ready to hear why Miss Vivee wanted to come to the diner.

Chapter Six

Momma Della may have replaced a bulb or two in her florescent light fixtures because the diner seemed a little brighter than it had been in a long while. But if it hadn't been for the large windows all along the side of the small eatery, it was still dim enough to make one think they were in a jazz bar.

The furniture in the diner was old, but always scrubbed clean. The mauve-colored vinyl covering on the booths was worn out and split in places. A pedestrian attempt had been made to repair them with duct tape. The Formica tabletops were scratched, the lights buzzed, the short swivel counter stools groaned if you turned them, and the wooden floor creaked as we walked over it. But the food was good, and people piled in for breakfast, lunch and dinner. And today, it seemed, was the place where Miss Vivee would reveal her dazzling abilities to us.

Momma Della, as per usual, even at six-thirty in the morning, was perched behind the cash register on her stool. She rarely left it, turning on it to bark out orders or point her guests to their seat.

She was a big woman—big eyes, big lips, big hands and big breasts. Her face and hands shiny, she looked like she was covered in enough grease to fry a chicken.

"Mornin' Babet" she said when we walked in, a wide grin on her face showing a mouthful of teeth. "I see you brought company."

"Sure did," Auntie Zanne said. "You got room for us?"

"Always got room for the First Lady of Roble." Momma Della counted us with one of her stubby fingers, swiveled around and yelled, "Put two of them tables together. Miss Babet needs enough room for her friends." She turned back and looked at us. "They here for your Boule?" she asked Auntie Zanne, nodding her head toward where Miss Vivee, Mac and Logan clustered together.

"Yes, they are. But they're leaving this afternoon," Auntie said. "They're going to Turkey."

"Turkey! Well we better fill them up good," she said and laughed. She pulled out a stack of menus and handed them to us. "They got a long way to go."

We headed over to our seats just as our server was placing the last chair under one of the two tables they'd pushed together.

"I'll be right back to get your drink order," she said.

"We think that Eugenia was murdered," Miss Vivee said even before we got into our seats properly. At least she waited until the server left.

"What?" Auntie Zanne said, still mid-air, she eased down into her chair. I could have sworn that there was a spark flickered in her sad eyes.

"I told you," Logan leaned in and whispered to me, giving me a nudge with her elbow. She reached inside her pants pocket, pulled out her phone and laid it on the table.

"Orville said she had a heart attack," Auntie said, searching Miss Vivee's face then turning to Mac.

"I don't care what her husband said," Miss Vivee said. "It was murder."

"It wasn't a heart attack," Mac said. He closed his eyes momentarily and shook his head. "I'm sorry to say, it was something more sinister."

"It was murder," Miss Vivee repeated.

"Okay, what y'all want to order?" The server was back leaving Auntie and me in the throes of anticipation.

I had suspected that might have been what Miss Vivee was going to tell us. But when she blurted it out, that feeling of anxiousness I'd tried to dispel earlier had come rushing back.

"I know you want an iced tea, Miss Babet," the server was

saying. "And what can I get everyone else?"

"Just bring everyone an iced tea," Miss Vivee said.

"She always does that." Logan was whispering toward me again. She looked at the waitress. "I'll have a Pepsi," she told her.

"Me too," I said. I knew I was going to need something stronger than tea. "And a cup of coffee."

"Coffee, too?" Auntie said and frowned.

"Haven't had any this morning. I want to be alert when I hear what Miss Vivee has to say."

"Shhh!" Auntie Zanne said and nodded her head toward the server.

I didn't know why she was shushing me. If Eugenia Elder really had been murdered, it wouldn't be long before everyone knew it. This was, after all, Typical-Small-Town-Gossip-Headquarters, USA.

"So murder," Auntie Zanne said more so than asked after the server left.

"We think so," Miss Vivee said. "I saw it, then told Mac what happened, didn't I, Mac?"

"I can't see any other explanation," Mac said. "Not with the condition of the body."

"What happened last night?" I asked Miss Vivee. I'd been there all night and I didn't see anything that would make me think murder.

"When that drink spilled on her," she said.

"The drink? Oh, the drink." I chewed on my bottom lip, blinking my eyes. I tried to remember exactly how it went. I hadn't thought about it might matter and I'd need to recall any of it. It had been a simple accident.

"Yes, the drink," Miss Vivee said, nodding like she understood.

I didn't. I glanced over at Logan one hand on her phone, poised, it seemed, to google on demand. I knew from our earlier conversation that she was all set to look up whatever fantastical explanation they came up with.

"I've got y'alls drinks." The waitress was back. She set them down in front of us, put the tray she had carried them over on under her arm and pulled out a pad and pen to take our orders. "Y'all wanna hear the specials?"

"No," Miss Vivee said. "Do you have egg salad?"

"Sure do." She looked up from her pad. "But we serving breakfast now. If'n you want some."

"I don't," Miss Vivee said. "I'll have egg salad and so will Mac and my granddaughter."

Her soon-to-be granddaughter spoke up again. "I'll have eggs, but make mine scrambled with cheese. White toast and bacon."

"Gotcha. Miss Babet, you and Romaine want anything?"

"Nothing for me," I said. I didn't want my stomach too upset. I already couldn't digest the news about how Miss Eugenia died.

"I'll have what she's having," Auntie Zanne said and pointed to Logan.

I turned to Mac. "And what was the condition of the body?" I asked.

"She looked green," Auntie Zanne said. "I noticed that. Did it mean something?" Her voice was low, and she leaned across the table.

"Green?" I scanned the nether reaches of my mind. I couldn't think of anything that could turn the body green. Certainly not a heart attack. So, why would anyone think it had been cardiac arrest?

"Didn't you say a heart attack?" I said to Mac. "She died from a heart attack. That was what her husband said, right?" Neither one of us were her primary physician, we'd have no idea what ailments she had. But with her age, and certainly no signs of illness that I noted, a heart attack was the most likely cause.

"A heart attack may have been the secondary cause of death," he said. "An underlying factor."

"But you *think* it was something else?" I queried. I folded my arms in front of me on the table and leaned it, almost mimicking Auntie's pose.

Logan had said Miss Vivee and Mac were able to ascertain

cause of death with just a look at the body. I wanted to hear just what they thought.

"We're sure it's something else," Miss Vivee said. She didn't flinch in her answer, there was no way it appeared that she felt she was wrong.

"Okay, what did she die from?" Logan asked, a smirk on her face. She held up her iPhone, as if saying "ready, set, go..."

"Hydrofluoric acid poisoning," Mac said.

"What the heck is that?" Auntie Zanne said.

Logan didn't ask. Didn't say a word. She swiped her phone without missing a beat and started typing.

Chapter Seven

"'Ingestion of hydrofluoric acid may cause corrosive injury to the mouth, throat and esophagus.'" Logan read from her phone's screen. "Inflammation of the stomach with bleeding occurs commonly. Nausea, vomiting diarrhea, and abdominal pain may occur."

I held up my hand and shook my head. "Eugenia didn't drink anything." I pointed my finger across the table, but Auntie, fast on the draw swatted it down reminding me it was impolite. "They said it was because the drink had been spilled, which it was," I kept talking, without the finger. But Logan hadn't been there. She was getting information wrong, and I didn't need anything interfering with getting to the right answer.

"It's true. She didn't ingest it," Mac said.

"It was spilled on her," Miss Vivee said.

"When the waitress spilled that drink on her?" Auntie Zanne said. "It was hydrofluoric acid?"

"Auntie," I said. "Do you even know what hydrofluoric acid is?"

"According to Vivee, it's what killed Eugenia," she answered.

"It didn't burn through her clothes or burn her," I said.

"Hydrofluoric acid is a weak acid," Mac said.

"Siri, is hydrofluoric acid caustic?" Logan spoke to her phone. She was double-checking everything they said, but it didn't seem like it was because she questioned their conclusions. It seemed more so she could keep up and learn from what they were saying.

"Here," Logan said, evidently finding what she was looking for. "This is from Wikipedia. 'Hydrofluoric acid is a highly corrosive liquid and is a contact poison.'"

"Oh," I said, popping up straight. "That means she would have felt it. It *would have* burned her." From what Logan was reading, I didn't think Miss Vivee and Mac could be right. Although I did remember Miss Eugenia feeling bad and that server saying it wasn't supposed to hurt.

"'Symptoms of exposure to hydrofluoric acid may not be immediately evident,'" Logan kept reading. "Poisoning can occur readily through exposure of skin.' And, it says that 'accidental exposures can go unnoticed.'"

She looked up from her phone, eyes wide, looking straight at me. "They're rarely wrong," she said, jerking her head to the side across the table at Miss Vivee and Mac.

"What makes you two think that was the way she died?" I asked.

"I remembered that drink had spilled on her," Miss Vivee said.

"I remember it too, but when you three came back to the car and said she'd died, I never thought the two were related."

"You didn't see her this morning," Mac said. He affirmed his words with a nod. "It was evident."

According to Logan, me seeing Miss Eugenia wouldn't have made a bit of difference. They knew because of their "sixth sense."

"What color is hydrofluoric acid?" I turned to Logan. "Does it say? I was almost sure that what had spilled on Miss Eugenia just looked like water.

"Clear."

I looked across the table. "So the clear liquid that spilled on Miss Eugenia was a...semi-caustic..." I shook my head. "Deadly acid that kills you over night?"

"Yes," Miss Vivee said, no hesitation in her voice.

"Well, we should find out about that server," I said, and stood up. "Maybe she's hurt." I looked at Auntie then back across the table at them. "Or maybe even dead."

"She had on plastic gloves," Miss Vivee said without one hint of skepticism.

Auntie put her hand on my arm, urging me to sit down. I looked down at her and slowly took my seat.

"Listen," she instructed me.

"Nooo..." I drew in a breath. "I don't think that server had on rubber gloves. I saw her.

"Hydrofluoric acid can eat through glass," Mac said. "It's even used in glass etching. So she couldn't have served it in anything or with anything but plastic."

"It can't eat through plastic?" Auntie Zanne asked.

"No," Miss Vivee said.

I was shaking my head, digesting this. "And because the server spilt something on her from a plastic cup and she was green this morning, you two think she was murdered with hydrofluoric acid?"

"Greenish," Mac corrected. "It interferes with the calcium in the body causing her to go into cardiac arrest."

That was about the only thing that I knew for a fact was a scientific fact. And from that I couldn't conclude murder unless I saw it in a toxicology report.

"So, it seeped in through her clothes?" I asked.

"Yes," Miss Vivee said.

"And maybe through her hands," Mac said. "Vivee told me how she brushed the liquid off of her dress."

"Yes, she had a cloth napkin," I said. But I'm sure some got on her hands."

"Here," Logan came up for air. She seemed to be able to keep up with our conversation and do her research at the same time. "'Once absorbed through the skin, it reacts with calcium in the blood and may cause cardiac arrest.'"

"The underlying cause," Mac said.

"Due to hydrofluoric acid poisoning," I said, still in disbelief.

"You got it," Miss Vivee said and placed her finger against her nose as if she were playing charades.

"So she did die from a heart attack? But," Auntie Zanne said, "it was because of the liquid that had been spilled on her."

"Listen to this," Logan said, interrupting. She looked up from her phone, no longer giving us verbatim answers from what she'd found in her google search. "You know that show *Breaking Bad*?"

No one at the table seemed to know it or understand her referencing to it in the middle of the conversation.

"In that show, they used hydrofluoric acid to get rid of a dead body."

"That wouldn't work," Mac interjected.

"I know," Logan said, smiling. "But in the show, the one guy poured it into a bath tub with the body and supposedly it ate through the body, the tub, and the floor."

"No," Mac said, frowning, he stroked his tongue over the roof of his mouth as if he was trying to get something off of it.

"Right. So *MythBusters*, that's a show, too," she said, "wanted to see if that could really happen."

"It wouldn't," Miss Vivee said.

"It didn't," Logan said. "And I saw a snippet of a video showing how hydrochloric acid works on the skin. The hydrochloric acid ate right through skin. But the hydro*fluoric* acid didn't. Even after eight hours. It just turned it green."

Mac's frown turned to a grin and he put up a finger as if he were about to say something, but I interjected.

"Someone tried putting acid on a person's skin?" I asked, dumbfounded. Everyone turned and frowned at me.

I was sure I wasn't making a good impression. Not that I was trying, I didn't mind so much being the dumb one out, as it were, because I really was having a hard time understanding this willy-nilly pronouncement of murder, and this knack Logan claimed Miss Vivee and Mac had, which was on full exhibit at the moment.

"No," Logan said. No condescension in her voice. I guess she was used to not following the elderly Whitcomb couple's conclusions. "They used pig's skin in one. A chicken leg in the other."

"And the acid didn't eat through? Disintegrate the fat and

muscle?" I asked.

"Nope," Logan said and shook her head. "Not the hydrofluoric acid. Just the hydro*choloric*."

"But Eugenia should have had some evidence of the burn, no matter how insignificant," I said. "Did you see it?" I looked at the three faces of the people that had gone in.

"She was in the bed," Auntie Zanne said. "Covered up. Waiting for the ambulance. She had on a sleeveless gown and her arms were outside the blanket. We could see just her upper body minus what was covered."

I thought about that for a moment. "Where were they taking her?" Most time bodies went to the coroner's office. But since I hadn't fully decided to take the job, I didn't know where she might go.

"Well, we have to get going," Miss Vivee said, brushing the crumbs from her hand. "I just wanted to let you know about the murder before we left." She looked over at me. "You think you could take us to the airport?"

Chapter Eight

Murder!

I didn't want to be excited about it, but I had a tingling that started in my toes and fingers and was moving up my body. And I knew I had a spark in my eye that matched the one I'd seen in Auntie Zanne's.

But, first things first. Before the server could even bring us the check, I took in a breath to calm down, excused myself from the table and went outside to call my cousin, Pogue Folsom. He was the law in these parts. Two murders under his belt, Auntie Zanne would still call him green, so I didn't let her know that I'd given him a call. But regardless to the fact that he was newly elected, he was the one that needed to be called.

As I had told Logan, there'd been two murders in Roble since I'd been back, and Auntie Zanne and I had had a hand in solving both of them. That was, unfortunately, to the chagrin of my cousin. He didn't like us poking our noses in, even when he wasn't sure about how to go about looking into the crime. But I respected Pogue and his position, and he needed to be the one to delve into an investigation, if one was warranted.

But more importantly, and to cure my curiosity and answer the murder question definitively, he needed to be sure that that body got over to the medical examiner's office.

While it was up in the air if that was me, I was going to be darn sure that I was the one that did the autopsy on Eugenia Elder, especially after the conversation I'd just had over breakfast.

In my seventy forty-five a.m. call to Pogue, I kept it brief. I was sure I'd woken him up. I didn't let on to him what all I had learned—how could I be sure it was true? And I didn't want to stay too long away from the table. Didn't know what other tidbits our visiting guests would share. I just asked him to see to Miss Eugenia's body and come over to the funeral home later in the afternoon so we could talk. After I hung up from him, I called Catfish so he could meet the body at the M.E. facility, let whoever delivered it in and get it stored.

When I got back to the table, everyone was ready to go. I'd have to drop Miss Vivee, Logan and Mac back at their hotel to get ready for their one o'clock flight out of Shreveport. It'd only take me thirty minutes to get them there, and they didn't need to be there to get through security until eleven. I'd have to come back and get them later.

So that's what I did. I dropped them off, then me and Auntie headed home. I hadn't said much on the drive to the hotel, but now that we were headed home, I couldn't keep quiet. I wanted to see what my auntie thought.

"Do you believe Miss Vivee?" I asked my auntie. I already knew the answer, the two women had been friends for more than a half century, but still I wanted to hear her say it.

"I'd trust her if she told me to go over a cliff and I'd be okay." Auntie Zanne wasn't looking at me as she spoke, her eyes were somewhere off in the distance. Her voice soft, hands folded in lap, she fiddled with her fingers. "You know she should have been the Most High."

"Over you?" I asked. I knew that out of all the auxiliaries and clubs my auntie was a part of, her position as the Most High Mambo of the Distinguished Ladies Society of Voodoo Herbalists was her most coveted.

"Yes. Over me," she said. "But she said she had another destiny. Said she was told about it when she was young, and she was just waiting for it to happen.

I knew about that. Logan had filled me in on how it was her

destiny was solving murders.

I still couldn't get my head around the fact that Miss Vivee could tell that Eugenia had been murdered by no more than looking at her, even if it was her destiny. I wondered had I ever done that. After all, I had been known to say that death was my legacy.

"This just couldn't be good," I said and glanced over at Auntie Zanne. "In the short amount of time that I've been home, this is the third murder that's happened in Roble."

"Well, don't get it into your head that it's *your* destiny." She smiled at me. "And, technically, this one happened in Yellowpine," Auntie Zanne said. "But I know what you mean since she lived in Roble."

"Pogue won't like this," I said. "You know, if it's true."

"It's definitely true," she said. "I just told you, I'd trust Vivienne Pennywell with my life."

"Vivienne Whitcomb," I corrected.

"Right. She is married now, bless her soul," Auntie said. "And what your dear little cousin Pogue won't like is not the murder, but us solving it."

"Whoa!" I said. "Who said anything about that?" I glanced over at her before pulling into our driveway.

"You know we're the dynamic duo," she said, grinning.

"I don't know about that." I could feel that tingling starting again as I put the gear in park. "That's Pogue's job."

"Ha!" She slapped my arm. "You know good and well you can't wait to delve into this whodunit." She nodded her head. "Don't think I don't know you were calling trying to get Eugenia's body transferred to your facility when you excused yourself from the table."

I grinned.

It had to be wrong to get excited about solving a murder. It just had to be.

"I'm not happy about anyone being murdered," Auntie Zanne said, seemingly knowing my thoughts. "Don't misunderstand. This one is bittersweet. Eugenia Elder was a dear friend to me. I was looking forward to serving on the Ladies Society with her."

"But..." I said.

"You know the but," she said, and unbuckled her seatbelt. "I love you being the Dr. Watson to my Sherlock Holmes."

I just shook my head. She was always giving herself top billing.

Chapter Nine

As soon as we walked into the door of the funeral home, Auntie Zanne headed right to the kitchen.

"I'm going to put some tea on," she called over her shoulder. "I need it."

I could understand that. I might even be tempted to drink some. Not any that she brewed, but something warm and soothing would help. Not getting enough sleep, rising before sunrise and the is-it-murder business could be taxing.

Auntie dealt with death and dead bodies every day, but I understood that seeing a friend go was hard business. I thought, instead of going to my room and falling out across the bed, as I had planned earlier. I'd go into the kitchen and hang out with my auntie.

When I got there, she was at the sink running water. She was holding the teapot in one hand, but her other hand was the one immersed in running water. Bubbling over her hand, it flowed over her wiggling fingers like a waterfall. Shoulders slumped, lips slightly parted, she had a distant gaze in her eyes

"Auntie," I said. "Would you like for me to make the tea?" I took the teapot out of her hand, placing a hand on her shoulder, I led her over to one of the kitchen chairs.

"I've buried a lot of friends and family," she said, her voice trailing off. "But this one I think is going to be hard."

"I understand," I said, going back to the sink and running water into the teapot.

"Well, I'm glad you do, because I don't." She turned in her seat so she could face me. "I've seen a person drop dead in front of my eyes. No kidding. How is seeing Eugenia alive last night and not so much this morning weighing so heavy on me?"

I shrugged. "Maybe because none of the other people had been murdered while you were there watching." I turned the gas on the eye of the stove and sat the teapot on top of it. "Whoever did it, if it was done like Miss Vivee said, did it right in front of a room full of people."

"Maybe..." she heaved the word out with an exasperated sigh.

"Don't worry, Pogue is coming over this afternoon." I was hesitant to tell her that, she wasn't too gung-ho on him being sheriff. But involving the law when there had been the possibility of a crime as brash as Eugenia's had been, had to make anyone more at ease.

"That boy is as much use as a glass hammer. Him coming here ain't no comfort to me, or Eugenia."

"That's not nice, Auntie Zanne."

"Don't matter so much that it ain't nice because it's true. Ain't talking about folks if you are telling the truth."

I shook my head. "He's still new in his position and the first murder we solved happened while he was away, and we just kind of took over that second one."

She waved her hand at me, dismissing me taking up for my cousin without saying a word. Gazing thoughtfully she said, "I wish Vivienne could stay here and help us solve this. Eugenia meant a lot to the both of us and she's got six solved murders under her belt."

"Six?" I said. "Doesn't Yasamee have the around the same number of residents. Like less than a thousand? Why are there so many murders?"

"Our murder rate is rising."

"Auntie! That is nothing to be proud of."

"I'm not." She shrugged. "She solved one in Fiji, too."

"I heard."

"She's quite gifted," Auntie Zanne said.

"I don't know that I'd call it gifted," I said, restraining from rolling my eyes. It couldn't be such a great thing that bodies were always turning up murdered. Granted, I'd been a medical examiner for Cook County for more than a decade, and grew up in a funeral home, but murdered people falling down in my path, even to me, was a bit much.

"Vivienne could probably get this solved in no time, it's going to leave such a stain on our Boule."

"The hundredth one marked by murder."

"Murder of a Mambo no less," Auntie Zanne said. "It couldn't be worse."

"I do have some ideas on where to start with Miss Eugenia's death. You know, once I confirm the cause after the autopsy.

"You and I made a pretty good team solving the last two murders," she said.

"I hooked a half-smile at her. "We could give it a go again this time, if you want."

"Aren't you worried about stepping on Pogue's toes?"

"I never step on his toes," I said. "I may solve the murder, but unlike you, I try to keep him in the loop."

There was a knock on the back door at the same time the teapot started whistling. We looked at each other. "I'll get the door," I said, "and you get the teapot."

"Who could it be?" Auntie said with a furrowed brow as she placed her palms on the tabletop and pushed herself up from the chair. It couldn't be that she thought it was an unusual occurrence for someone to be visiting. Her house was the Grand Central Station of East Texas.

"Babet!" Delphine Griffith rushed through the door, blowing past me, waving her spindly arms wildly through the air. I made myself flush with the wall and raised my arms so as not to get bowled over. "Babet!" she said again.

"Oh, Delphine," Auntie Zanne said. "I'm so sorry about how you had to find out. I just didn't have time to come and tell you personally this morning at the Sunrise Breakfast." She opened her arms to embrace Delphine. "Who knew she was sick?"

Auntie had definitely gotten on board with the murder diagnosis as soon as Miss Vivee proclaimed it at Momma Della's place. Now what was she doing pretending like she thought it was a heart attack that killed Miss Eugenia?

Delphine smacked her hands away. "She was the picture of health. You have to help."

"Help with what?" Auntie Zanne sounded coy. I guess she wasn't going to give away the conclusion we'd come to, not that she'd be able to keep it secret for long.

"Eugenia was murdered!" Delphine spat out the words.

Auntie put a fake shocked look on her face. "No!" she said and shook her head. "She died from a heart attack."

"Heart attack my foot," Delphine said and stomped her foot. She brushed the gray hair that had fallen in her face away. "She was murdered, and I know who did it."

"Who?" Auntie and I both said at the same time.

"Orville Elder," she said.

Auntie's eyes got big. "Her husband?"

Chapter Ten

Delphine Griffith had been the one to supply the murder weapon for the last person killed in Roble. Michael "Bumper" Hackett.

Although, her complicity in the murder wasn't as bad as it sounded. She did supply the murder weapon—ricin, a very deadly poison—only she did it unwittingly. She hadn't even been reprimanded by the law, it appeared that her part in the whole thing was completely legal.

She, along with five other herbalists, had been cultivating the castor bean, the source of ricin for Doc Westin, the former medical examiner for Roble and the entire tri-county area. He'd heard that ricin, used sparingly, wouldn't kill a person but may be a cure for cancer. He died before he had a chance to find out.

It had also been discovered by a few of the Voodoo herbalists around that ricin was in fact hard to extract. Not for Delphine. She figured it out, and with Doc Westin not needing it any more, she bottled it and put it on a kitchen shelf. Easy access for a wanna-be murderer.

Now here she stood perched, exaggerating her bird-like features, hands on hips, looking down her long nose, her barreled-shaped chest pocking out, accusing someone of a crime that hadn't officially been determined or announced.

"Calm down, Delphine," Auntie Zanne said. "What do you mean Orville killed her?"

"Just what I said is what I mean."

Auntie and I turned and looked at each other.

"No one has said Miss Eugenia was *killed*," I said. It seemed that determining Miss Eugenia's cause of death was contagious. Everyone was thinking the same thing. "She had a heart attack as far as we know," I continued, "and although I didn't call her death, that's my opinion until I talk to her doctor or do an autopsy."

"You can autopsy all you like," Delphine said. "Won't change the fact that Orville killed her."

"If she *was* killed," Auntie Zanne said, "how do you know it was Orville who did it?'

Delphine flapped her arms at her side and her voice want up another octave. "Because she told me he was going to kill her."

"She told you that?" I asked.

Delphine flopped down in a chair. "You asking me questions ain't gonna change my words or solve this case." She looked at Auntie Zanne. "Are you going to do something about it?"

"Me?"

"Yes. Aren't you the Justice of the Peace?"

"That's not quite what they do," I said. I didn't need anyone adding to Auntie's job description, she had an inflated opinion of what her duties were as it was.

There was another knock on the back door. This time it was me flapping arms. "If this is another person with the news of a murder," I said.

"Murder!" came a voice from out back. The screen door swung opened and a large woman pushed her way through.

"Avoyelles!" Delphine said and rushed over to the woman before she'd gotten halfway in the door. "Tell them."

"Tell them what?" our new visitor said. I didn't remember seeing her before, but she seemed familiar with our house. She knew to come to the back door. That told me she'd probably been there before.

"What Eugenia said about Orville."

"What she said...Oh, that?" Avoyelles waved a hand. "She didn't mean it. She couldn't have meant it. They loved each other." She pointed a finger at Delphine. "It's not good to spread rumors at a time like this."

"Hello, Avoyelles," Auntie Zanne said. "Come on in."

"Didn't mean to barge in, but after I heard 'murder' I panicked. I've heard about what's been happening down here in Roble."

"Don't worry about it," Auntie Zanne said, seemingly glad for the interruption.

"I just stopped by to see what I can do. I'll be going back home tomorrow."

"That's sweet of you, Avoyelles," Auntie Zanne said. "C'mon. Have a seat." She pointed to a chair. "I'll put on some tea." The woman sat next to me and nodded a hello. "I don't think you ever met my niece, have you?"

"The doctor? No, but I've heard you talk about her enough," she said and smiled. "Feels like I know her."

"Avoyelles Kalty this is my niece, Romaine Wilder." Auntie nodded her head. "Dr. Wilder."

"Nice to meet you," I said.

"Same here," she said then looked over toward Delphine. "I didn't know that Delphine was here spreading gossip." She shook her head at her. "It's not like you."

"You know Eugenia said it," Delphine said. She was standing over the sink, still looking frantic but wasn't being as boisterous. "And now she's dead."

"One doesn't have anything to do with the other," Avoyelles Kalty said. "Eugenia might have said it, but she didn't mean it."

Avoyelles Kalty was tall and stocky. Her skin was plump and smooth, she had caramel colored skin and full head of gray hair. Crow's feet etched the corner of her dark eyes. Her beet red lipstick was the only splash of color of her dark attire. Her breathing was heavy and noisy and she smelled like liniment.

"So," I spoke up. "Miss Eugenia told the both of you that her husband was going to kill her?"

"Yes!" Delphine said. "It's what I've been telling you."

"I don't think it's true," Avoyelles said. "Eugenia would just get upset with him about his gambling and spending her money."

"And now who's going to get that money?" Delphine put a hand on her hip and cocked her head to the side.

"Orville will get the money," Auntie Zanne said slowly, the realization hitting her.

"Exactly." Delphine said and turned toward Auntie Zanne. "Babet, you've got to do something about this. I feel so bad that my nephew got ahold of that ricin that killed the Hackett boy. My fault." Auntie opened her mouth to say something, but Delphine held up her hand. "I shouldn't have had it where someone could get to it so easily and I shouldn't have kept quiet about being able to extract it. For that I am truly sorry."

The room grew quiet and the three of us looked at each other.

"But I am not going to keep quiet about this." She stopped, sucked in a breath and shook her head. "Although I should have said something to someone when Eugenia first told me."

"She told me, too," Avoyelles said. "It wasn't something to do anything about. If she really felt like that about Orville, she wouldn't have stayed with him."

"Maybe she couldn't leave," Delphine said. "You ever thought about that? Maybe he was forcing her to stay with him."

"Eugenia?" Both Auntie Zanne and Avoyelles said at the same time. It was evident that they both thought he couldn't have done that to her.

"Yes. Eugenia. She may have been tough at one time, but she was older, we are all older now. We can't do the same things we used to do."

"I don't know about that," Avoyelles said shaking her head.

"Well, I do," Delphine said, her blue eyes on fire. "And we need Babet to find the evidence on that no-good," she shook her fist in the air, "wife-murdering, gambling-halfwit Orville and solve this case before he gets away with it."

Avoyelles and I looked over at Auntie, but she looked as if she was at a loss for words. It was already what she was planning on doing—solving the murder, if there really had been one. We had just talked about it. Working together. Solving the murder. But with it being expected by Delphine, instead of her doing it because of her intrusive nature, the suggestion seemed to have taken her aback.

"Solve it?" Auntie said.

"Yes," Delphine said. "You have to solve it."

"I don't know—"

"Who's solving what?

Crap! It was Pogue. I glanced up at the kitchen wall clock. He was hours early. I didn't expect him until I'd gotten back from taking Miss Vivee and her crew to the airport. I didn't need him in on this conversation.

"Pogue, is that the way you come into people's houses?" Auntie Zanne said. "No 'hello.' No 'how you doing.' Where's your manners?"

Pogue looked around the room. He was here as the sheriff and that did bring some authority with it. And knowing that and Auntie still fussing at him, it made me cringe. It wasn't good, I thought, for Auntie not to show respect for him and his office especially in front of other people.

"Sorry, Babet." He pulled off his hat and looked around the room. "Morning, ladies."

"Morning," came a round of greetings.

"Pogue," Auntie Zanne said. "That's Avoyelles Kalty, she's from Angelina County. And that's Delphine Griffith. She lives over in Shelby County. They're here for the Boule.

Then I remembered who Avoyelles Kalty was. I hadn't ever met her, but I had heard of her. I don't what made it click, but she'd been one of the Voodoo herbalists who had helped Auntie grow castor beans for Doc Westin. Her efforts had been useless, she had been one of the ones who couldn't extract the ricin.

"What are you ladies talking about in here?" Pogue asked. He turned and looked at me. "Is this what you wanted to talk to me about? Why you wanted the body?"

"What body?" Delphine asked. "Eugenia's?" She looked at me. "You're going to do the autopsy on Eugenia?"

"Probably," I said, though I knew I was.

"If you're not, why would you have me send it to the medical examiner's office?" Pogue asked.

"Oh! Thank goodness!" Delphine Griffith said, laying a hand on her chest, she pulled out a seat and plopped down in it. "Now I don't have to worry anymore."

"What is she worried about?" Pogue asked.

"That Orville killed Eugenia," Auntie Zanne said.

Pogue looked at Auntie Zanne with disbelief on his face. Then he let his eyes drift from her to Delphine and by the time they reached me, that look had changed to amusement.

"Don't tell me it's happened again?" Pogue said, looking back at Auntie Zanne. "Just don't tell me that there has been another murder."

"Okay. I won't tell you," Auntie Zanne said, she put her hand over her heart like she'd taken a solemn oath. "It's only right I don't since Romaine called you and asked you to stop by." She held up both hands as if she was surrendering and took a step back. "So we're gonna let her be the one to tell you all about how Eugenia Elder was murdered sometime during the night."

Chapter Eleven

I needed to talk to my stunned cousin in private. I excused us from the room, took him by the hand and walked with him to one of the chapel rooms. It was occupied. An old man in a gray suit, a gray metal casket with an egg shell-colored bedding was using it presently, but I knew he'd never repeat a word we'd say.

Pogue and I had always been close, even before I moved to Roble. His mother, my Aunt Julep and my father were brother and sister. And after my father died, they were the only family on my paternal side I had left. Even though I sometimes didn't act like it, family meant a lot to me.

"You wanna tell me what's going on?" Pogue said.

"I'm not sure, but I think maybe it's bad," I said. "Miss Eugenia had some kind of clear liquid, that was...well, I don't know what it was. Not yet. Anyway, *something* spilled on her last night and this morning, she woke up dead."

"How does that make her murdered?"

"It doesn't. Necessarily. But Miss Vivee and her husband—"

"Wait. The Miss Vivee that used to come and visit when were younger? The one from Georgia?"

"One and the same."

"She's here?"

"Yes."

"She's still alive?" He scrunched up his nose.

"Evidently."

"Oh wow," Pogue said. "She must be a hundred by now. I remember her visiting even before you moved here. She was old back then."

"You want me to tell you what she said, or should we just stand around and speculate on her age?"

"Did you say her *husband*?"

It seemed he wasn't ever going to let me get around to answering his question.

"She got married," I said, thinking I'd better just fill him in on Miss Vivee all in one breath so we could get past her and on to the reason I'd called him over. "Her husband looks as old as she, and his name is Mac. He's a doctor." My voice went up an octave and I titled my head to the side as I finished my recitation. "Her grandson, Bay is engaged. His fiancée, Logan, came with Miss Vivee and her husband and they're leaving," I looked down at my watch, "in a few hours to go to Turkey where Logan is going to excavate some plot of land because she's an archaeologist."

"An archeo—"

I put a finger up to his mouth. "You want to hear about the murder?"

"Can't you tell," he said swatting my hand out of the way. "That I don't."

"Okay," I said. "Probably better for you not to hear about it until I get confirmation anyway."

"How are you going to do that?"

"Autopsy," I said, and bucked my eyes. "Duh."

"Oh yeah," he said.

"Did you have the body sent over to the facility?"

"I did," he said. "You'll run all the tests and find the cause of death?"

"I will."

"So tell me then."

"Okay," I said.

He started to walk out of the chapel room, but when he got to the door, he turned back to me. "Do either of those women know anything about it supposedly being a murder?" he asked.

"They were there when the spill happened. Although, they don't seem to know to relate the two."

"And the liquid that spilled may have something to do with the cause of death?"

"It might."

"Anything else?"

"Only that they think they know who did it."

"Mr. Elder."

"That's what they said."

He filled up his cheeks with air, puffed them up, then blew it out. "And they don't live here in Roble, do they?"

"No," I said, "they don't."

"And if I don't talk to them now, and it turns out it was murder…"

"You'd miss out talking to two valuable witnesses. And you'd end up having to make a drive to get the chance to talk to them and see what they know."

Pogue looked up toward the ceiling and let out a groan. He raked his fingers over the stubble on his throat. "You know," he said looking at me, "I used to be happy that you came back home."

"But now?"

"Yeah. Not so much." He walked back toward me and took a seat in the first row of white folding chairs. "Tell me what you know so when I talk to the ladies, I'll have a clue about what in the world is going on."

I filled him in. I told him about what happened at the Boule, but he seemed more interested in why I was there. "Good question," I told him because I had wondered the same thing myself. I proceeded to tell him what had happened that morning—the visit to Miss Eugenia's, the conversation at the diner and how Delphine thought the culprit was Orville Elder, Miss Eugenia's wayward husband, and that even though Avoyelles had heard her say it, she didn't believe he did it.

"Does she believe it was murder?"

"Who?"

"Avoy. Whatever her name is."

"She doesn't seem to think so."

"Did you see Orville Elder this morning?" he asked.

"No. Like I told you, I didn't go in the house, and he didn't come out," I said. "All I noticed was that the house was dark. At first I thought no one was even awake in there."

"Well, it appears that only one person was," he said.

"Yep. It appears that way."

"Did Mrs. Elder have a bad heart? That's what the other doctor said, right?" Pogue scratched his head. "What's his name? Mac?"

"Dr. Macomber Whitson," I said. "Mac for short. He said that that was what Mr. Elder had said. But Mac didn't believe it. He was the one who noticed she was greenish."

He frowned. "Green?"

"Ish."

"Greenish," he put the words together and made a face like he had a bad taste in his mouth. He sat quiet for a moment, then blew out a breath before he spoke. "Does any of this mean anything to you?"

"No," I said, and nothing else. I was sure that Pogue didn't want to hear about Miss Vivee and Mac's proclivities for calling the manner of death before a doctor had. He just wanted the facts. And I didn't know enough about hydrofluoric acid to formulate a decision. So, for me, there were no facts that pointed to murder. Not yet.

"Okay," he said and stood up. "I'll go talk to the ladies and see what they know."

"Okay," I said.

He started walking out of the chapel, and I followed behind him. "But I don't want to put any thoughts in their heads about the spilt liquid having anything to do with anything until you check it out," he said, talking over his shoulder. "The power of suggestion is pretty strong."

"I agree," I said. "What are you going to ask them?"

"Don't know," he said, he stopped and turned to face me. "I guess I'll just figure that out as I go."

Chapter Twelve

"He murdered her!" I guessed Delphine thought that repeating the same exact thing again and again, only louder each time would make Pogue run out and arrest Orville Elder.

By the time the two of us got back into the kitchen, Auntie Zanne and Avoyelles Kalty were sitting around the table having tea—or whatever it was Auntie Zanne had brewed up. Delphine was still leaning against the sink. Arms folded across her torso. A determined look on her face.

I had pulled out a chair from under the table and had sat down. Pogue had stood in the doorway, pulled out his notebook, ready to start his interrogation. He had looked at me, then at Delphine.

He had tried asking her a few questions, but the only answer she'd given to every question he asked was to point a finger at Orville Elder being the murderer.

"We don't even know if it's murder yet," Pogue said.

"I know it is," Delphine said, she gave a firm nod.

Pogue, exasperated with Delphine, turned to Avoyelles. He turned to a clean sheet of paper in his notebook. "Please, Ms. Kalty, would you spell your name for me."

"My first name, pronounced Ah-vo-yell, is French," she said. "The 's' at the end is silent. And Kalty is actually a very old name of the region I'm from—Angelina County. We Kaltys have a rich and grand history."

Pogue sat with his pen poised hovering over the paper, waiting for Miss Kalty to get to the spelling. It was evident in his face he was sorry he hadn't waited until later to come. I'm sure he realized then he would have missed all the drama.

"Would you spell that for me?" he asked again. "First name, then last."

"Avoyelles. A-V-O-Y-E-L-L-E-S. And Kalty is just like it sounds."

"Which is?" he asked, there was forced politeness in his voice.

"K-A-L-T-Y."

"Thank you," Pogue said. "Now did you hear Mrs. Elder say that..." Pogue flipped back through his notebook, "If anything happens to me, Orville will be to blame."

"Yes, I did," she said.

"And did you think she meant he would kill her?"

"When? When she said it, or now?"

"Either one," Pogue said.

"No," she said.

"To which time?" he asked.

"Both."

I could see Pogue restraining from rolling his eyes. "When you heard her say it, what did you think she meant?" Pogue asked.

"That all of his womanizing and spending was at some point going to wear her down. We all say things like that, you know," she said.

"Like what?" he asked.

"Like saying someone is 'going to be the death of me.' We don't mean they'll kill us literally. Just that they're hard to take."

Pogue nodded and scribbled something in his notebook.

"I've got a letter," Delphine interrupted. She pulled out a folded piece of paper from the pocket of her dress.

"A letter?" asked Auntie Zanne, who'd been standing by the stove, surprisingly quiet for the entire interrogation.

"From Eugenia," Delphine said. "She gave it to me for safe keeping."

"What does it say?" Auntie Zanne asked. "Let me see it," she walked over to Delphine to get it.

"It's proof," Delphine said.

Pogue stood up from the table and intercepted "the proof" before Auntie could get to it. He opened it up and stared down at it.

"Well what does it say?" Auntie Zanne said. She went and stood next to him.

Delphine spoke up before Pogue had a chance. "It says, *'If anything out of the ordinary happens to me, it'll be because of Orville. He wants my money and my life. I have no more strength left to fight him. I bought a burial plot next to my parents at Field Memorial Cemetery. Send me to my heavenly home in my rose-colored dress. You know the one I love. Have Babet take care of my arrangements. She'll know what to do.'* Then she signed it, *'Your Friend, Eugenia.'*"

Pogue looked up from the letter. "That's exactly what it says," he said. "Word for word."

"I memorized it," Delphine said. "After Nola made the announcement at breakfast this morning, I went right home and got it. I had put it in the Bible when Eugenia gave it to me. For safekeeping." I saw her swipe at the edge of a misty eye. "I reread it must've been a hundred times to make sure I understood it right before I came over here. Then I did just what she'd said." She turned and looked at Auntie Zanne. "I came to you. Eugenia said you'd know what to do."

Auntie Zanne looked at me. I looked at Pogue. There was an awkward silence in the room long enough to make everyone feel uncomfortable. A shifting in seats, a cough into balled fist, rubbing a hand across furrowed brow showed it. Then Pogue spoke. "Did anyone see Orville at the dinner last night?"

"No," the answer came in chorus from each of us.

"He wasn't there," Auntie Zanne said.

"No he wasn't. But he didn't kill her there," Delphine said understanding why Pogue had asked that question. "He killed her after she left the dinner. She went home early," she looked at Auntie wide eyed. "Maybe she caught him doing something and he killed her."

"Caught him doing what?" Avoyelles asked.

"I don't know," Delphine said. "Maybe Babet and the Sheriff can figure that out."

"We won't know what happened, if anything, until Romaine finishes up with what she has to do," Pogue said.

"Are you saying you don't believe me?" Delphine said. Her voice was strong, raised up a couple octaves.

"I'm not saying that," Pogue said, "but I can't go around investigating a murder when I'm not even sure one's been committed or how it was done. From what I've heard, Mr. Elder said she had a heart attack."

"Well, she didn't," Delphine said.

"I don't know that," Pogue said.

"Ha!" Delphine said. "Well, I do." She walked over to Pogue and tried pulling the letter from Pogue's hand, but he didn't let go.

"Evidence," he said.

Delphine huffed again and stormed toward the back door. Before she left, she turned to Auntie Zanne. "Eugenia is counting on you." She held up a finger. "Don't let her down."

"She sure is upset," Pogue said after the screen door slammed behind her.

"And not completely truthful, either," Avoyelles said.

"What do you mean?" Auntie Zanne asked.

She looked at the door, like she was making sure Delphine was gone. "That part Delphine quoted," she nodded toward the paper, "was the second page of the letter she got from Eugenia."

"The second page?" Pogue said, he flipped the letter over and looked at the back.

"Yes, there's another page to it. I've seen it before."

"Why wouldn't she show me the entire thing?" Pogue asked.

"What I want to know is why did she only bring it out after you got here?" I said. "She hadn't mentioned the letter before."

Pogue held the letter up to Avoyelles. "Is this Eugenia's handwriting?" he asked.

"Sure is," Avoyelles said. Auntie Zanne nodded her agreement. "And her words," Avoyelles closed her eyes for a moment seemingly in thought. "It just wasn't all she had to say."

Chapter Thirteen

"What did the other page say?" Pogue asked.

"I don't know if I should say..." Avoyelles said, looking down at her hands. "It was personal and maybe that's why Delphine didn't share it."

"Personal how?" he asked.

"Avoyelles shook her head. It was easy to see she felt uncomfortable. "I wish I hadn't said anything," she said. "But if it turned out to be...you know...I can't even say the word out loud. But if it turned out to be that and I didn't speak up. I'd never forgive myself." She looked at Babet and huffed.

"It's okay, Avoyelles," Auntie Zanne said.

"One of the women Orville supposedly was cheating with was Delphine's sister," Avoyelles spat out. "Eugenia and Delphine were on the outs for a while after that—Eugenia saying that Delphine knew about it and didn't tell her. Delphine tried, but she couldn't get Eugenia to believe that she didn't know if it was true and if it had that Delphine didn't know anything about it."

"They didn't seem on the outs to me," Auntie Zanne said. "Last night they were as friendly as I'd ever seen them."

"They made up. Been a good little while know. I think that letter was the beginning of them mending their friendship."

"Delphine's sister that died?" Auntie Zanne asked. "Was she the one?"

"Yes. That's the one. All water under the bridge now. I don't even know if was true. Delphine, if she did in fact know, would have to tell you for sure." Avoyelles got up to leave. "Babet, you know Eugenia used to come up and get her hair done by me. For more than thirty years."

"I remember that," Auntie Zanne said. "She loved the way you did it."

"Then you probably remember that she had to stop coming once she wasn't able to drive all the way to Angelina County anymore." Avoyelles swiped at the corner of her eye and seemed to sniff back a tear. She had to find a local hairdresser."

"I know," Auntie said, trying to calm Avoyelles.

"But I did it for her for last night."

"You did?"

"Yes, I did." She smiled warmly at the thought. "Got to town a couple of days early, and we spent some time together. It was like old times. But it was the last time."

"You didn't know that, Avoyelles," Auntie said.

She didn't respond to Auntie, kept talking like she was reliving it again. "We talked," she said. "I did her hair, just like I used to. Then she showed me what she was going to wear. That pretty yellow pantsuit..." The tears pooled in her eyes.

"Avoyelles," Auntie said and nothing more. It seemed like my auntie was at a loss for words. An unusual occurrence.

"What I want to say, Babet, if it's okay with you," she lowered her head, and wiped a tear from her cheek. "I'd like to be the one who does her hair for the funeral."

"That'll be nice of you, Avoyelles," Auntie Zanne said, she smiled softly. "I'll let you know when the time comes."

"Please do. I'm going back home day after tomorrow. But I'll come back. See to it being done right."

She left out the back door. Same way she came in. Pogue wanted to do the same. He picked up his hat off the table and walked to the doorway that led from the kitchen to the front of the house. He stopped, turned around and looked over at Auntie Zanne, but didn't say anything. A silent warning, perhaps? It didn't matter, no one could stop her once she set her mind to something. Especially after she got being elected a Texas Justice of the Peace.

Pogue turned to me. "Romaine." He put his hat on his head,

pulled down on the brim and put a hand into his pants pocket. "When you get the autopsy done, call me. Meanwhile, let's keep this between the three of us."

"What about Delphine and Avoyelles?" Auntie Zanne said. "They already know."

'They're only speculating. And they didn't seem to know anything about the spill possibly having something to do with Mrs. Elder's death," Pogue said. "They didn't even mention it happening. We can't give away our hand."

Auntie Zanne drew a line across her lips with her finger, gave it a twist as if she was locking them and tossed the imaginary key over her shoulder.

That seemed to satisfy Pogue. He headed out, and we followed. Auntie probably to her office to take care of funeral business, so she could get back to her Boule goings-ons. Me upstairs. Whatever was on the itinerary for this afternoon, she'd have to count me out. I had to make the run to the airport to take Miss Vivee and her clan then perform an autopsy. I still had a couple of hours, so I thought perhaps I could catch forty-winks.

But before we could get halfway through to the front exit, Orville Elder walked through the door.

I cringed.

Anyone who knew my Auntie Zanne, even slightly, knew she couldn't hold her tongue despite just promising she would. She was one to spill the beans on any information given to her. I could just picture her grabbing one of the large vases filled with flowers that sat on the pedestals in the lobby and whacking Mr. Elder over the head with it all while asking, "Why did you do it? Why did you kill your wife?"

Instead, to Pogue and my surprise, she stretched out her arms and walked to Mr. Elder, embracing him in a hug.

"So glad you're here," she said. "I saw how upset you were this morning and I hoped you'd come by. I want to give my deepest condolences once again."

"Yes. Yes," he said. "Thank you. Thank you. It is all quite

unreal. I just don't know what I'm going to do without my Eugenia."

Auntie Zanne looped her arm through his and turned to face us, as if to say, "Okay guys, get a good look at him. He might just be a murderer."

Orville Elder stood only an inch or two taller than my five-foot three auntie. His wingtip shoes were as shiny as his bald head and out of place suit. I was thinking the suit was sharkskin, but I couldn't be sure, I'd never seen one in real life only on television. Tailor made, teal blue, it had a sheen to it and looked expensive.

"I need to talk to you about the arrangements," Orville said. "Should we go into your office?" He looked around the foyer. "I don't think I've ever been inside here before."

"Well, that's obvious," Auntie Zanne said, "because I rarely conduct business in there."

That certainly wasn't the truth. I didn't know what game she was playing with Mr. Elder, but she evidently wanted us to play along—she was keeping us all together.

"This is my niece, Romaine Wilder, and you know Pogue."

"The sheriff," Mr. Elder said and nodded. "Yes, I know him, and it's nice to meet you, Ms. Wilder."

Auntie leaned in toward him and lowered her voice. "It's Doctor Wilder."

"Oh, well nice to meet you, Doctor." He licked his lips and looked at Auntie Zanne. "I needed to discuss the arrangements."

He wanted to get right down to business.

"Yes, you said that," Auntie Zanne said. "And I'm listening."

He looked at Pogue then me.

"Oh. Don't worry about them. This is a family business." She waved a hand toward us. "They're family."

"Sheriff looks like he's on duty."

"Not in my house he's not," Auntie Zanne said. "When he's here, he's my nephew nothing more. He was just here to help supervise the delivery of new caskets. Thanks to him, we'll be able to look at one of those for Eugenia."

"I'm not sure how this works," Mr. Elder said looking at us then back over at Auntie Zanne. "If I need a casket or not." He reached inside his jacket pocket and pulled out a folded sheet of paper. "This is the life insurance policy on Eugenia."

"How what works?" At the same time she took paper from him and read over it, and then let out a low whistle. "Fifty thousand dollars," she said and looked up from the paper over at us. "Orville," she turned to speak to him, "this will be more than enough for a casket and the funeral Eugenia wanted."

"That's the thing," he said. "She didn't want a funeral."

"Who didn't?" I said. I couldn't resist asking. It seemed as if he was set to say something other than what we'd just learned about Miss Eugenia's final wishes.

"Eugenia."

"She didn't want a funeral?" Auntie Zanne asked.

"No. She always said that she wanted to be cremated," he looked at Auntie Zanne. "I was thinking that I wouldn't need to get a casket or anything."

Auntie nodded, seemingly amused, she baited him. "No service or anything? Straight from the hospital morgue and into the furnace?"

"Yes," he said. He lowered his head, it seemed to display some sort of mock sorrow. "Just like she wanted."

"To be cremated?" Auntie asked.

"It's what she always said, and I want to follow her wishes. 'I don't want a big fuss after I'm gone,'" he said imitating her voice. "That's what she always told me."

"She did?" Auntie Zanne asked.

"Yes. 'Just throw my ashes in my rose garden.'" He did his imitation again.

"In her rose garden?" Auntie said.

"You know how she loved those roses," he said. "I was wondering what the cost of that would be." He pointed to the paper. "Then with what's left, after you take out your fee, would you just write me a check?"

"Eugenia's has lots of friends," Auntie Zanne said. "I could put together a little something to give her a proper send off."

"I'd hate to go against her wishes," he said.

"Wouldn't cost a penny more than just the cremation," Auntie Zanne said.

"No?" His eyebrows hiked up. "Same price as just the cremation?"

"Same price," she said.

He smiled. A slick smile. "We could do that then. I'm sure her friends would want to come to pay their respect."

"I would think so," Auntie Zanne said. "All I'd need is to get her some clothes and things. I can stop over this afternoon and pick them up."

"That'll be fine," he said. "I think she'd want her blue dress. It was her favorite."

"The blue one?"

"Yes. I've packed up most of her things already." He lowered his eyes again, the smile disappeared. "I just couldn't stand to be around them. Too many memories, they were just painful. Very painful."

"You couldn't stand being around them? Just since this morning?" I said.

"Too painful," he repeated and hung his head.

"I understand," Auntie Zanne said and rubbed his back. "It was a lot to take," she shook her head, "being there. Watching her slip away."

"No." He looked at her. "Don't you remember I told you I'd just come home? I wasn't there, but," he added, "that was just as painful, to see my beloved lying there. Dead from a heart attack."

"A heart attack?" Auntie said.

"Had to be," he said. "If only I'd been there."

"Oh, I do remember you saying you weren't home," Auntie Zanne said and glanced over at Pogue, telling him it seemed, to pay attention. "I think I remember you telling us that you'd dropped Eugenia off last night at the Boule."

"Right," he said.

"So that was the last time you saw her? When you dropped her off?" Auntie Zanne asked.

"Yes, it was. So sad. So sad." He looked around the foyer and back at Auntie Zanne. "So, we're set? You'll get her and the things you need from the house and make arrangements for the service? A small service," he emphasized.

"I will," she said.

"And then you can get me the check from the insurance—for what's left over. Right?"

"Sure," Auntie Zanne said, sweet as pie. Then her voice changed. It became stern. "But first, there's has to be an autopsy."

"What!" he said. He stepped back from Auntie and shook his head so hard his jaws wiggled. "No! No autopsy. I forbid it."

"Why?" Pogue asked, his first words in the conversation.

"Well, b-because…It's not…I don't want…S-she… Eugenia. My Eugenia. My dear sweet wife…" He cleared his throat. "She wouldn't want that." He sputtered out the words, then flung an accusatory finger my way. "Is that why the doctor is here? Is that what you do to your clients, Babet? Is this how you treat the grieving families?"

"Not all of them," she said.

"Well, I don't want it done to Eugenia," he stammered. "She would *not*," his arm came down hard with the word, "have wanted that. All she wants is to be with her roses."

"You don't have any say in it. I'm the justice of peace in these parts, and I can make the call on whether they'll be an autopsy or not."

"I'm sorry I voted for you," he said with a huff.

"I won't be cremating your dear sweet Eugenia, either," Auntie Zanne said.

"What!" he clamored.

"After the service, where she'll be wearing her favorite dress— the rose-colored one, she'll be buried in the plot she bought over at Field Memorial."

"She bought a plot?"

"Next to her parents," she said.

"Did she buy one for me?"

"I don't think so," Auntie Zanne said.

His mouth dropped opened and a series of grunts and groans came out before any words. "I'll just take my business somewhere else," he finally said. He tried to pull the paper from Auntie Zanne's hands, but she held it behind her back before he had the chance to.

"That's mine."

"Not anymore," she said. "Doesn't look like you're the beneficiary anyway. This money won't be paid out to you."

"What are you talking about?" he said. "My name is right there." He jabbed a finger at the paper. "Right at the bottom."

"Says you're the second beneficiary. You only get the money if the first beneficiary isn't around."

"What? No."

"Yes," Auntie nodded, this time she smiled.

"I'm her husband. *Was* her husband. It's my right to get it. Texas state law says so."

"Not on this. A life insurance policy is just like a contract. What's in it is what has to be done. And you ain't in this. Not first anyway." She gave him her funeral smile. "You can go to court and contest it if you want."

"Well...I...I can't...This is just..." And with that he turned and stormed out.

"Maybe, Delphine was right," I said after he left. "He sure did seem awfully suspicious."

"He did," Auntie Zanne said. "But, I'm not sure if he's the number one suspect." She pulled the paper from behind her back and handed it to Pogue. "Look who's the first beneficiary and gets the fifty thousand dollars."

Pogue took the paper, looked at it and back up at Auntie Zanne. A smirk on his face.

"Who?" I said. "Who gets the money?"

"Delphine Griffith," they said in unison.

Chapter Fourteen

"This is looking more and more fishy," I said. "Even without confirmation of it being a murder."

"I would say I'd have to agree," Pogue said. "As much as I hate to admit it." He shook his head and dug his hand in his pocket. "What is going on around here? I swear! We hadn't had a murder ever in Roble, and then you come home, Romie."

"And what?" I asked.

"And now there's a murder every other week," he said.

I held up my hands. "Don't blame me!"

"It's not every other week, Pogue," Auntie Zanne said. "This will *only* make the third one."

"You say that like three murders is no big deal," he said.

"And," she continued, "it wasn't just *after* Romaine came home that it started," Auntie Zanne said, "it was also *after* you became sheriff."

"See," I said and punched his arm. "Maybe all of this is happening because of you being sheriff."

"Whatever happened, this is bad," he said, rubbing the spot where I landed a punch as if it really hurt. "One murder after another."

"I know," I said. "It's like being in Chicago."

Pogue sucked his teeth. "I hope we never get that bad. He turned and looked at Auntie Zanne. "You know I want to tell you not to get involved, Babet," he said.

"But?" we both asked.

"But I'm not going to say it. It seems like people are coming to you, giving you unsolicited information on this one."

"They are," she said, a sly grin spreading across her face.

"Doesn't mean for you to go poking your nose into anything extra, though," Pogue said.

"I don't poke my nose in—"

He didn't let her finish her sentence. "You do. So just don't. That's all I'm asking. That and to tell me when anyone else comes spilling the beans or you find out anything else that might help button this down."

"Done," she said.

Pogue looked toward the door where Mr. Elder had stalked out. "You did a good job getting information out of him, Babet. Without confirmation of a murder, though, all it appears is that he is just a big liar."

"Romaine will confirm it," she said.

"You act as if you want it to be a murder," Pogue said.

"Vivienne Pennywell is never wrong," she said. "I trust her. She said it was murder. I believe that'll be just what Romaine will find."

"Even if it's not murder," Pogue said. "All the people I've talked to today are definitely up to something. They all are acting awfully suspicious."

"You think so?" I said.

"Yeah, I do. Why else are they lying? No one even has to ask them a question, they just spout out lies on their own volition."

"Doesn't mean it's anything illegal," I said. "The reason that they're lying."

"Didn't say it was illegal. I just said suspicious."

Pogue left and I knew I was going to be unable to sleep. I had so much information spinning around in my head. Too much stuff to sort out about who did or said what, so I took a shower instead.

A nice long one so I could think. But by the time I stepped out of it, I just had more questions.

If Orville Elder did kill his wife, how did he do it? According to him, he dropped her off way before the spill happened. Could it really have been hydrofluoric acid in that plastic tumbler? And if it was, was it what killed her?

The husband was the killer. Cliché, but often the best first and best person to look at for the deed.

Was it for the fifty-thousand dollars? Or did perhaps...I took my towel and swiped the condensation off of the bathroom mirror. "Perhaps," I said out loud, "Delphine's the one who's got murder in her blood."

I wrapped the towel around me and walked into my bedroom, grabbed my Nivea lotion off the top of the chest of drawers and plopped down on the bed.

Delphine's nephew, Boone Alouette, I thought as I smoothed the cool cream up my leg, had just killed someone using the ricin she had. I remember after I saw her, I realized she and Boone had the same eyes. Maybe the same evil was behind them.

The thought made me sit up straight. Why had she kept something so deadly right in her kitchen cabinet?

Maybe. Just maybe...I squirted another dollop of lotion into my hand and spread it over my arms and hands. Maybe Delphine had been planning murder all along. Planning to kill Eugenia because she accused her sister of infidelity. Or because she'd found out that she was the beneficiary of a fifty-thousand-dollar life insurance policy...

That's a reason to kill.

So, maybe...Delphine had used hydrofluoric acid because her murderous nephew Boone had used up all the ricin leaving her without her weapon of choice. She had to improvise.

And, I thought and tilted my head to the side, she did point to her cabinet and tell me she had lots of deadly herbs in them. Maybe she meant herbs and acids.

I walked back over the dresser, put the lotion back on top and pulled open a drawer. I found clean underwear in the top one, and a pair a jeans and a t-shirt in another one. I pushed it shut with my hip.

But where had Delphine gotten hydrofluoric acid from to put in her cabinet? Surely, she couldn't have grown it in her garden right next to the nightshade and foxglove.

I decided to look it up.

I slipped into my underwear, grabbed my phone from the nightstand and sat on the side of the bed. I'd learned from Logan it was a handy little instrument for furthering your knowledge on anything.

I typed in hydrofluoric acid and scrolled down past pictures and videos, one entitled *"Flesh-Eating Acid,"* which according to Mac it wasn't, and found a "People Also Ask" section. The first question listed was, "What hydrofluoric acid is used for?" And the answer was authored by Medscape. A reputable go-to place for people of my profession, so I figured I could trust what they had say. *"Hydrofluoric (HF) acid,"* it read:

one of the strongest inorganic acids, is used mainly for industrial purposes (e.g., glass etching, metal cleaning, electronics manufacturing). Hydrofluoric acid also may be found in home rust removers. Exposure usually is unintentional and often is due to inadequate use of protective measures.

"Is it in common household cleaners?" I said aloud. I scrunched my nose. "Just found around the house?" I couldn't believe something so deadly was a staple in people's under-the-sink stash of cleaning products.

I googled household cleaners with hydrofluoric acid and an ad for Lysol was the first result. "Oh my goodness! Lysol has hydrofluoric acid in it?"

"What is hydrofluoric acid?" A voice came from behind me. I turned and saw Rhett standing at my door. I screeched, jumped then slid onto the floor in one movement.

"What are you doing here?"

"Your Auntie Zanne sent me up to make sure you hadn't fallen asleep and would miss getting her guests to the airport."

Rhett Remmiere was Auntie Zanne's employee of sorts. The black Frenchman who wasn't French at all. I wasn't quite sure what he did around the funeral home, he just would seem to always show up and irritate me. Although, it seemed that I had suddenly discovered his eyes. Behind those wire-rimmed glasses he always wore, he had beautiful light-colored eyes with specks of gold that danced and twinkled, especially when he smiled.

Auntie Zanne said he was ex-FBI, even suggesting he was a spy. He had thought that part funny. Either way, I didn't believe he was an agent, although he did seem to have a knack for showing up to help when I needed it. If he were FBI, it would seem to me that he would've shown some interest in the murder investigations and Auntie and I had conducted right under his nose. He hadn't. Never even offered help or much advice.

Still, even with him not being forthcoming about his personal life, and me unsure of his purpose in Roble, I wasn't sure how I felt about him. He was the man that was getting tangled up with my thoughts of Alex. A man I felt myself possibly being drawn to.

I was sure that couldn't be good.

"Why are you standing there?" I said peeking over atop of the bed from where I was perched on the floor.

"I just told you," he said, his eyes seemingly twinkling more than usual, "I came to make sure you weren't going to be late for your assignment."

"An assignment is what it is," I said with a groan. I grabbed my watch off the nightstand. 10:10. I was okay on time. I strapped it on and looked at Rhett. "Auntie Zanne just thinks I'm back here with nothing to do and on her beck and call."

"You are here with nothing to do," he said.

"I have things to do."

"Yeah. Right," he said and smiled. "You could get a job though, you know." He shrugged. "She couldn't pick on you if you're weren't here."

"I could say the same thing to you."

"This is my job."

"What? Delivering messages for Auntie Zanne?"

"Yep."

"So you've officially quit the FBI?" He had never admitted to me that he actually worked for the agency.

"You're always bringing that up?" he said.

"What?"

"Did I tell you I worked for the FBI?"

"You evidently told Auntie Zanne, and she has told everyone else." I raised an eyebrow. "You're wasting your FBI skills here."

"I'm here because of you," he said.

"You are not," I said, my heart unsuspectedly starting to flutter. "You're always trying to flirt with me. Can't you see it's not working?"

"I'm going to keep trying until it does."

"Is that what they teach during FBI training? Always get your man? Or in my case, woman."

He laughed. "Even a non-FBI trained person could see that I'm wearing you down."

"You wish."

"I'd show you," he said, raising his head like he was peeking over the bed, "but right now you are off task. Like I said, I'm here to remind you not to be late."

He changed the subject, but not my heart rate. I did believe he was wearing me down. But he was right, I had to get to the airport, and I wanted to get to Eugenia Elder's autopsy. I didn't have time to think about what he did to my blood pressure.

"If you'd leave so I could get dressed," I said, "I could get to what I need to do."

"You need any help?" he asked, a smirk on his face.

"No."

"I meant with what you need to do."

"Yeah. I'm sure that's what you meant. All I need is for you to go."

He grabbed the doorknob and started to pull the door shut. "You know you should probably keep this closed when you're getting dressed. It can be distracting for passersby."

"No one lives in this house but me and Auntie Zanne," I said. "Its other periodic occupants don't go roaming around."

Those darn eyes of his started twinkling even more. "They might," he said, "if they knew they'd find you."

Chapter Fifteen

I threw on my jeans and t-shirt, flew down the steps and went out the front door without stopping to speak to anyone. I didn't need any more distractions.

I didn't talk much when Miss Vivee and her crew piled into the car. I didn't know if they'd want to talk murder and I didn't want anyone influencing my conclusions when I did the autopsy. But murder wasn't on their minds. Logan spent the time explaining to me, with me throwing in some "ohs," and "okays," to her discourse, about what she was looking for on her dig.

I glanced more than a couple of times down at her sparkling ring. Each time it made me sigh.

On the way back to the medical facility where I had Eugenia waiting for me, I thought about what Rhett had said. The part about me finding a job. Not about him flirting with me.

It did take a lot of effort to keep my mind off that, though...

Much to my Auntie Zanne's chagrin, I turned down the medical examiner's job after Doc Westin, the tri-county ME, died. It had been not long after I arrived back in Roble, making my auntie think it was a sign.

Although I didn't take the job, I did have the opportunity to oversee the completion of the new medical examiner's facility. It had been started long before I got there, and even with serving the populous of three counties, it was going to be, in my eyes, just adequate. So I stepped in and helped them choose all the state-of-the-art bells and whistles to furnish it with. Then, after it was completed, I fell in love with it.

I'd only done three autopsies there, utilizing my skills each time a murder occurred in Roble. But, why not take it on as a full-time job? Then when it was time to do my sleuthing (God forbid murdered bodies kept popping up), I wouldn't feel so bad with my newly formed obsession.

I pulled up in the parking lot and saw that Catfish was already there. His beat-up truck parked right by the door, him standing outside of it waiting for me. I had called him on the way back from the airport, just to make sure Miss Eugenia had arrived okay and there hadn't been any hiccups. A childhood friend he had turned into my right-hand man when I performed autopsies.

Auntie had told me that I didn't have any friends. She must have forgotten about Catfish.

"Hey, you," I said and smiled.

"Romie!" he said, a smile spreading on his face. He was always happy to see me.

"You didn't have to come," I said.

"I wanted to make sure you got in okay. It's getting kind of late in the day."

I looked up at the bright blue sky, sun shining in the sky. Catfish woke up with the chickens. Late for him was any time after ten a.m. "Looks like it'll be a while before it gets dark," I said.

"Can't never be too sure," he said.

I had to chuckle. If there was one thing that was predictable, it was the setting of the sun.

"Glad you're here," I said. "You gonna come in?" I pointed to the glass doors of the facility.

"Sure thing," he said grinning.

I knew that Catfish had a thing for me, and I loved him more than I cared to admit but my feelings for him were more like for a brother than a lover. I'd never express that out loud. I wouldn't have

He'd been my protector since the day I arrived in Roble—seeing after the pretentious black girl who spoke French. He even took up the language when we got to high school, but by then, I'd given up speaking it anywhere other than at home with Auntie Zanne.

"So sorry to hear about Miss Eugenia," Catfish said as he followed me down the hallway to the office.

"Me too," I said. "Miss Vivee said she was murdered."

"Aww. No," he said and shook his head. "How did she know? She was here?"

"You remember Miss Vivee?" I asked.

"Of course I do," he said. "Weren't a lot of people around here back then that had a black son-in-law."

"Guess that's right." I nodded. "She came for the Boule."

"She had a dog named Cat," Catfish said still reminiscing.

"Still does, I'm told. I think she must name all her dogs Cat. No way one could live that long."

"She lived that long," Catfish said.

"Yep. Sure did."

"Good. I liked her," he said. "She knew more about plants than anybody I'd ever met. Even Babet. I remember once she just looked at me and knew exactly what was wrong with me. Gave me a plant to make some tea."

"She did?"

"Yep, she did."

"And was something wrong?"

"Yeah, it was. I had a rash." He pointed to his arm. "Scared my little young self to the point of crying."

"You cried?"

"Sure did." He shook his head. "I never told anybody about that."

"Miss Vivee fixed you?"

"Yep, whatever she gave me cured it right up."

"Why wouldn't you tell somebody about a rash? What's the big deal?"

"I had just kissed Louise Higgins. You remember her?"

I laughed. "Yes. I remember her."

"Yeah, and I thought I might have caught it from doing that."

"A rash from kissing a girl? And on your arm? Why would it be there?"

"I don't know. I was too scared to be rational. It was my first kiss. I did it then I got a rash." He chuckled. "I didn't know any better, I guess."

I punched him in the chest. "I thought I was your first kiss."

"You were my first peck," he said backing up. "She was the first kiss." He blushed like I was embarrassing him. He was the one who'd brought it up.

"Well, I hope you've learned you can't get a rash from kissing."

"Guess I have. Probably wouldn't have ever thought that if it had of been you I kissed." He gave a single nod of his head. "But I know if I do, I can just get some of that tea Miss Vivee brewed up for me."

"I wouldn't drink anything those women cooked up."

"It's just natural ingredients. Natural healing medicine," he said. "I'd think you'd be for all of that."

"I'm not in to healing too much," I said. "All the patients I see are way past that."

"Yeah." He chuckled. "I guess they are," he said.

We walked into the medical examiner's office and I sat at the desk.

"You going to perform the autopsy now?" he asked.

"Yeah, I am," I said, and fired up my computer. "But she might have been exposed to some kind of chemical that may still be present once I open her up." I pointed at the screen. "I thought I'd better look up what kind of extra precautions I need to adhere to."

"You want me to wait around and help?"

I smiled at him. "I'm good. Unless you want to stay."

"I always want to be around you, Romie." His grin grew wider and he tucked his head. "But I was thinking I'd go out to catch some crawfish in a bit. I thought maybe," he wiggled his head back and forth, a blush coming on his face, "I could get a certain someone to come over and use it to make me some étouffée."

"And who is that certain someone? Louise Higgins?"

"Haha!" He bent over with laughter, his eyes lit up, and he shook his head at me. "I'm still afraid of her kisses," he said once his laughing subsided.

"Well, I might come over and cook, but there won't be any kissing."

"Alright then," he said. "I'll take that."

"Okay, then," I said. "It's a date."

He nodded. "I'ma take my leave then."

"Alright," I said. He walked toward the door. "Catfish," I said before he could get away.

"Yeah?"

"Wait for me to come to catch the crawfish."

"Yeah?"

"It'll be fun," I said.

"Sure will," he said. "But what I'm supposed to do in the meantime? You're gonna be here for a while."

"Clean up that kitchen," I said. "I know it's too messy for me to cook in."

That made him laugh almost as hard as me asking was he having Louise Higgins over.

Chapter Sixteen

Once Catfish left, I found the website for the CDC. I needed information on handling a decedent exposed to deadly chemicals. I was sure whatever measures they prescribed I had it in the facility. I had the place well stocked with all the essentials when it first opened. And I'd have to be sure to tell Auntie all I found too. Didn't want her exposing herself to anything during the embalming.

I found that my usual precautions were adequate, still I didn't want to take anything for granted. I grabbed a poly laminated protective gown from the cabinet. I pushed my hands through the elastic cuffs and tied it at the neck and waist. The gown had a repellent surface, keeping me dry and stain-free. Then to be safe, I put on a second one. Then I slipped boot covers on, got a full-face splash shield that fastened with adjustable Velcro straps and for my hands, two pair of Nitrile gloves.

I got Miss Eugenia from the cooler, rolled her to a station and took the sheet off of her. Pulling down the mic and setting out all of my instruments, situating them close at hand, I started to recite my preliminary information when I heard a commotion at the door.

"What the heck," I said. I went out of the room, down the hallway and peeked around the corner into the main lobby. I felt like the woman on the television show *Romper Room* looking through my magic mirror—surely this couldn't be happening. I could see Auntie and Mark and Leonard and Nola and Avoyelles and Delphine.

Delphine? *Romper, stomper, bomper boo!*

An entourage of Voodoo herbalists had entered the building. One quite possibly a murderess. What in the world did they want?

"Oh my goodness," I huffed and marched over to the horde of herbalists.

"Hi Romaine," they all said in some form or fashion, waving, smiling at me. Happy to be there.

I said, "Hello," nodded and smiled politely before I jerked Auntie Zanne by her hand and dragged her behind me to a corner.

"What is wrong with you?" she asked, a frown on her face. She pulled her arm from my grasp.

"I'm wondering the same thing about you," I said in a strained whisper. "Why are you here with all of these people?" I flung an arm toward the intruding interlopers.

"We came to help with the autopsy," she said.

"To do what?" I shrieked, it seemed I was no longer able to keep my voice low.

"Well, not really help," she said by way of a correction. "I know you're quite capable of doing that." She waved her hand in the air. "We just came more to oversee."

"Oversee? Me?" I yelped.

"Okay, maybe that wasn't the right word."

I turned and looked at the overseers. The only ones who came crashing the autopsy that I knew more than in passing was my auntie and the twins, Mark and Leonard.

Mark and Leonard Wilson were in their seventies and identical in every way, even down to their wrinkles. Technically spinsters, the sisters were kind and devoted to each other. They'd changed their names after their father passed away when they were seventeen, taking on his first and middle names as their own. They lived next door to us, and I couldn't remember a single time when I saw one without the other.

Delphine I'd only met because I needed to get information from her about a murder—certainly not a way to glean a good first impression. Now, I was considering her as the culprit.

And other than knowing Nola Landry from the Boule and

Avoyelles Kalty from our house earlier, I knew nothing about them. And while I wasn't going to have final autopsy results for Miss Eugenia right away, those kinds of reports were not public records.

"Auntie, you can't be here," I said. "How in the world did you all get here anyway?" I pictured a caravan of cars each being driven by an old woman—two hands on the wheel, eyes straight ahead, oblivious to everything else on the road. Mark and Leonard both probably trying to drive the car.

How much road rage and blaring of horns had they incited on the twenty-minute ride over?

"We came in Avoyelles' car."

"All of you?"

"Yes."

"In one car?" That was hard to believe.

"It's a big car."

"Oh my," I said and shut my eyes. Were they on each other's laps?

"It's a 1970 Buick Electric 225," Auntie Zanne said in answer to my unspoken question. "White. Beautiful. Still looks new," she continued. "We called it a deuce and a quarter back in the day." She spoke in a conversational tone like I had asked her to dump all this information on me. "The gear shift is behind the wheel. They didn't make it in the floor back then unless the car was a stick. So three in the front, three in the back. Plenty of room—"

"Auntie!" I said.

"What?" she stopped her explanation and looked at me.

"What are you doing?"

"Explaining how we all got here in one car."

"What are you *doing* here?

"Oh," she stopped and looked up at me. "I've already explained that."

"Ugh!" I blew out a breath. "Well explain this to me. Why would you bring Delphine? Because if it is murder, don't we think it's her who did it?"

"That's why I brought her," she said nodding her head. A sly smile curling up her lips. "I wanted to see if we can't trip her up. Catch her in a lie. Well, more lies." She was wiggling her head around like she was wrapping up the investigation in a neat little bow with her clever plan. "We can get proof that will show she's the culprit. Maybe even get a confession from her."

"We?"

"Me. You. The girls."

I assumed "the girls" were the senior citizen light brigade that was standing in the lobby. Minus Delphine of course.

"I don't think this is a good idea," I said.

"Pshaw," she said and dismissed me with a wave. "It's a brilliant idea. We'll get information, put our heads together on the clues and ferret out the killer all in one fell swoop."

"Auntie—"

"But if we don't start at the beginning—clue one—we won't be able to effectively do our job. That's why we're here."

"It's not your job. Or the job of your 'girls.' It's Pogue's job."

This time she sucked her teeth with the dismissive wave. "It'll be fine," she said. "We won't get in your way. I helped you last time. I was there when you did the autopsy. Don't you remember?"

"I remember."

"And everything was fine. I was very helpful."

"That's not what I remember."

"We'll be quiet."

"You'll leave. That's what you'll do." I pointed toward the door. "Back the way you came in. I don't want you here."

"What will I tell the girls?"

"That I don't want them here either." I gave her a look that said I meant business. "I'll let you know what I find when I get back to the house." I started walking back to the autopsy room. I got halfway down the hallway and turned around. She was still standing where I'd left her. "Bye," I said and threw up a wave.

She mimicked my gesture.

I went into the autopsy room, determined not to look back. I took in a shaky breath. Not used to telling the woman who raised me what to do. But I knew if I hadn't put my foot down, she and her crew would have come piling into my autopsy room.

"Eugenia Elder," I said speaking into the microphone after I calmed my nerves. "Eighty-year-old female. Caucasian. 124 lbs. All tattoos, scars and identifying marks will be documented photographically...

"Oh my God, she's naked! Eugenia's naked!"

I turned to see those six merry marauders, despite my warning to their leader, standing in the doorway, smiling. All except Delphine, evidently unaware decedents didn't wear clothes during an autopsy. She was bug-eyed, pointing to her exposed friend, her mouth wide open in disbelief.

Chapter Seventeen

It took me five hours to do a two-hour autopsy due to all my "help."

They giggled and fumbled their way into the protective gear—putting gowns on backwards, shields on upside down, Nola Landry spilling hand sanitizer everywhere. I had to stop the initial incision three times because it was "jarring." Their words. I offered them an out several times, but of course each time they declined.

"Just give us a minute." They all agreed that was all the time they needed to collect themselves and to see their good friend autopsied. Auntie laughed at them, she was used to doing procedures on the dead.

I just huffed my way through getting them acclimated. Then they had me to explain everything I did, my recording was going to be sorely littered with their voices—all their exclamations and squeals—forever preserved. On the record. And then, as I recited my conclusions into the mic in medical-*ese*, they all wanted me to tell them what it all meant.

I didn't do that.

I did, in the course of my work, give them a mini lesson on the anatomy. But that's all they got. I couldn't give information out willy-nilly on a murder investigation.

Yep. Murder investigation. That was what it was. Eugenia Elder did die from a myocardial infarction—a heart attack in layman's terms, but it was only secondary to the poisoning which had been easy for me to see with just a cursory look inside.

And that was exactly what I told Pogue when I finally finished and had shooed those pesky peepers out of my examination room.

"I have to send the samples off, but Miss Vivee was right," I told him.

"Murder?"

"Murder," I said.

"Goddarn it!" he said. "When is this going to stop?"

"I don't know," I said. "I don't know why it started."

"What is wrong with people? Killing other folks. And in these diabolical ways." I heard him suck his tongue. "What happened to our peaceful little Roble?"

"I guess that it's finally catching up with the rest of the world."

"Is this what's going on in the rest of the world?"

"Pretty much," I said.

"Wow. I guess that's why I stayed here and didn't venture out too far. So did you see what Miss Vivee saw?"

"If you mean could I have called it before the autopsy, I would have to say no," I said, wondering how in the world Miss Vivee and Mac did it. "I did notice the greenish tinge to her skin, but I don't think I would have known what that meant. I surely wouldn't have thought she'd been poisoned by hydrofluoric acid."

"Well, it's a good thing they gave you a heads up. We might not have gotten the autopsy done and found out what really happened."

"I agree," I said. "It's not official though, not until I get everything back, but I'm calling it homicide. I'm releasing her body to the Ball Funeral Home and Crematorium."

"Babet?"

"Yes. Our funeral home. Even though we got that information from part of a letter, I think it was what Miss Eugenia wanted," I said. "It's what Delphine wants and she's the one in charge of the money."

I heard him suck in a breath. "Okay," he said. "That'll be okay, I guess. Mr. Elder might have other ideas. I think first thing I need to do is see the other page to that letter Delphine Griffith had. Hiding things is always some admission of guilt about something."

"Good idea," I said, and didn't mention Delphine was cleaning up in the bathroom right down the hall from where I sat.

"Alright. Get back to me once you get the results back."

"Will do," I said.

"And Romaine..."

"Yeah?"

"No snooping," he said. "If someone comes to you or Babet with some information, talk to them and let me know what they said. But don't go out seeking any."

"Gotcha," I said.

"Thanks, Cousin," he said in a softer tone. The one I was used to hearing from him. "I couldn't have gotten through all of these without you."

"No problem. That's what family is for."

Chapter Eighteen

"This is not what family is for," I said to Auntie Zanne. She had insisted that she get in the car with me instead of going back home the way she came. I had other plans and she was getting in the way.

"I have to stop at Eugenia's and get her things for burial," she said. "I can't ask them all to go and do that with me."

"Why not? You had no problem inviting them in on your hostile takeover...your...heist...or whatever it was of the medical examiner's facility." I couldn't even find the words I wanted to use to describe her actions.

"Did you find anything that pointed to Delphine as the murderer?" she asked.

"Is that why you wanted to ride with me?" I asked. "You didn't get anything from the autopsy, so you figured you'd question me now?"

"You were using all those big words."

"It's medical terminology."

"Doesn't help me to understand it one bit. I need it in regular English."

"I didn't find anything that pointed to Delphine necessarily," I said.

"There you go again," she said. "What's with the 'necessarily'?"

"It means that I don't know that she did it from what I found," I said. "Pogue will have to follow the clues."

"I don't think she did it," she said and locking her eyes on me. I would have stared back but I needed to keep my eyes on the road.

"You said at the medical facility that's why you brought her with you. So you could snake her out, catch her."

"I changed my mind."

"You can't decide who did it," I said, not wanting to know her reasons for a change of heart. "You have a knack for that, you know?"

"I do not," she said and scrunched her nose at me.

"You have to follow the clues," I said.

"You always say that. And I am following them," she said, "and the clues tell me that Delphine didn't do it."

"Are you getting these clues from some kind of 'hocus pocus' source?" I asked.

"No. It's Delphine. She's a healer, this wouldn't be like her. Not in her realm," Auntie said. "It's not the kind of herbalist she is."

"Are there those kinds of herbalists?" I asked. "The kind that have killing in their *realm*? Whatever that means."

"Sure there are. It's what they're known for. It's easy to tell their handiwork. People come to them or fear them because of it," she said. "But doing harm? No, that's just not Delphine's style. She helps people. She teaches those classes at her house."

"The herbology classes?" It was more of a statement than a question. I remembered Delphine telling me about how she taught a steady stream of students that flowed into her home.

"Yes," Auntie said. "She's into natural remedies. She's into healing."

"She had the ricin that killed Bumper," I reminded her.

"If you'd take the time to remember the story correctly," Auntie Zanne said, "instead of giving it your own spin, you'd know she used it as a natural remedy."

"For cancer." I nodded my head toward her. "I remember."

"One murderer in the family does not make a family of murderers," Auntie Zanne said.

"She did lie about the letter."

"No she didn't," Auntie Zanne said. "She never said it was or was not another part to it. She only shared the one part with us."

"That's an omission."

"Oh please," Auntie Zanne said.

"And what about the insurance money?" I asked.

"I was thinking," Auntie Zanne said, completely ignoring my question, "we shouldn't count Orville out."

"Oh you think he's capable?"

"I do."

"What reason would he have for wanting his wife dead?"

"You mean other than him lying about the arrangements Eugenia wanted. Him trying to cremate her to get rid of the evidence? And him being the last one to see her alive?" She raised one eyebrow. "Other than those things?"

"Those are reasons for us to consider him a suspect," I said. "But none of those things tell us the *reason* he would have done it."

"Money," she said. "You heard Delphine same as I did. He was all about the money."

"Seems to me, he had more access to her money when she was alive." I mimicked her expression and raised an eyebrow of my own.

"He was the last person to see her," she said.

"You already said that, and we don't know that for sure. He said he didn't come home until this morning. She was already dead by then."

"We do know for sure," Auntie Zanne said, "that the deed was done at the dinner. That part is certain. But we don't know that he wasn't responsible for what happened at the dinner or, maybe, that he did something once she got home."

"Did something? Like what?" I asked. "It had already been spilled on her."

"Maybe he put more on her." Auntie Zanne said holding her hand out and shaking her hand, indicating there was a multitude of things he could have done. "Maybe," she continued, "he wouldn't let her get undressed until it was all soaked into her skin to his satisfaction. Maybe," she clung onto the word, "when she got sick, he held her down and wouldn't let her call for help."

"Auntie—"

"You don't know," she said. "It's possible. You didn't see her. Lying there. Posed. Looked like she'd been placed in a casket by a skilled mortician. Who dies like that?"

"Maybe he put her like that because...he...loved her." I could barely get the words out of my mouth. He certainly hadn't appeared to be the loving, caring type when he showed up at the funeral home. Still, people love and grieve in different ways.

"You know what time she died?" Auntie asked.

"Approximately. She'd already been put in the cooler at the hospital morgue when I got her. No temperature taken beforehand." I looked at Auntie. "Why? What do you know about his whereabouts last night?"

"Nothing. Yet." Her eyes looked forward, but I could see the firm nod she gave. It meant that she was going to find out.

"Don't go trying to force him into a confession," I said. "Follow the clues."

"He knows something." Her thoughts were miles away from my warning. "Did you see him practically go into convulsions when we mentioned an autopsy?" She turned to me.

"No," I said.

"*Tsk*," she sucked her teeth. "Yes you did," she said. "We've got to investigate." She rocked her head back and forth. "Maybe the both of them. Orville and Delphine. So we don't look biased."

Now she wanted to carry on a fake investigation side-by-side with the real one. I had to chuckle, anyone could see who her pick as the murderer was. The only thing I could do was try to stop her from going too far, although that was almost an impossible task.

"Pogue said—" I started to say.

"For me not to go poking my nose in anything," she finished my sentence. "I already know that. But you can't expect me to sit idly by with my dear friend, Eugenia, murdered and another friend and Eugenia's husband as the murder suspects. I'm too far in."

"You're not *in* at all, Auntie Zanne."

"I can't do it," she said, shaking her head so vigorously I

thought she'd rattle her brains. "I have to do something."

"Pogue expects you to not do anything."

"I don't know how many times or how many ways I'll have to tell you that Pogue ain't got the sense God gave a watermelon. He can't solve a murder. He needs me whether he knows it or not."

"Watermelons don't have any sense," I said. "They don't have a brain."

"Exactly," she said and lifted her eyebrows. "And I wouldn't have to go around asking a whole bunch of questions," she continued, "if you would share with me—in English—what you found at the autopsy." She swiped her hand across her forehead. "So now I have to ask questions to put the pieces together."

There wasn't anything I could say about Pogue to make her change her mind. She'd thought something was wrong with Pogue's head from the time he was born.

What the heck. I always ended up sharing what I knew with Auntie anyway, I had even told her when I tried to get her to leave that I'd tell her what I found when we got home. I had to share. I knew that. I did it to both keep her from harassing—what she called "interrogating" people—and to keep her from going down the wrong road when it came to the right suspect. Which she did often.

"So," I said, trying to slow her impending inquest, "I didn't see anything in the autopsy that gave me any kind of clue about who did it." I nodded and glanced at her, wanting for her to not go off the deep end. "All I know now is that she was poisoned. And from what I learned this morning about hydrofluoric acid, that's probably what did it."

"Now was that so hard to tell me?" she asked. "Plain English is always best."

"No. But you shouldn't have hijacked the medical examiner's office and have me drive you to do errands to prod me for information. I can't give out autopsy results to just anybody. I said. "We live in the same house. You could have just asked me later."

"You don't have anything else to do," she said. "Why should you mind helping me see to my friend? Or helping all of us do that?"

That made me pause. Not the part about seeing to their friend. The rest of what she'd said was the part that cut. It wasn't too long ago that she'd told me that I didn't have any friends. And evidently, she had a slew of them. Now, added to that, it was I didn't have anything to do. Just what Rhett had said to me earlier.

I guess I really did need to get a life.

"I do have something to do," I said defensively.

"What?"

"I'm going over Catfish's. We're catching crawfish, drinking beer and making étouffée."

"Does Rhett know you're going over there for a date?" she said, an eyebrow arched.

"Rhett?" I glanced over at her. "Why would I tell Rhett that I'm going over Catfish's house?" I shook my head. "And it's not a date."

"I thought you and Rhett were an item," she said.

"No you didn't," I said. There was no reason for her to think that. At least I hoped I hadn't outwardly shown what I'd been internally thinking about that man. "Now you're just fishing."

"Just trying to keep up with you," she said. "You lose your job up north, come home and then you just do... nothing." She looked over at me, it seemed it was concern that was emanating from her brown eyes. "I just want to know what's going on with you."

"I'm fine," I said.

"You heard from Alex?"

"Fishing." I looked at her and put on a fake smile. Then I put my eyes back on the road and chewed on my bottom lip. I couldn't even believe what I was about to say.

"I do have something to do, Auntie," I said in earnest. "I've decided to be the medical examiner for Sabine, Shelby and St. Augustine counties."

"What?" She reached over, took ahold of my arm and jerked it so hard that I almost lost control of the car. "You're going to be the tri-county medical examiner?" She shook my arm with each word.

"Whoa!" I said. "You're gonna make me have an accident."

"When did you decide that?" She turned my arm loose and rocked back in her seat, a big smile across her face. "When do you start?" Excitement in her voice. "I'll pack you a lunch every day and a thermos of tea. Maybe I can come help out sometime. You know when I'm not busy." She slapped her hand against her forehead. "What am I saying, I'm always busy." She grabbed my arm again. "How much are they going to pay you?"

I laughed and rubbed my arm. She had had a firm grip. She was more excited than I was about my revelation. "You're awfully nosey," I told her.

"I'm going to need you to pay rent, just wondering what would be fair."

"The house is paid for," I said. "Why do you need rent from me?"

"I can't just let people stay in my house free of charge. It'll make people think I'm running a flophouse."

"It's my home, Auntie." I shook my head. "And I can't answer any of those questions now, anyway," I said, "because I don't know."

"They didn't tell you?"

"I didn't tell them. Not yet, anyway, that I'd take the job."

"Oh my goodness!" she said. She grabbed my purse and dug down in it.

"Get out of my purse!" I said.

"I need your phone," she said still digging. "*You* need your phone. You need to call them now."

"No I don't." I put my hand down on my purse so she couldn't rummage through it.

"Yes you do," she said in a huff. "How do you know they even still want you?"

I hadn't thought about that. Guess it was kind of arrogant for me to think they'd just wait for me to make up my mind. Especially since whenever I got the chance, I told everyone how much I hated being home and couldn't wait to get back to Chicago.

But then it hit me. Auntie reading me my life. Me happy about the autopsy although I could hardly get through it with all the cackling from the girls going on. Spending time with family—even if it was on a murder investigation.

Pogue, Aunt Julep and Auntie Zanne were the only family I had, and I had missed them. I needed them. And with Alex being divorced and me discovering that maybe I didn't care as much as I thought I would...It had all been a catalyst, I guess, to making up my mind.

Just like that. Just in that moment I decided. And I felt good about my decision.

I pulled my arm away from my purse and put my hand back on the steering wheel. No, I decided, putting a smile on my face, I felt *really* good about my decision.

I looked at Auntie holding my purse, poised ready to assault it so she could search for my cellphone if I gave the word.

I shook my head. "I can't call Auntie, it's Saturday. I'll call them Monday."

"You should call now."

"No one is there."

"You can leave a message."

"No time," I said. "We're almost here," I pointed out the window. "We'll be pulling up at Miss Eugenia's house any second."

She looked out the window as I turned the corner onto Maple Grove where the Elders' house set mid-block.

"Oh good," she said, lifting herself up and squinting her eyes to get a better look. "They're there."

As I got closer to the house, I saw who the "they" were. There was a big car sitting in the driveway that I knew didn't belong to the Elders. I knew because it hadn't been there this morning.

It was a gleaming white, Buick Electric 225.

A deuce and a quarter according to my Auntie Zanne. And I knew I had been duped.

"I thought you said you needed me to bring you because they couldn't?" I said. I could see her partners in crime mingling around boxes that sat in front of the Elder home.

"Did I say that?" Auntie Zanne said, a confused look on her face. "I don't think those were my exact words."

"You know," I said, "if we are identifying killers based on their omissions and lies, you would be the number one suspect."

Chapter Nineteen

Auntie waved off my assessment and had the car door open before I even came to a complete stop.

"Hey!" she said waving an arm. She hopped out the car and walked with purpose over to her buddies. They all stood conversing around boxes and bags that were on the tree lawn. All except Nola and Avoyelles.

Nola stood several feet back, reaching into the purse she carried, she pulled out hand sanitizer. She joined in the conversation, but not the search. She was dressed for afternoon tea with a Queen, so probably, with no protective covering like there had been at the autopsy, she was above going through trash.

Avoyelles was sitting in the car. Door opened, legs swinging out of it. She seemed out of breath. Sweat running down her face. Probably the heat, but it might've been she just didn't want to look, either. For that I couldn't blame either one of them.

Before I could park and get out of the car to talk to Auntie about dragging me there under false pretenses, another car came rolling down the street. A black sedan moving at a snail's pace obviously observing Auntie and her girls. I watched as it pulled up, taking everyone's attention away from the pile up of trash, and stopped in front of the house. Auntie walked up to the car.

That's when I got out of the car. Auntie acted as if she'd never heard of the term "stranger danger." She was always being friendly to strangers, offering her help and her home to them. I'd always been afraid someone might snatch her up.

"What are you doing, Auntie?" I called out walking toward her.

"Hi, Romaine," Leonard said, as if I hadn't just seen her at the medical facility.

"Hi, Romaine," Mark said, mimicking her twin.

"You remember Hailey, don't you?" Auntie Zanne said, reaching her hand out gesturing for me to come to her.

I took in a deep breath. "Yes, I remember her." I lowered my head and looked into the window of the car. I threw on a fake smile for good measure.

She was an FBI friend of Rhett's. A close friend from what I remembered. Her hair pulled back, she had on a button up shirt, a blazer and dark aviator sunglasses. Trying to look the part, I guessed.

"What are you ladies doing here?" she asked.

"Came over to get a dress to bury my friend in and found all her things out here."

Hailey surveyed the landscape looking over the top of her sunglasses. "You talking about Eugenia Elder?" she asked.

"Yes," Auntie Zanne said. "You know her?"

"No. Afraid not." She pursed her lips and gave a nod. "You seen Orville?" she asked.

"No," Auntie said. "Not since this morning."

"Okay, well you ladies take care," she said, rolling up the window. "Good seeing you again."

"Well. Where did she come from?" Auntie said as she turned and walked back to the sidewalk. "Haven't seen her in a long time. Didn't know she was back around."

"Me either," I said.

"Don't you worry about her," Auntie said and started looking through one of the boxes on the curb.

"Auntie," I said and pulled her a few feet away. "I thought you were going into the house to find that rose-colored dress."

"These are Eugenia's things out here."

"And?" I said.

"And? What do you mean 'and?' I can't believe this," Delphine said, she had tears in her eyes. I took it that she overheard me even with me trying to be discreet. "She hasn't been dead a whole day and he's throwing her things away. She never treated her things like this. She took good care of them."

"I'm sure she did," I said. "I didn't mean anything by it."

"She was very particular," Delphine continued. "Very meticulous with her clothes."

"I thought he said he had given them away," I said to Auntie. It seemed like a lot for Delphine to digest.

I looked at the boxes. They opened the lid on several of them and it was clear to see they were filled with a woman's belongings thrown in haphazardly.

"He said?" Delphine said. "You saw him?" Her face was red, her beak-like nose snotty, and her words making bubbles as each one came out of her mouth.

"He came over to the funeral parlor this morning," Auntie Zanne gave the answer, her voice gentle. She reached in her purse and pulled out a tissue. "To make arrangements."

"He doesn't know what she wanted," Delphine said, dabbing her eyes.

"Don't worry none about that," Auntie said. "Romaine released the body to me. I'll make sure that letter you have is followed to a T."

Delphine sniffed back her tears and ran a sleeve over her nose. "You will?"

"Of course I will," she said. "And Avoyelles is coming to do her hair."

That made Delphine smile. "Eugenia would have liked that."

"So let's see which one of these boxes has that dress in it."

It was rare seeing Auntie Zanne so loving and caring. She usually just bullied and pushed people into doing what she wanted.

With her in that mood, I knew I wasn't going to be able to stop them from going through the boxes or rush them along. And I was going to have to wait because I was Auntie's ride home. I decided to see about Avoyelles.

"Are you okay?" I said as I walked across the grass toward her.

"I'm fine," she said, rubbing her fingertips into her chest. "It's the heat, I think."

"You feeling a tightness in your chest or dizziness?" I asked. Didn't want her having a heart attack on me.

"Not really," she said. "Just hot."

"Would you like me to get you some water?" I asked and pointed toward the house. Most people around Roble didn't lock their doors.

"No. Thank you," she smiled. "I just didn't take my medicine is all."

"You take medicine?" I asked.

"Yes. Got a couple things wrong with me." She looked at me. "Why do you seem surprised?"

"Because you're a Voodoo herbalist," I said. "I thought you guys were all natural."

She chuckled. "Little extra never hurt anybody."

"I guess not," I said.

"Maybe if Eugenia had seen a doctor, she'd still be around."

I leaned my head to the side and looked at her. Was she still not believing that Miss Eugenia had been murdered? I wanted to say it was the spill that did her in. I hadn't said out loud the manner of death during the autopsy, but it was written clearly in my report.

Then I thought about that spill, and my heart leapt into my throat. Miss Eugenia's canary yellow pantsuit. It was covered in hydrofluoric acid.

I jerked my head around and looked at the pilfers. If they laid a hand on Miss Eugenia's pantsuit—it wouldn't be good for them.

"I'll be right back," I said over my shoulder, and took off trotting back toward the tree lawn bandits. And that's when the car I did recognize pulled up in the driveway. It was a Buick, too. A much later model, not one that had gone extinct.

Orville Elder, the driver of said vehicle, didn't seem too happy about the people in his yard. I could see the steam coming from his anger fogging up his car windows.

His shiny dark green Lacrosse matched the shininess I noticed on him earlier perfectly. We all gathered on the lawn. Even Avoyelles and Nola.

"What are you doing here?" Orville shouted. He scooted out of the car pointing a finger, at whom I couldn't tell.

"Why are Eugenia's things out here in the trash?" Delphine said, her sadness switching over to anger. "You couldn't wait to get rid of her or her things, could you? Already spending her money."

"What are you talking about?" he said, his anger matching hers. His eyes had narrowed and looked on fire. "I want you people to get out of here, and you," he did the errant pointing thing again, now the finger wagging bac and forth. "Move that piece of junk out of my driveway."

He pointed his finger at Avoyelles.

"I am not the one to mess with," Avoyelles said. "Watch how you talk to me."

"I'll say just what I want at my house." He was wiggling his finger, but not coming any closer. "And you'll do good not to get me any more riled up than I already am!"

"Hold on," Auntie Zanne put her hands up. She walked over and stood next to Delphine. "We came to get the clothes for the burial and saw these things out here. It just shocked us, that's all."

"I don't know why," Orville said. "I told you this morning that all that stuff—her things," he corrected himself and flung an arm at the tree lawn, "were just upsetting to me."

"I didn't think you meant putting them out here," Auntie Zanne said.

Delphine had been inching her way over toward Orville every time she'd say something back to him. She'd gotten as far as the middle of the grass. "You don't even care that she's dead." She was back to crying. "You're probably the reason she is."

"You are a crazy woman!" he said. "All of you are. I want all of you off my property, now!" He stomped a foot.

"This is Eugenia's property," Delphine said and took a step closer to him. "And you better watch those shoes."

He looked down at his shoes, and then shook his whole body as if he realized he might have messed them up with his antics. He bent down and brushed them off with a handkerchief he pulled from his jacket pocket. "This house is mine now," he said standing back up, "and I don't have to tolerate the likes of you people anymore." He slung another accusatory finger. "I know you're the ones up to something. Not me!" He turned that finger around and jabbed it into his chest.

Then Delphine took off running. Not very fast, she was after all probably close to eighty. So it was more like her shoulders and arms hunched and swung back and forth intimating that the rest of her body was in a full dash across the lawn. But her feet were barely moving. Shuffling along, they didn't no way near match the speed of her arms.

It didn't take much for me to get in front of Delphine.

"Hold up there," I said, and stood in front of her. "What are you doing?"

"I'm going to take him down a peg or two!" She shook her little fist at him, reminding me of how she reacted when she discovered her nephew Boone had taken the ricin from her to kill Bumper.

With those words I had to look away so she wouldn't see the smile on my face. I didn't think she could muster enough force to bowl over a pyramid of apples.

Mr. Elder stuffed his handkerchief back down in his suit jacket pocket and scrambled back in the car, started it and rolled down the window. "I'll be back in in fifteen minutes. If you aren't all gone by then, I'm calling the sheriff."

"You should call them on yourself!" Delphine said, she leaned to the side so she could see around me. "This is all your fault!"

"Wait," I said and held up an arm. I walked over to his window and leaned in. "Where are the clothes Eugenia wore last night?"

"What?" he said, a frown on his face.

"She had on a yellow pantsuit at the Boule dinner last night. She spilled something on it," I said. "Do you know what she did with it?"

"How would I know? I told you I wasn't here when she got home. She left me a note to take out the trash because she was going to bed. That's all I know about last night."

"Where is that trash bag?" I asked.

"In the trash. Where else?" He pointed toward the back of the house. "No get out of my way!"

He jerked the car into gear, the wrong way at first, almost running into the back of Avoyelles car. "Move that piece of junk!" he called out at the same time he threw the car into reverse, his tires squealing as he tried to get out of the driveway. I had to chuckle at his quick getaway, he nearly hit a car parked across the street.

"Do you see that?" Delphine said. "He's spending the insurance money already. Probably not even saving one cent for the funeral."

Auntie and I looked at each other. As far as we knew, he didn't have any insurance money those funds belonged to her.

"Why do you say that?" Auntie said.

"Didn't you see those new shoes?" she asked.

"New shoes?" I asked and turned to look toward the car as if I could see them then.

"Bottom of them clean as a whistle. I saw them when he was getting out of the car," she said.

That was something I wouldn't have ever noticed, but she evidently had her reasons to take note.

Delphine nodded her head. "Eugenia told me she always knew when he'd come up on some money. That was his tell, he'd buy new shoes." She looked down the street where he driven down. "That and go down to Naskila."

"Naskila Gaming down in Livingston?" Auntie Zanne asked.

"Yep. That's the one. She said when he really had come into big bucks, he'd gamble all up and down I-20. That always prompted her to check her bank account."

"What? Where'd he get money from?" Nola Landry had walked over to us. The first one of the crew to move or say anything after

Orville's outburst. The others seemed frozen in place.

"He'd steal it from Eugenia," Delphine said, her voice loud.

"You don't know that," Avoyelles said. She'd walked toward her car. "But whatever he's going to do, and wherever he got the money to do it, isn't our concern."

"Yes. I think we should go," Nola said.

"Why?" Delphine said. "He doesn't have any right to tell me what to do."

"He kind of does," Auntie Zanne said.

"Well, I'm not leaving all of Eugenia's things here," Delphine said.

"What are you going to do with them?" I asked.

"Take them with me."

"All of that is not going to fit into my car," Avoyelles said. "And I just had my nephew detail it."

"It's not like it's junk," Delphine squawked. "It's our friend's belongings."

"I understand that," Avoyelles said. "But it's enough of us in the car already. There's no room."

Auntie Zanne looked at me.

"No," I said, without her even asking the question. I held up my hand. "No way." I turned and looked at Delphine. "Why don't you go through it and take things that are special to you."

"Orville said he'll be back," Mark spoke her first words.

"In thirty minutes," Leonard said, finishing her twin's thought.

"We'd better hurry then," Auntie Zanne said. "C'mon, Delphine." She looped her arm through Delphine's. "You can only pick out one or two things. Keepsakes. I'll see if I can find that rose-colored dress she wanted." Auntie looked at Avoyelles. "Is that okay? We'll put it in the trunk."

Avoyelles closed her eyes momentarily, sucked in a breath and nodded her head. "Sure," she said. "You all go through it. Maybe take a box or two. That'll be okay. I can take it back to the hotel Delphine's staying at, but it's up to her to get it back to Shelby county."

"A box or two..." Delphine repeated and set her gaze on the front lawn.

"We'll help," Leonard said.

"We're happy to help you," Mark said

"We loved her too," they said together.

"I'm not touching any of it," Nola Landry said. She waved her hands and backed up even though she wasn't anywhere near the pile. "I'll stay over by the car with Avoyelles."

"Our real memory of her," Auntie Zanne said, unlooping her arm from Delphine's and wrapping it around her friend's shoulder, "is in our hearts. We'll always hold those good memories fast and close."

While they divvied up their friend's belonging, I went around the back. I found two metal trashcans lined up against the house. One was empty. The other had a black plastic bag in it. Even though it was a large 33-gallon bag, it wasn't anywhere near full. I was thinking it was Miss Eugenia's pantsuit she'd worn the night before.

The night she was murdered.

I called Pogue so he could come over and secure the evidence. I'd have to tag it and send it off for testing, but I wasn't prepared to deal with hazardous waste and I didn't know what else we might find in that bag.

Chapter Twenty

I finally made it to Catfish's. It was close to seven and I had been dealing with death all day. I couldn't wait to kick back and relax.

He was sitting on his front porch waiting for me. Two pails sitting at his feet. Probably the same ones we had used as kids. His green bucket hat pulled down, nearly covering his eyes, his head leaned on the back of the chair, his arms folded in his lap.

I wondered how long he'd been sitting there.

Catfish owned a large spread—house, a couple of barns—all pushed up against a creek that followed the property line in the pinelands not far from the Sabine River. He fished, hunted and farmed all by himself. He seemed content living his life away from all the hustle and bustle I had always seemed to crave.

"Nothing to do?" I asked as I walked up on the porch.

"Doing just what I like doing," he said.

"And what's that?"

"Waiting on you."

I smiled. "You need to find something else to do. No telling how long I'd make you wait. I had to deal with Auntie Zanne, and her plans never mesh with mine."

"She got you running around?"

"All the time," I said and sat next to him. The makeshift furniture was old and familiar. "But I had a little surprise for her today."

"Did you now?" he said, his eyes sparkling. He looked toward me a slight grin on his face. "I bet I can guess what that was." He pushed his hat up on his forehead.

"You'll never guess," I said.

"You decided to stay."

"What?" I said surprised. "How in the world did you guess that?"

"I know you, Romie." He gave me that smile, the one, it seemed, reserved for me. The one that made his hazel eyes and his caramel-colored skin light up.

"And what is it that you know?" I said, returning his contagious smile.

"That you're happy here."

I sucked my tongue. "No way you could've known that," I said. "I've been complaining since I've been here. How much I hate it."

"Not the way you used to complain about leaving," he said, and shook his head. "And I've never seen you hang out so much with Babet."

"She makes me!" I said, scooting up to the edge of my chair, holding out my hands. "I don't want to go and do all these things she wants me to do. But how can I tell her no?"

"Oh, I remember a younger version of you that didn't have so much of a problem doing that."

"My rebellious days," I said thoughtfully, I sat back in the chair. "*Disrespectful* rebellious days." I shook my head. "But she never let me get away with it. I'd have to dodge the big wallop she was aiming to give me over the head when I talked back, and I still had to do what she said."

"Reluctantly. You did it reluctantly. Now you do it willingly."

I smiled as I thought about what he said. It probably was true, even though I'd never admit it out loud. "I'm still reluctant," I told him.

"Sure you are," he said. "So what turned you around?"

"I don't know." I pulled in a breath and looked out past the gravel area he called a driveway and across the front of Catfish's property. "I always thought there was more out there. Living in a small town—I don't know, I just railed against it. I felt it just couldn't give me all the things I needed. You know?"

He nodded but didn't say anything.

"And I had hung on to that hope," I continued, "that all the things out there in the world—all the big and wonderful things could be mine if I was there with them."

"But now?" he said.

"I don't know."

"I think you do," he said.

"Things have just changed for me. People here..." I licked my lips and thought about how to put my feelings into words. "The people here love me, always cared about me and miss me. Still, I wanted to get back to Chicago where I'm not sure if I had even one true friend."

"What about Alex?" Catfish said.

"What about Alex..." My voice drifted off as I repeated his question. I didn't say anything for a long time. I couldn't. I didn't know what to say about Alex. I loved him, so I thought. So I *think*. But I was ready to get past that.

I looked over at Catfish, he sat waiting for my answer.

"When Auntie Zanne first met him," I finally said, "she said she didn't raise me to be the kind of person that dated a married man."

"You didn't know he was married."

"Yeah. That's true. But..."

"And he's not married now," Catfish said.

I took in a deep breath. I looked at Catfish. Into his eyes. "He'll be okay without me."

"Will you be okay without him?"

I chuckled. "You just said I'm doing good."

This time he chuckled. "Guess I did."

"So remember when I told you Miss Vivee just looked at Miss Eugenia and knew she'd been murdered?"

"Yeah."

"Yeah well I didn't tell you that she just looked at Miss Eugenia and knew *how* she was killed."

"Did you do that?" he asked.

"Just look at her and know what killed her?"

"Yeah."

"No. I had to do the autopsy."

"You know I would have stayed and kept you company," he said. He looked out at the sky. "'Cause now it looks like we're gonna be doing some night trapping for those crawfish."

"Auntie Zanne and about fifteen of her Voodoo sisters came to the medical facility and wanted to sit in on the autopsy with me. That's why I'm late getting here."

"Oh," he said. "Fifteen?"

"Okay, maybe it was only actually about five. Six including Auntie Zanne. But with all the confusion they caused me, it seemed like fifteen."

He laughed. "Guess that wasn't so good."

"I would say no."

"Okay. Go ahead you were telling me that because..."

"Because, I think that's one of the reasons I want to stay."

"Because of all of Babet's society ladies?"

"No," I closed my eyes and shook my head. "Because of the murders that have been happening. I know that's bad to say. But each one piqued my curiosity and excited me about my job in ways I'd never been before." I'm sure he could hear the passion in my voice. "I enjoyed solving the murders. Following the clues. Investigating." I sat on the edge of my seat and shifted toward Catfish. He must have seen in my eyes how I felt, because he turned to me and looked into my eyes, letting me know I had his full attention. "Actually," I continued, "I relished every clue I found and...I don't know...I like...eagerly...Yeah, eagerly anticipated the next one."

"And all those things are why you're staying?"

"Yes. And because I think...Finally..." I tilted my head, not having to give it too much thought. "And because I'm happy. I like it here. I'm liking my life."

"And then there's Rhett," Catfish said.

"So," I said and stood up, ignoring that comment. He was fishing just like Auntie Zanne had been. "Are we going out to catch crawfish? That setting sun ain't gonna wait for us."

Catfish laughed. "I see you are back home, bad English and all."

Chapter Twenty-One

I rolled up the pants leg on my jeans and took off my shoes and socks. Catfish had taught me a long time ago how to walk in the creek and catch crawfish.

And that's what we did until it got dark. We snagged buckets full of crawfish. We laughed. We reminisced. And Catfish had to catch me a few times as I slipped on the rocks. I felt like a young teenager all over again.

This time a happy one.

"I see you cleaned up," I said as I stepped through the back door, letting the screen slam shut behind me.

"You told me to."

"You always do what people tell you to do?" I said, knowing he didn't. One thing about Catfish, he was his own man. A loner—strong and independent.

"I always do what you tell me to do." He took the pail from my hand and put it in the sink. I pulled out a kitchen chair and plopped down, sliding into a comfortable position.

"So you were telling me before about Miss Vivee calling the cause of death for Miss Eugenia."

"Yeah. Don't know how she did it."

"How did she die?"

"Hydrofluoric acid."

"What's that?"

"Apparently a deadly acid that can spill on you and not cause enough damage for you to notice. And," I said, "it's in household cleaners."

"So it was an accident?" he said. He went to the fridge, took out two beers and popped the caps off. "She was cleaning with it?" He handed me one and walked over to the sink.

"Nope." I said and took a swig of my drink. I shook my head. "I already told you it was murder. Somebody poured it on her at the Boule dinner."

"What?" He turned from the sink and looked at me. "At the dinner. In front of everyone?"

"Yep."

He poured the crawfish from both pails into the plastic tub and poured salt on top of them, adding water from the sink. "How diabolical," he said, shaking his head. He picked up a small wooden paddle stirring in the salt in to purge the little mudbugs.

"That was the exact word that Pogue used." I stood up from the chair. "Diabolical." I walked over to the pantry to get a pot to cook the crawfish in. "And I guess they were," I said ducking inside.

"Who?"

"Who what?" I said emerging out of the pantry.

"Who spilled the acid on her?"

"Who spilled the acid..." I repeated it. I hadn't thought of the actual deed. I held on to the pot while I did. I had in fact done what my Auntie Zanne always did. Something I had scolded her about a few times. I picked a person I thought was the murderer and tried to make the facts fit her.

I had decided it was Delphine. But was it? I set the pot I was holding next to the sink, walked back to my chair and sat down.

How could it be? She wasn't the one who poured the acid on Miss Eugenia.

As much as I was attributing my new-found love of home to following the clues, I wasn't actually doing that.

So, I replayed last night's event over in my mind. In slow motion...

The girl.

That server.

She had been the one that walked up to Miss Eugenia's table. Just like she was supposed to be there. But was she? Had she only been there to commit a murder?

What do I remember about her? What did I remember about the whole incident?

I hadn't really seen it happen.

Or had I?

Maybe I did. I tilted my head and looked up at the ceiling. Maybe I saw Eugenia smile at the server as she approached her. Unexpectedly. Moving slightly aside so the girl could serve her. The server then smiling back.

No...I shook my head. I didn't see that. I only saw afterwards. After I came over. After Auntie gave me the eye. That's when I saw that plastic tumbler laying on its side on the silver tray.

Why did the server even have a silver tray? They'd already passed out the absinthe frappes and that was the only thing they'd been used for.

Absinthe frappes. I scrunched my nose. "I hadn't thought of that," I mumbled. "That's why that acid didn't burn so much. Other than it not being so caustic, Miss Eugenia had turned that tall glass filled with a liquor made from wormwood and full of crushed ice into her lap right after the acid had been poured.

The ice probably slowed the caustic reaction.

Wormwood, I knew from living with Auntie, was used to reduce pain...

She stood there, the server, in plain sight and...

I remember the servers were picking up the salad plates. That girl must have leaned over Miss Eugenia under the pretense of getting the salad plate. I squinted, trying to see that tray in my mind. No. There were no plates on it. No salads.

The server had only come out from...where? Had she been in the kitchen? She'd come out just to pour the acid? The tumbler turned over...I tilted my head to the other side. Maybe...she just pick it up and poured it. The clear liquid slushing out, splashing into Eugenia's lap and...and killed her.

I do remember seeing Eugenia's expression. Nothing like the one I was used to seeing on her face. Her usual smile had melted. Eyes widening and mouth dropping open then after the second slush of liquid she had popped up out of her chair. Wet. Pantsuit ruined. Angry. Then I remember it looked as if she felt faint. That's when the server said...

"Hey!" Catfish's face was right in front of mine. He was yelling the word.

I backed my face up. "What?" I said, confused. "Why are you yelling?"

"You were lost," he said and walked back over to the sink.

"Oh," I said and shook my head. "I was thinking about what happened to Eugenia."

"And?" He turned on the water to wash off the crawfish.

"I've been going about this all wrong." I went over and stood next to him at the sink, leaning up against it and crossing my arms.

"Tell me what you mean?"

"That server said to me, 'it wasn't supposed to hurt.'"

"It wasn't supposed to hurt?" Catfish said, eyebrows arched, he looked up from his rinsing. "What does that mean?"

"That she knew something," I said, narrowing my eyes and thinking about the incident. "That's what it meant." I looked at him. "That's what it has to mean. That she's the killer."

"Where is she now?"

"That's a good question," I said. "I don't know." I looked at Catfish. "But I know who should know."

"Who?"

"Rayanne Chambers. One of Auntie's many friends and club members. She owns the Grandview Motor Lodge."

"Out in Yellowpine?"

"Yep. That's the one. It's where the Boule dinner was. Well, actually that's where all the events so far have been."

Yellowpine was a small-town leftover from the timber boom of the early part of the last century. The town hadn't even had a post office since the early 1950s, and I didn't think there could be more than a hundred people that lived there. But it was the second time a murder that I was involved in had occurred there.

Remembering how we'd gone out to Yellowpine to find a murderer before, I added, "I'm sure it's where I should be looking for clues and for the server."

"So are you going to go out there?" he asked.

"I sure am." I gave an affirmative nod. "I can't believe that I didn't think of that before," I said. "I swear, maybe I should rethink this whole staying home thing."

"Why?" Catfish said and chuckled.

"Because Auntie Zanne is rubbing off on me. I don't want to turn out to be just like her."

"I hate to tell you this, Romie," Catfish said, "but you've been like Babet for a long time. Your apple didn't fall far from her tree."

"That is a terrible thing to say," I said. I picked up a crawfish out of the purge water and threw it at him.

"See? That's exactly what Babet would do," he said laughing. "Resort to violence."

"Yes. That she would." I hung my hand. "Sorry."

"So what are you going to do when you find this server?"

"I'm going to question her," I said. "What else would I do?" I shook my head. "I need to find out why she killed Miss Eugenia."

"And what she did with it after she spilt it on Eugenia?" Catfish asked. "'Cause that stuff is deadly."

"Oooh." I took a handful of the crawfish and dumped them into my pot. "That's true," I said. "She couldn't have taken it far." I bumped Catfish out of the way with my hip so I could finish filling the pot. "What about..." I turned to face him. "What if the hydrofluoric acid is still at the motel? Maybe sitting inconspicuously under the sink in the kitchen or in a maid's storage closet?"

"You said it was used for household cleaning."

"Right." I nodded and turned the water on filling the pot. "I need to go over there," I said. I took the pot to the stove and started a flame under it. I looked down at my watch.

"Now?" Catfish asked.

"Okay. Maybe not now. But first thing in the morning."

"Isn't that something that Pogue should do?" Catfish asked, a glint of mischief in his eyes. "I mean if you've identified the killer and possibly the location of what was used to murder Eugenia Elder."

"No!" I said. I walked over from the stove and took my seat back at the table. Then I sighed. Long and hard. "Okay, maybe it is." I slid my arms across the table, leaning in, I looked at Catfish. His eyes dancing with amusement. I knew what he was thinking—that I was going to find a way to do it anyway just like Auntie Zanne would do. But I didn't want to be like her…if I could help it. "What am I gonna do? I want to go and find out what happened."

"How about this?" he said, a playful smile curling around the edge of his lips. "You're the scientific person, right?"

"Right."

"And you would know better than Pogue what to look for."

"Yeah," I said slowly nodding my head in semi-agreement. "I would."

"And looking for it will take up so much time," Catfish said. "Searching that big ole' motel." I nodded. "And time is really something he doesn't have with everything else he has to do."

"Like what?" I said. "Pogue does nothing."

"You want to be the one to tell him that."

"You're right. Go on."

"And you have plenty of time on your hands."

"Watch it," I said, remembering how everyone lately was accusing me of having nothing to do.

"It's just that you'd need to be the one," he said, "if you did find anything, to send it to the lab to see if it matched what was found on Miss Eugenia's clothes. Plus, you have a friend," he placed his hand on his chest, "who is more than willing to help—he too, has nothing to do. And the more manpower the better to do an exhaustive sweep of the place helping Pogue to solve the case that much quicker." He held up his hands and smiled.

I sat back in my seat and smiled at Catfish. "Man. You're good. I probably wouldn't have ever come up with a cover story that good."

"Oh, I think you could've Miss Babet, Jr."

I had to restrain myself from hitting him, it would have just proved his point.

Chapter Twenty-Two

I was exhausted by the time I got home. I'd been gone all day. Since *before* day. And my day had been stuffed with nothing fun, except for the time I'd spent with Catfish.

I wanted to just fall across the bed, close my eyes and not do another thing until at least ten o'clock the next day. But I had on the same clothes I'd wore for an autopsy and for catching crawfish. I probably needed to do with them what Miss Eugenia had done with her yellow pantsuit. Toss them in the trash.

I stripped, dropped the clothes on the floor and kicked them into a corner. I'd find a hamper to deposit them in in the morning. I crawled under the cover and was sleep before my head hit the pillow. I dreamt of little hydrofluoric acid filled crawfish jumping up out of salted water, their acid purge squirting on all who tried to eat them.

I woke up to J.R. licking my face.

"Hey, little buddy. Where'd you come from?" I said. I pushed up on my elbows and looked around the room

J.R., Auntie's little Jack Russell terrier barked at me. "You back from the sitters? Who picked you up?" I looked at the clock on my nightstand. "Oh. I slept longer than I thought."

Auntie Zanne had taken J.R. to a sitter while the Boule was going on. She said we'd be spending too much time away from the house to keep him happy.

He was a spoiled little puppy, but I envied him being able to get away from all of Auntie's activities. I was pulled right into them.

Although things had slowed up because of Miss Eugenia's death. Not as many herbalists traipsing through the house as I expected, and me not being called upon to do as many missions. That was the only good thing about it.

I pulled the cover off me and sat on the side of the bed. J.R. jumped down and sat in front of me, tilting his head, tail wagging.

I tilted my head at an angle to match his. "What are your plans today, little buddy?" I reached down and scratched him behind the ears. "I'm supposed to hang out with Catfish." I stood up, stretched and headed to the bathroom with J.R. in tow. "I wonder why he hasn't called yet."

Catfish and I had planned to go out to the Grandview Motor Lodge and investigate. We also had decided not to tell my cousin the sheriff about it until I found something—*if* I something.

I pulled the covers back and noticed that I had neglected to put on a gown. I looked over at the door and it was opened. I remembered how Rhett has just come in the day before.

"Let me up, little buddy," I said. "I gotta put some clothes on, we've got peeping Toms roaming this abode."

I showered, got dressed and went downstairs. Figured I'd get me a cup of coffee and talk to Auntie Zanne. I knew she'd been in the kitchen. It was the first place she went every morning.

I found a microcosm of the Distinguished Voodoo Ladies swarming around the kitchen.

They were brewing up their concoctions.

I stood in the doorway and watched. There was the big lobster pot on the stove. Steam swirling over it, I could hear the boiling bubbles. It may as well have been a cauldron.

There were dried plants, mortars and pestles of varying sizes and shapes, leather-bound "recipe" books opened to handwritten pages, lit candles giving off smelly aromas, crystals scattered about and a striped cat sitting in J.R.'s corner.

"No wonder he came upstairs," I muttered.

"Good morning," the herbalists chirped.

"Is it still morning?" Auntie Zanne said and looked at me down her nose.

"Good morning," I said, wishing this was one of those mornings when I couldn't hold an eye open. This was one sight I could do without seeing.

"What you cooking?" I asked, although I was unsure of why I had, and pretty sure I'd regret it.

"We're going to snuff out the killer," Mark said, lowering her voice making it sound sinister.

"Make them present themselves to us," Leonard added.

The Wilson twins were present. Hair alike. Dressed alike. Even the same pattern of wrinkles in their seventy-year-old faces.

"Then what?" I asked.

"We'll make him pay," Leonard said.

"For what he did," Mark finished.

"Oh," I said, and nodded. I wondered if it took all these people to do that.

There was Delphine and Avoyelles with their heads together over a page in a book. The only person missing from yesterday's crew was Nola Landry. She was replaced by Flannery Poole. Roble's own beauty queen. She was much younger than most of the other ladies in the Ladies Society, she must have been newly inducted. She was a member of the Roble Belle, the high school football booster club and one of the people that prompted me to leave Roble in the first place. I had always wondered with her beauty, couldn't she had done so much more somewhere else? Be someone better, someone different.

I looked at her now, big smile on her face, grinding up something. She looked more like their helper, with no real skills of her own.

Wait. Did I just say these women had skills?

I definitely needed a cup of coffee.

I looked across the room at my Keurig sitting on the counter. Unplugged, it had been pushed back. I'm guessing it had been in their way.

"I'll just grab an apple," I said to no one in particular. I got one out the fridge and headed to the back porch. I'd eat it out there, out of their way, then I'd call Catfish to see what time he wanted to meet up at the Grandview Motor Lodge.

I opened the screen and ran smack into Rhett.

"Good morning," he said holding my arms keeping me close.

"Don't you have a home?" I asked pulling away—slowly.

"I feel at home when I'm around you."

"Oh brother," I rolled my eyes, making it appear he and his comments were a bother to me. But after sitting on the step, out of his eyesight, I smiled. I couldn't help it. "Why are you out here?" I asked over my shoulder.

"Kitchen was full," he said and nodded that way.

"You should probably call it Murder Central."

He chuckled. "And why is that?" he asked.

"They're in there cooking up deadly spells. Best to steer clear of them and their work." I chomped into my shiny Red Delicious.

Rhett let out a loud hearty laugh. "I thought they were making potpourri."

"Yeah, well I'd suggest that you not use their brand of potpourri to make your house smell better. You might end up turning into a pig." I took another bite of my apple.

He let out another laugh. "You're so cute."

"My point exactly," I said with a nod, chewing on my bite and swallowing. "You probably only think that because you've been drinking some of Auntie's tea. She wants you to feel like that. I warned you against drinking it."

"What about you? She doesn't want you to feel like that about me?" he asked.

I looked up at him. Standing over me smiling. His jeans and t-shirt fitting him even better than usual. "Probably," I said, turning my head away from him. "But I don't drink anything she brews."

"So you don't think I'm cute? Even without her tea?"

"You're cute enough," I said.

"I'll take that," he said, and sat down on the step next to me. "What are you doing right now?" Rhett asked.

"Eating an apple." I held up the half-eaten fruit.

"After you finish eating the apple."

"Why?" I asked and took another bite.

"I wanted you to take a ride with me?"

"A ride?" I chuckled, the apple in my mouth almost getting stuck in my throat. I looked at him. He didn't appear to be joking. "And go where?" I asked.

"To visit a friend."

"A friend of whose?" I asked. I didn't think we knew any of the same people other than those that came to the funeral home.

"Of mine." He dug his hands down in his jean pockets. "Maybe she'll become a friend of yours, too."

She?

My heart leapt. Then I swallowed hard to try to make that feeling go away. I hated when I had any kind of emotion about Rhett. I didn't want to like him. I was trying hard to resist him. I mean, that's not what deciding to stay home meant, did it? Jumping out of one relationship and into another? I was sure that wasn't a good thing to do.

But thinking that he wanted to introduce me to a girl—maybe his girl—made me feel...I don't know...jealous. Or something. I knew neither my stomach nor my heart liked it.

"You sure are taking a long time to think about it," he said.

"I was, uh..."

"We won't be gone long," he said.

I looked at him, sitting next to me. Eyes doing their twinkling dance, his smile soft and gentle.

"Sure," I said, although I wasn't keen on going to meet any *girl* of his I was liking the idea of spending time with him. "When do you want to go?"

"You ready now?" he asked.

"Aren't you supposed to be working?"

"There's nothing going on here," he said. "No funerals today. Babet is enjoying time with her friends and I think they have a run to make later. I know she said she was going out."

"Well, I have to go over to Yellowpine with Catfish for about an hour."

"Catfish, huh?"

"Yes, Catfish," I said.

"Am I always going to have competition?" he asked.

"Competition?" I stretched my neck to look at his face.

"Yes. First Dr. Chicago and now Catfish. Or was it always Catfish?" he said. He sat down on the step next to me. Too close to keep my heart at its usual pace.

"I don't know what you mean," I said.

"You know exactly what I mean," he said, his voice low. I could feel his warm breath on my neck.

"Am I going to have to worry about you being this close on our little road trip," I said and scooted over, away from him.

"Yes," he said and scooted over, too.

I stood up. I was finding it hard to breathe. "How about I call you when I finish up with Catfish?"

"How about I come out to the Grandview with you and Catfish?"

I smiled. "No," I said. "I think we're good."

"We're good," Catfish said. He was standing on the walkway in front of us, a grin on his face, his hands stuffed down into his pants pocket, his eyes nearly hidden under his bucket hat.

"Morning," Rhett said and stood up. He stuck out his hand as a greeting.

Catfish grabbed it, but he looked at me the entire time they shook hands, a big smirk on his face.

"Okay," Rhett said, standing, "I'll meet up with you when you get back?"

"Yep," I said and gave him a nod. "When I get back."

"Can you bring your medical bag with you?" Rhett asked.

"When?"

"When we go to see my friend."

"Is she sick?"

"She'll feel better after she meets you. But I'd like for you to reassure her of that."

"Okay," I said. His comment made me even more curious about this girl."

Rhett nodded at Catfish, tugged on the hem of his with t-shirt and walked inside the back door.

"What's up with you two?" Catfish said.

"I told you yesterday, nothing."

"I don't think that's how *he* feels."

"He's been drinking some of Auntie's concoctions," I said.

"Oh," he said, seemingly understanding. "Must've been a love potion because that guy is smitten."

Chapter Twenty-Three

I rode in Catfish's truck. No need of us taking two cars, plus, I didn't own one. I was going to have to get one soon if I was truly planning on staying in Roble.

On the way to our investigation in Yellowpine, we swung by the medical examiner's office. I wanted to get a couple pairs of Nitrile gloves for me and Catfish. We might end up handling the murder weapon on our little trip. Then we stopped at Momma Della's so I could get a cup of coffee and ended up getting a bite to eat. We must have sat there over an hour just laughing and talking.

After leaving there, Catfish needed to go by his house, for what I don't know, but he spent forever inside and came back out looking the same way he did when he went in. I only take that long to do anything when I'm getting dressed up to go out. We finally got on our way to Yellowpine nearly three hours after I'd left home

I hadn't let Auntie know where I was going. She would have wanted to tag along, and with Rayanne Chambers being her good friend, I'm sure I wouldn't have gotten a word in edgewise when I started questioning her.

I hadn't told Pogue where I was going either.

It wasn't such a bad thing, I figured. If he was conducting his investigation properly, he would have already thought to go there to see what he could find out. He didn't have Auntie in his ear all the time like I did trying to steer the investigation the way she wanted. His brain had room to think on its own.

Well, he did have her in his ear, but he knew how to ignore her better than I did. So, I was pretty certain he'd have thought of questioning the server first thing.

Yep, my focus was now on the server.

"I think I was way off track thinking it was Delphine," I said out loud, letting Catfish in on my thoughts. He glanced over at me and returned his gaze. He was calm, his bucket hat pulled way down on his forehead, his stubby fingers drumming on the steering wheel as he drove. Catfish was a way better investigating partner than Auntie, if nothing else he didn't talk all the time.

"Why?" he asked. "Having that letter would probably make anyone think she might have done it. Even Babet did, isn't that what you told me?"

"Yeah, but she changed her mind and so have I."

"Is it because of Babet you changed your mind?"

"No. Well maybe. She did say something that made me think she might be right."

"What was that?"

"She said, which ended up being Delphine's own words—using an acid isn't Delphine's tell."

"And what does that mean?"

"Delphine is a healer. It's not the way she does things."

"Healers don't kill?" he asked, glancing over at me, doubt in his voice.

"I don't know," I said, I let my head roll back. "Maybe I'm letting Auntie get into my head again."

"What's *your* reason for thinking it's not Delphine?" Catfish asked. "Babet might get into your head sometimes, but you never let her do your thinking for you."

"I was thinking..." I started, appreciating Catfish's words, "if Delphine did it, it was one big elaborate scheme. A production number. Hiring the girl and everything. Pouring it on Miss Eugenia in front of everyone. Getting her out of there before anyone knew."

"You think that whole thing was planned?"

I drew in a breath. "I don't know." I looked at him. "Yeah, I think I'm starting to think that."

"And Delphine couldn't have planned it?"

"I don't think so. She just doesn't seem like the kind. She's simple." I saw Catfish raise an eyebrow. "I don't mean not smart, I mean, I went to her house. She welcomes everyone over, leaves them to roam around while she merrily goes into the kitchen to brew coffee. She teaches people how to heal using natural methods."

"Who do you think did it now? Orville?"

"I don't want to guess," I said. "I mean I don't really have anything other than he-said-she-said accusations." I tapped my finger on the dashboard. "Let's just see what we can find out at Grandview."

As we drove down the road to the Grandview, a garbage truck passed us going in the opposite direction.

"Catfish," I said turning in my seat to watch as the truck got lost from my view. "You think maybe that girl threw that stuff away?"

"What stuff?"

"That plastic tumbler she used. I don't know," I said turning to face forward again. "The tray. The acid."

"She'd have to get rid of it," he said.

"Maybe she put it in the motel's dumpster."

"The motel has fed a hundred women dinner and breakfast since then," Catfish said. "I don't know what you'd be able to find. It'd be like a needle in a haystack."

"Probably," I said. "Luckily we don't have to do it." I chuckled. "But I think it needs to be done."

Catfish pointed out of his window to two large dumpsters lined up against a cement wall in the back of the motel. "They look pretty full," he said.

"Must be from the Boule," I said. "Has to be. I don't think this motel is popular enough to generate that much trash."

"Pogue will have to get out here before they come to take it away," Catfish said.

"Look," I said, and pointed to a sign on the side of the

dumpster. "There's the name of the waste management company that handles the trash. All the information is there." I dug down in my purse. "I'll take a picture. Maybe call them later and find out what day and time they pick up from here."

"You could ask the owner of the motel."

"I could, but I still want to get a picture. Never know, it might come in handy."

I got out of the truck and walked over to the dumpster. I waved my hand in front of my face. The smell was thick, taking up all the air surrounding the two big containers.

If the server did throw any evidence in either one of those, I thought to myself, Pogue would never be able to find it. I brought up the camera on my phone, looking through the screen and getting the signage on the dumpster in view, I thought this was probably a waste of time.

"What are you doing?"

Uh-oh. Hearing that voice meant my investigative plans were about to go south.

I turned and saw Auntie Zanne getting out of that white deuce and a quarter that had been serving as her ride ever since I got busied by the murder. She and her posse had arrived on the scene.

"What are you doing here?" I said. "I thought you were making up a brew to catch the killer."

"What?" she said and frowned, then her face cleared as she realized what I was saying. "You mean this morning? We were making potpourri."

"That's not what Mark and Leonard told me," I said.

"Well, if they said anything different, they were joking with you." She turned and looked back toward the car, presumably where they were. "And we came to see about setting up a room with Rayanne where the Ladies Society could come back to vote in. Much as it pains me, we have to find a replacement for Eugenia." She pointed at the dumpster. "Now you want to tell me what you're doing?"

"Taking a picture of the dumpster," I said.

"I can see that," she said. "The question is why?"

"Because I want to give it to Pogue."

"For what? Spit it out," she said. "Stop giving me evasive answers."

I knew there was no need trying to hide anything from her. If I didn't tell her, she'd get it out of Catfish. One thing for sure, I wasn't going to get rid of her before her curiosity was satisfied.

"I was thinking that maybe that server threw away the tumbler or the hydrofluoric acid in here."

Auntie looked at the dumpster then back at me. "That could be dangerous if someone touched it," she said. "You shouldn't touch it."

"I'm not," I said. "And I know that. I came prepared." I pulled the Nitrile gloves out of my purse." I flapped them at her. "Plus, if I found anything, I would call Pogue so he could get someone who knows how to handle waste out here."

Auntie pointed to the sign I'd come over to take a picture of. "Wouldn't they know how to do it?" she asked.

"I guess," I said. "I was getting their information."

"But what if nothing's in there?"

I hunched my shoulder. I didn't understand her point. If it wasn't there, it wasn't there.

"I mean if we call them over to go through it," Auntie Zanne said, evidently reading my thoughts. "And nothing's there, they'd be quite upset with us."

"I don't think that matters," I said. "It has to be done."

"I think we should check it first," she said.

"What?" I said, my voice going up an octave.

"Now," she said. "We can check it out first before we call anyone in."

"No," I said backing up. "I don't think that's a good idea."

"Oh pshaw," she said, giving me one of her dismissive hand waves. "We'll get Catfish in there. He can look around."

"No," I said, but she wasn't listening, she'd already started a march over to his truck. I could hear him screech when she opened the door and pulled him out.

"Babet!" he said. "What's going on?"

"I need you to help Romaine," Auntie Zanne said.

"What is going on?" Delphine was out of the car, asking the same thing. And behind her came Mark and Leonard. I saw Avoyelles pulling over and parking her car away from the dumpsters. I was guessing there was one more person—Flannery Poole—in the car with her. Poor woman didn't know what she was getting herself into hanging out with them.

"We're going to take a look in this dumpster to see if we can't find that cup that spilled on Eugenia," Auntie yelled over to Delphine while still tugging on Catfish.

I turned to see Delphine put up her hand as if she was saying, "Amen." Then she broke into a little trot—it was really a faster walk—Mark and Leonard close behind.

Then it hit me. No one was supposed to know the cause of death. No one in this crowd but Catfish, Auntie and me.

That meant Auntie had spilled the beans.

"Auntie," I said and grabbed the sleeve of her blouse. I gave it a yank telling her to follow me. I walked her back over to the dumpster area and stepped to the side of it.

"No one but us knew that she'd died from that spill at the Boule dinner," I said.

Auntie eye's widened and her eyeballs went from side-to-side. She may as well have voiced that "oops" that was on the tip of her tongue. I just didn't know whether her reaction was because she'd told them when she wasn't supposed to or because I found out she had.

"None of them killed Eugenia," Auntie said and threw a hand back toward her girls. "It didn't hurt to fill them in."

"Auntie, they may not have done it, but they may know something important. We won't know if they already knew that or assumed it because you'd told them facts about the case."

"It slipped."

"If you're going to be a part of this investigation, which is against Pogue's better judgment, then you're going to have to be still."

"You told Catfish," she said, throwing my logic right back at me.

"Catfish is helping me. He helps down at the morgue and he isn't going to tell anyone. He doesn't even talk to anyone else."

"My girls are helping me," she said, "just like he's helping you."

"I don't think they are the kind of help that's needed."

"What does that mean?" she said. She slapped hands on hips, and she stood up a little taller.

"Nothing bad," I said. "But Mark and Leonard said you were using your magic, hocus pocus to snuff out the killer."

"That wouldn't have been a bad thing if we had, but we weren't," Auntie Zanne said. "And I think we are more useful than you think." She snatched the gloves out of my hand, ending up with three of them, turned around and marched back over to Catfish. She dragged him back to the dumpster and gave him a push. "Bend over."

"What?" he said. He looked back at me.

"I'm going to see what's in that dumpster," she said. She went behind him and holding to his shoulders started to try and climb up on him. I didn't know if she was trying to bend him over to get on his back, or if she figured his shoulders would do. "C'mon Catfish, you gotta give me a hand here."

With Auntie's firm hold on him, Catfish tried to turn to talk to me, his eyes pleading. "I thought we were going to talk to the owner about this trash." His words came out in grunts and spurts.

"We need to see what's in there," Auntie said, answering for me. "We can talk to Rayanne later. I don't want this dumpster to be emptied of its contents before we know what's inside."

"If it hasn't been emptied already," Delphine said, her lips pursed. She was on Auntie's side.

"Delphine," I said as I started walking over to see if I couldn't free Catfish of Auntie's grasp, "the thing is full. It hasn't been emptied." I tugged at Auntie's leg, it was wrapped around Catfish's, her fingers digging into his shoulders trying to get leverage and move up his back. "Auntie," I said, as calmly as I could. I didn't want to add fuel to her fire by making her even more upset. "I didn't mean you and the girls couldn't help."

"Help with what?" Avoyelles had parked her car and wanted in on the conversation.

"I'm sure you didn't," Auntie said. As I spoke, she thrusted the extra glove toward Delphine. She started putting on the pair she had. "Romaine doesn't think we can help find out what's in that dumpster." She directed her words to Avoyelles. Holding onto Catfish, it looked like she'd only taken a break from trying to get over into the dumpster long enough to get protective gear on.

"What's in the dumpster?" Avoyelles asked.

"The cup that spilled that deadly stuff on Eugenia," Mark said.

"The killer agent," Leonard added her spy-like response.

"Oh," Avoyelles said. "You think it might be in there."

"Romaine thought so," Auntie Zanne said. "Now she doesn't want to go in it."

"I never wanted to go in it," I said. "I just wanted to take a picture of it."

"It's too much garbage in that can for you to go dumpster diving, Babet," Catfish said. Auntie was still holding on to him. He turned around to face her so she couldn't climb up his back again.

"You want to do it?" Auntie asked Catfish. She had handed over the gloves to Delphine who pulled one onto Auntie's free hand snapping the rubber at her wrist.

"Nope. Definitely too much trash for me," he answered.

"What's going on?" Rayanne Chambers came walking across the parking lot.

Another inquisitive mind.

"I've been keeping myself amused watching all y'all's fascination with my dumpster from my office window," Rayanne said and jerked a thumb over her shoulder toward the motel, "but when it appeared that Babet was going in, I thought I'd better come on out and see what in the blazes is going on."

Rayanne Chambers looked her part. As the owner/operator of the Grandview Motor Lodge she wore a pink raw silk suit with black piping. She walked deftly in her 5-inch black pumps. Her auburn hair was high on top of her head, like Auntie wore hers, but Rayanne sported a French roll instead of the back being cut short and tapered. She had a Texas twang, wore a frosty red lipstick and had a mouth full of pearly whites that she loved to display.

"Babet needs to get into your dumpster," Mark said in answer to Rayanne's question. As she spoke, I looked to Leonard, I knew she'd say something next.

"There's evidence in there," Leonard said, nodding toward the dumpster with her head. She was right on cue.

"Evidence of what?" Rayanne said.

"Of the acid that was poured on Eugenia."

"Auntie!" I said

Eyes bucked, she slapped a hand over her mouth.

"Too late now," I said.

Chapter Twenty-Four

Avoyelles got out of the car when Rayanne arrived on the scene. It appeared that there wasn't a sixth passenger. Flannery is smarter than I had given her credit for.

Now the eight of us were standing around just looking at each other, Auntie Zanne's hand still over her mouth. Auntie's girls probably didn't know what the problem was, she had shared the information about Miss Eugenia's manner of death so freely, they wouldn't see a problem.

Although I hadn't told Catfish not to go spreading it around, he was not one to talk much—about anything to anyone—and gossip certainly was against every part of his moral fiber.

"What in the world are you talking about?" Rayanne said, her voice high, her accent pitchy. "No one spilled hydrofluoric acid on anyone in my establishment."

Hydrofluoric, I thought. Auntie hadn't said what kind of acid it was...

"How about we talk in your office," Auntie Zanne said, taking her hand down from her mouth. She looped her arm around Rayanne's. "C'mon Romaine. You come with us." She looked over her shoulder as she led Rayanne away, "Avoyelles maybe you should park the car and wait. You too, Catfish. We'll be back soon."

I guessed this was her way of making up for setting off her small-town gossip wheel. Taking Rayanne inside for a private conversation. I was glad it was going to happen, I did need to talk to her. But Auntie couldn't take back what she'd done. Good thing I was no longer thinking of Delphine as the culprit.

I didn't know what Pogue thought, or whether he'd even spoken to Delphine yet.

"Have you talked to Sheriff Folsom yet?" I asked Rayanne as we made our way down the hallway to her office.

"Who?" she asked. She waved us inside. "Sit down anywhere. Make yourselves comfortable."

Her office didn't match the rest of the yellow motel. This one was classy and luxe. The floors and column that were posted on either side of her mahogany desk were white marble. The desk sat on a hand-tufted, triple border, multi-colored Persian rug. There was a crystal, teardrop chandelier hanging from the ceiling that were nearly as big as the ones in the banquet hall.

Auntie and I each settled into floral upholstered Queen Anne chairs that faced her desk. I was able to see through the large window flanked by the American and Texas flags that Avoyelles and the girls, as well as Catfish had moved their vehicles. It was so contradictory that such an opulent looking office would have a view of garbage dumpsters.

"Now let me just get my head together," Rayanne said. "Y'all bombarding me with all sorts of craziness all at one time." She pointed to Auntie Zanne. "Now, you said that Eugenia had acid poured on her. Are you sure? I heard she was fine when she left here. And you," she pointed at me, "whom I haven't seen in forever, wants to know if some sheriff has been here to talk to me?" She threw up her hands. "What in the tarnation is going on?"

"My Auntie Zanne didn't—"

Auntie cut me off before I could finish. "I can talk," she said at to me. "She asked me a question." Auntie turned to Rayanne, then shot me another warning look before she started speaking. "This is a very sensitive matter." She put a finger up to her lips saying, "mums the word," which was quite ironic since she seemed set to spill the beans. Again. "You can't say a word."

"Of course not," Rayanne said and clamped her lips tightly together.

"Eugenia might have been working for a secret government agency."

My eyes and mouth both popped open. What in the world was she doing? Auntie looked at me, slid her foot next to mine and gave it a kick. I shut my mouth, and batting my eyes, I tried to blink away the look of shock

"She what?" Rayanne's face matched mine—wide-eyed and slack jawed.

"I hate to say it," Auntie went on matter-of-factly, "but she may have been killed in response to sensitive information that she knew."

"Oh no!" Rayanne slapped her hands on either side of her face and dragged them down leaving streaks in her porcelain-colored makeup. "I wouldn't have ever thought Eugenia Elder was capable of doing such a thing." She shook her head slowly. "A spy!"

Auntie nodded as if to say it were true. She leaned in close to whisper. Rayanne leaned in to hear. "Perhaps," Auntie's one-word response seemed to give Rayanne a chill.

"It's what happens to spies," Rayanne said and sat back in her chair. A smug look on her face, she took an imaginary dagger jabbed it in the air and gave it a twist.

That gave me a chill.

I think it gave Auntie one too, she straightened up and slid back in her seat. "Yes, well, that's why they used her," she said. "No one would ever suspect her."

"They picked the right person," Rayanne agreed.

"We're here to try and circumvent the sheriff from coming," Auntie Zanne said gaining her composure back.

Rayanne pointed to me. "The sheriff she asked me about?"

"Same one," Auntie said and scooted up in her chair again. "It probably would be best if that didn't happen."

"Why would they come here?" Rayanne asked. "I don't know anything."

"Sometimes you know more than you think," Auntie said leveraging a finger at her. "You just have to think about it. Go over an incident in your mind and make yourself remember. Sometime clues that mean a lot to the trained eye seem small and inconsequential to the average person."

Rayanne was nodding. Soaking up everything Auntie was saying. Believing every word of it. "You know I'm the Justice of the Peace over in Sabine County."

"Yes, of course I know," she said. "That's why I trust what you say. Other than the fact that I've known you for more than forty years. I know you'd never steer me wrong. Never lie to me."

"No I wouldn't," Auntie said.

I coughed into my fist. Auntie kicked me again.

"And if I can talk to you about what happened here at our Boule," Auntie said, "and we can keep whatever we discuss between the three of us, then I can guarantee that the Sheriff won't be coming this way."

"Well, you know I'm willing to help anyway I can," Rayanne said. She rubbed her hands together, and licked her lips, that frosty red coloring staying true.

"Romaine's the new medical examiner over in Roble."

"She is?" Rayanne gave me a nervous smile.

"Yes. She's finally agreed to the job." I looked at Auntie. How in the world did Rayanne know anything about me taking a job or not taking it? "And due to her position, she has questions for you."

That jerked me out of my wandering thoughts. I looked at Auntie, I was so shocked with her made up story about a government-asset-assassination-plot that when she tossed the ball to me, I fumbled. "Uh...uhm..." I looked at Auntie.

"The dumpster..." Auntie Zanne said, trying to help me find my way.

"Oh yes, you were at that dumpster," Rayanne said. "Were there some clues in that nasty thing?"

"That's what we wanted to ask you," I said, my words falling in place. "There was a server who spilled something in Eugenia's lap."

"I don't know who she was," Rayanne said, her response quicker than expected. "Never saw her before."

"Remember how Auntie Zanne said you'd have to think about it."

"I thought about it," she said. She gave a quick nod. "I didn't hire her."

"How do you know?" I asked. I didn't remember seeing Rayanne anywhere about when the incident happened.

"Because I asked about it," she said, another quick response. "All my servers were accounted for and hers was not a face in my hired hands."

"You weren't out there," I said, still wondering how she could pick out the servers absent in her kitchen-help-line-up.

"Nola Landry told me."

"Nola Landry?" I said.

"You know," Auntie said. "Our Sergeant-at-Arms."

"I know who she is," I said. "I remember her from the autopsy."

"She was at the autopsy?" Rayanne asked, excitement sparked in her eyes. "I've always wanted to see one performed."

"Autopsies are closed," I said.

Rayanne shot Auntie an eye, then narrowed it at me. "Nola was there."

"What have you and Nola discussed?" I said, ignoring her observation. It wasn't that I'd told them anything during the autopsy, although it appeared Auntie filled them in on what she knew.

"Discussed? Nothing. I hardly know the woman."

"Nola Landry is the one who had the table cleared, isn't she?" I asked.

"Was she?" Rayanne asked.

Rayanne was confusing me. "Can we back up?" I asked. "I think I'm missing something."

"What are you missing?"

"You said that the server who spilled the liquid on Eugenia wasn't hired by you?"

"Right."

"And you hired everyone who worked at the dinner?"

"I did."

"And you didn't talk to Nola about anything that happened that night?"

"I did not," she said.

"But isn't she the person who told you about the spilled drink—"

"The hydrofluoric acid," she corrected.

"How do you know what kind of acid it was?" I asked, stopping my current line of questioning to get an answer about something I had wondered about since we first sat down.

"You told me," she said, seemingly surprised that I didn't know that.

"No, I didn't," I said.

Without missing a beat, she turned to Auntie. "Then Babet told me."

"No, she didn't," I said.

"Well goodness sake, how else would I know?" Rayanne laughed.

I didn't answer that question. I looked at Auntie, though, mentally telling her that we need to find out how she knew.

I shook my head. "Back to my question—"

"Which was?" Rayanne asked as if she was testing me to see if I remembered.

"Nola Landry told you that the person who spilled the drink was not one of the servers in the room when you questioned them."

"Right," she nodded in the affirmative.

"Did she tell you anything else when you didn't talk to her?" I asked. I'm sure the sarcasm was evident in my voice.

"Nope," Rayanne said, either unaware of my disbelief at her statement or not caring.

"Nothing?"

"Nothing."

"What else did you have to do with the Boule other than hiring the wait staff?"

"Oh everything!" She threw up her hands, a big smile lit up her face, her cheeks became rosy. "And other than the one little mishap with Eugenia," she cupped one hand at the side of her mouth and looked at Auntie, "the *spy*," she put her hand down and turned her eyes back to me, "everything went off without a hitch. Beautiful event."

Something about Rayanne was off. She wasn't telling me the truth, and she wasn't a good liar.

"Why did Nola Landry have the table cleared instead of you?" I asked.

"I was busy. I had a lot of things going on," she said. "You were there. You witnessed it." She locked eyes with me. "Everything had to be timed perfectly. The food had to be served on time. The frappes had to be presented a certain way. It cost me a lot of money and time. Plus," she added, lowering her voice as if someone else might be listening, "you have to watch the help. Things might come up missing. If you know what I mean."

"What happened to the place settings and linen that was on that table?" I asked.

"Oh, I don't know," Rayanne waved her hand up in the air, like that may have been where they disappeared to. "You'd have to ask Nola that."

Chapter Twenty-Five

I walked out of Rayanne Chambers office and felt like she might have something to do with what happened.

I stood in the hallway and waited for Auntie. She still needed to speak to Rayanne about using a room large enough to hold all the herbalists of the Ladies Society so they could redo the vote for the Lessor Mambo.

And my thoughts weren't too far away from that Boule either. If Rayanne Chambers hadn't spoken to Nola Landry about anything she sure did defer to Nola when she explained how she got information about what happened. And if she was the one who'd taken care of "everything" at the dinner, keeping a "watchful eye" so things didn't disappear, why was it that only Nola knew where the linen and things that came off the table were?

"Whew! That was close," Auntie said, swiping her hand across her forehead. She grabbed my arm and held onto it as she started walking down the hallway.

"What in the world was that all about?" I asked. Auntie Zanne was always putting her nose in the middle of things, but that what she did, coming up with a spy story about Miss Eugenia, was a performance worthy of an Oscar.

"Vivienne schooled me on how to get information out of people."

"Miss Vivee?" I asked. "You two talked about interrogation techniques?" I had to giggle.

"Yes." Auntie Zanne nodded. "And I think it worked."

"Probably nothing's as bad as the bully techniques you usually employ."

"I do not bully," she said and smacked me on my arm. "And it was necessary. Rayanne is the biggest gossip in the tri-county."

"Yellowpine isn't part of the tri-county," I said.

"Did I say tri-county? I meant tri-state area. Texas, Louisiana and Arkansas."

"If she's such a big gossiper, why would you tell her all those lies that she'll start spreading around?"

"Rayanne doesn't want any part of any government investigation. Didn't you see the chandeliers and marble in her office?"

"I couldn't've missed it."

"No one could. I'm sure you also couldn't miss the fact that that motel doesn't do much in the way of business." Auntie lifted her eyebrows and gave a curt nod. "Put those things together and you'd know that Rayanne don't want no part of any official, whether it be sheriff or tax collector, coming out to her place of business."

"And how are you supposed to keep Pogue from coming out here?" I asked. "This is where everything happened."

"Pogue said that whatever we find out, share with him," Auntie said. "So we'll tell him. He won't need to come this way and question anyone."

"He'll have to come and go through the trash," I said.

"If I know Nola Landry, there's nothing left of that stuff."

"What does that mean?" I asked. But Auntie was gone. Out the front door and to the car with her girls. When she got to the car, she waved back at me.

"We'll go question," she put her hands near her mouth, "you know who," she mouthed then returned to her regular voice, "when I get back."

I was sure, "you know who," was Nola Landry. I was thinking I should go and question her by myself, but didn't see how I could ever get away with that.

I watched Auntie Zanne as she got into the car and she and the girls drove off. Then I looked over and saw Catfish's truck. It looked deserted sitting in a space across the lot, and when I looked around, I saw why. He had gotten out and was talking to Rhett. They were standing in the parking lot and both were looking my way.

"What are you doing here?" I asked Rhett when I got over to them. "How did you even know I was here?"

"You told me," he said.

I couldn't remember doing that, and it made me wonder if I'd been the one to tell Rayanne that it was hydrofluoric acid. "Nah," I said and shook my head. I was sure I hadn't told her that.

"Yeah, you did," he said. "When we were on the back porch this morning."

"I was saying no to something else," I said and pointed behind me to the motel.

"Did you find out anything while you were here?" Rhett aske.

"What happened in there?" Catfish asked at the same time.

"All I found out is that Rayanne Chambers, like so many of Auntie's friends, likes to lie." I looked at Rhett and tilted my head. "And when did you get interested in the happenings around here?"

"What does that mean?" he looked at Catfish then back at me, that twinkle in his eye flickering. "I'm always interested in the things you do."

"Time for me to go," Catfish said and pretended to tip his hat. "I'll catch you later."

"Bye, Catfish," I said. I watched him walk over to his truck

"C'mon," Rhett said. He pulled his hands out of his pocket. I saw a slight smile curl up the edge of his lips. "You can fill me in in the car." He took off walking toward it.

"Fill you in about what?" I said and started after him.

Rhett walked toward a light blue Ford Thunderbird convertible. I knew it wasn't a late model car, not because I can tell these things by looking at a car, but because I knew Ford wasn't making Thunderbirds anymore. But the car was in immaculate condition. But what I didn't know was who it belonged to.

Rhett always drove cars that belonged to the funeral home,

mostly the hearse. He was Auntie's funeral boy, as I called him. Always at her beck and call. At least that's what I used to say about him. Now it seemed that a better word to describe him was dedicated.

He stood on the passenger side of the car and opened the door.

"Is this your car?" I asked.

"You're always asking me personal questions," he said holding the door while I got in. "Are you interested in me or are you just nosy."

That question gave me pause. I didn't know quite how to answer. If I said I wasn't interested in him, it meant I was nosy, which after growing up in a small town I never wanted to be described as. Being surrounded by, or part of, a rumor mill was one of things that had made me want to go away in the first place. And if I told him I was interested in him, he might think I really was.

Actually, I was beginning to think that I was...

"Watch your medical bag down there on the floor," he said. Inside there were white leather seats that were smooth and soft. I slid in and they seemed to cuddle me. It's was nice. I couldn't imagine him with this car. I'd never seen him in anything but ripped jeans and sneakers.

"You got my medical bag?" I said looking up at him

"That's why it's on the floor," he said and shut the door.

He was starting to act like Auntie. Always with a snappy comeback. I looked down at , as he came around the car and got in the driver's side. I pushed it over with my foot.

"Nice car," I said, circumventing the question of who owned it.

"Thank you," he said and started the engine. It purred. He adjusted the volume down on the music coming from the radio and smiled at me.

"So why do I need my medical bag?" I asked. "Is it for your girl?" I asked playfully, but those were my thoughts. I realized once I let the words out, I really didn't want him to tell me that she was. I glanced over at him, flinching waiting for the answer.

He gave me a quick look then put his eyes back on the road.

No hesitating, he said, "Yep. It's for my girl."

I think my heart stopped after he said those words.

I didn't want to die in his car. It wasn't how I had pictured leaving this world, but I was sure I had no pulse.

Why did it even bother me?

I knew why it bothered me. It bothered me he was always flirting with me. Telling me he was interested in me. That he liked being where I was. And whether I wanted to admit it or not, I enjoyed him saying those things. Maybe hoping down deep, or not so deep down, they were true even though I liked to act as if it annoyed me.

Had he just been playing with me? Was it no more than him just flirting? Figures, now that I was taking it to heart.

Rhett Remmiere had skin the color of honey and just as smooth. He was tall and well-built, nonplussed and it seemed, not attached to any drama. He was something, I'd come to realize, I needed it my life.

I looked over at him and waited for him to say something more. To tell me he was joking. To tell me that he didn't have a girl. And that he'd asked me along to be with me...

He didn't say a word.

I bobbled my head from side to side. I really knew how to pick 'em. The way he always flirted with me, I thought he was single. Maybe if I'd paid attention instead of being so wrapped up in Alex— a man two thousand miles away and not the man that was right in front of me—I wouldn't have made that mistake. Or was it I had just waited too long?

"She's not feeling well," he said. "Thought maybe you could take a look at her."

"Doesn't she have a doctor?" I asked. Doctors nowadays I knew didn't make house calls, even in rural areas, but he could have gotten her to one instead of asking me to see about. "Plus, I'm not one to give a good diagnosis. All my patients are usually dead."

"I trust you," he said, not taking his eyes off the road. "I know you'll take good care of her for me."

Chapter Twenty-Six

Rhett didn't give me a clue as to where we were going.

He headed down SR-96 toward Beaumont, the place I'd lived up until the age twelve. The place I lived with my parents. I didn't recognize one thing about it anymore, yet just being close to it pulled on my heartstrings.

He drove through the city and then alongside I-10 until we came to the downtown area of Peterson. There were bright lights on along the street and people mulling around. As we slowed, I could hear music coming from bars on the street, it gave me the feel of being on Bourbon Street in New Orleans.

Before we turned off the main street, I caught a glimpse of a faded neon sign shaped like a saxophone that flickered over a wooden and glass door. It read: The Lady Frankie's Juke Joint.

Rhett pulled the car through a narrow alley between two brick buildings. I drew my shoulders together, as if that would help, thinking that it wasn't wide enough for us to make it through.

"Is this where we're going?" I asked. "A juke joint?"

I always felt that Rhett tried to impress me with his musical knowledge and love of the blues and zydeco—he knew it reminded me of my dad. My father, Earle Wilder, a man that wouldn't be caught without his Les Gibson Guitar, taught me a true and special appreciation of music.

And then there was the whole French thing. When Auntie first made mention of him the day I arrived back in Roble, she said he was French. He may have spoken it, but French he was not. He did seem to have a grasp of the language, although I'd never heard him attempt Louisiana Creole. That would have impressed me.

I hoped tonight wasn't another attempt for him to compare those things I held dear in my life to his knowledge, however true, of the same. If that was what he wanted, I wouldn't have needed my medical bag.

"Yep," this is where we're going," he said. "A juke joint." He turned the key in the ignition off. "You ready?"

"I guess," I said. "Although I don't know for what."

"Hold on," he said and pointed. "Let me get that door for you." He didn't even venture a response for my statement about why I was there.

I reached down and grabbed my bag while I waited for him to come around the car. When I went to step out of the car, he took my hand and held it a little longer than he needed to as we made our way back to a rusty steel door.

"What will your girl say about this?" I said and pulled my hand away.

"I don't think she'll mind." He put his hand in the small of my back and guided me toward the door. "We have the same taste," he said.

I pulled my head back. "Really?"

"Really," he said. "That means she's gonna love you."

I couldn't help but to blush, which was ridiculous. Why would I be happy about his girl liking me?

He took a key out of his pants pocket, a different ring than the ones his car keys were on and opened the door. He stood back and gestured for me to go in.

He led me down a back hallway. I could hear music and people talking from what must've been the bar area. The music wasn't live, it sounded like it was coming from a jukebox. We passed the kitchen area then went down a small hallway to a set of stairs.

I followed Rhett up the steps to a door that he again had a key to fit. He pushed it open and stood waiting for me to enter. "After you," he said.

I entered into a small living room. It was dark, quiet and the air smelled of medicine and incense. The music coming from somewhere in the back was low but familiar. It was the blues.

Rhett walked over to an old dark brown wooden buffet. He turned on a lamp that sat atop. There was a doily, the old lace kind, covering most of it. Beautiful gold and silver frames housed pictures that looked to be from the 1950s and 60s.

"Your girlfriend lives here?" I asked, wondering why everything seemed old.

"Not my girlfriend," he said. "My *girl*."

"Oh," I said and nodded.

Maybe this wasn't what I thought it was.

"Come on back this way," he said. I left the buffet and the pictures and wended my way around a couch that had a folded quilt slung over the back and a recliner and television set that both had seen better days.

"Is that you, Rhett?" I heard a voice call out.

"It's me," he said, but stood at the door and waited for me before he went in.

"Hey, Frankie." Rhett walked through the door and over to a woman sitting on the side of a bed. She was dressed in a nightgown and turquoise chenille bathrobe that had a raised floral design. Rhett bent down and kissed her. She smiled and held onto his face.

"Hi, baby," she said. I could hear in her voice that she wasn't doing well. It was low, scratchy and fragile. But there was a twinkle in her eye that reminded me of Rhett. It exuded warmth and laughter. She had to be in her late eighties or early nineties, her hair cut low, she was thin. She smiled at me. Rhett noticed and it made him smile, too.

"You brought your girl," she said. She did seem happy about it, just like he had said.

Rhett turned and looked at me. I smiled at her.

"He told me *you* were his girl," I said.

"Aww," she waved a weak hand at him. "He just fancies himself debonair enough to have two girls. I'm too much for him to handle," she said, and tried to laugh, instead she coughed into a closed fist.

"I told you I was going to bring her," Rhett said. "I wanted you to meet her first," he said.

"First?" I said, although I couldn't keep my smile silent. "Before what?"

"Before I made you my girl," he said, those eyes twinkling in the dim light, even from behind those wire rimmed glasses.

He'd flirted with me before, but these words seemed real. They left me at a loss for words, but I knew the rosy glow coming off my cheeks served as my answer.

"This is Romaine Wilder." Rhett said, finally getting around to the actual introduction.

"Hi, Romaine," she said and held a slight hand out for me to take. "It's so good to meet you."

"It's nice to meet you too, Frankie." I said her name with hesitation. It's what he called her, but I didn't know if that was how I should address her. I took the hand she offered and held onto it for a moment. It felt like a feather.

She patted the seat next to her, and I sat down. She held my hand in hers, patting it. "So, you're the one that's got my Rhett all smitten," she said.

I chuckled. It was the second time in one day I'd heard that word.

"She is," Rhett said, not shying away from admitting his feelings for me, even without having ever telling me about them. "But right now she's gonna take a look at you," Rhett said. "Maybe she can convince you that you need to go into a hospital."

"Not unless she's got some kind of magical powers," she said. "I want to be right here at home." She pointed through the walls. "Close to both my homes."

"If it's magic you want, he brought the wrong girl for that," I said and smiled at her. "For that he would've needed to bring my Auntie Zanne."

"She knows magic?" she said, amusement in her eyes.

"So she thinks," I said.

"And everyone else in Roble thinks it too," Rhett said and chuckled. He looked at me and then down. I followed his eyes and saw that he was looking at my bag that I'd sat at the foot of the bed when I came in.

"How about I take a look at you?" I said. I stood up and got the bag.

My medical bag was really something I just kept. I rarely used it, except for when I came to Roble. People there didn't care that I was a medical examiner.

"What kind of doctor are you?" Frankie said, as if she'd read my mind.

"The kind that went to medical school?" Rhett said.

I took out my stethoscope and cupped it in my hands to get the metal warm to the touch.

I listened to her heart, had her take a deep breath once or twice so I could listen to her lungs. She sat still and let me play doctor, a smile on her face.

As I took her pulse, she asked, "Do you like music?"

"I do," I said. "Same music as you."

"You do?" she said, surprise in her voice. "How do you know what kind of music I like?"

"Isn't that your name on the front of this place?"

She pursed her lips and nodded. "That's me. Lady Frankie. Ironic, huh? Seeing that Frankie is a man's name."

"I like it," I said.

"Me too," she said.

"I have a man's name," I said.

She chuckled. "You do. And I like it."

"Me too," I said. "And, thank you."

"I like the blues," she said.

"And so do I."

"Don't hear many young people that like the blues," she said.

"I'm not so young, Miss Frankie."

"Just call me Frankie."

"Okay," I said and smiled.

"How do you know about the blues?" she asked.

"My father," I said. "He loved the blues. He taught me to love it too."

"Remember, I told you that," Rhett chimed in. "I told you she played the fiddle for the Zydeco contest we had."

"You did?" she asked and squinted her eyes. "Oh yeah," she lifted her hand and pointed a limp finger at Rhett. "I do remember that. Zydeco girl!" She smacked my hand, seemingly happy about recalling the memory and associating it with someone.

I laughed, then looked up at Rhett. He was standing there an approving smile plastered on his face, apparently happy with the two of us together.

"Did your father play Zydeco?" Frankie asked.

"Oh no. My love from that came from my mother."

"She's from Louisiana?"

"Yep." I nodded. "She was French Creole."

"Oh!" She clapped her hands together. "I see you two do have so much in common. Rhett loves everything French. Don't you?" Her eyes, the only spark it seemed left in her, gleamed at Rhett. "And he speaks it beautifully."

"I do," he said. "Thanks to you."

"You earned it, I just made sure you got to go." Frankie turned to me. "He earned a scholarship to go to study *Institut d'Art et d'Archéologie* at the Sorbonne University. Didn't you?"

"Yes, I did," he said.

"But even though he got that scholarship," she said, "we soon figured out that living in Paris ain't cheap."

I looked at Rhett. He was smiling at Frankie, seemingly engrossed with how the memory made her feel, and not how it was he that had accomplished those things.

"I have pictures of him back then, you want to see them?" she asked.

"No, Frankie," Rhett said. "She didn't come here for you to bombard her with pictures of me."

"I'd love to see them," I said. And honestly, that was how I felt.

She pointed to an armoire. "Rhett," she waggled her finger, "look in the bottom of my chifforobe and get my albums."

"Frankie-" Rhett started.

"Don't Frankie me," she interrupted. "Just do like I tell you to do." She looked at me, after ensuring that Rhett dutifully complied with her directive. "You ever been to France?"

"Me?" I shook my head. "No. Never made it there."

"She speaks French," Rhett said.

"You do?" Frankie asked, and a seemingly proud smile erupted on her face. "I know French Creole is a dialect, not the same though, right?"

"No, not the same. But I speak both," I said, now it felt like I was the one bragging. "My mother taught me."

"That's so nice." She smiled. "Have you met her parents yet, Rhett?"

"Both my parents are gone." I didn't let Rhett answer that question for me. "Died when I was twelve," I said. "My Auntie Zanne raised me, she's the closet thing I have to a parent and," I looked over at Rhett, "she's met him and thinks he's the best thing going."

"Oh, you poor baby." She gave my hand a pat. "I'm sorry to hear that. At least they left you something wonderful to remember them by. Music and language. Both are powerful things. Music can soothe you when you facing a whole heap of trouble. I know." She smiled at me. "And your Auntie is right, Rhett is the best thing going."

Just as Rhett sat the photo albums on the bed next to her, my phone rang. I pulled it out of my purse and saw it was Auntie. "Speak of the devil," I said.

"Babet?" Rhett asked.

"Yes," I said. "No telling what she's up to." I turned to Frankie. "I have to take this." I stood up and walked a couple of feet away from the bed.

Chapter Twenty-Seven

"I'm in jail." The words didn't stick. They hung somewhere on the edge of my comprehension, tethered to an obligatory disbelief.

"Where are you?" I asked, a question mark inserted after each word, my voice up a couple of octaves.

Coupled with the doubt I heard her correctly, she was doing that whispering thing she does and I could barely hear her. There was some sort of loud racket going on in the background that could probably drown out screaming.

At least I didn't think I had understood her.

"You have to speak up," I prompted her.

I heard her huff into the phone. "In jail," she repeated, this time shouting, she enunciated each word and syllable. "I said, I'm in jail."

That's what I thought she'd said.

I looked over at Rhett sitting next to Frankie, looking at pictures I'm sure he'd seen a thousand times. Still he sat patiently and looked at each one she held. I didn't want to interrupt him with this crazy conversation. I turned my back, stuck a finger in one ear, and tried to whisper into the phone. "Auntie, what in the world are you doing in jail?"

"I got arrested?" she yelled. "How else do you end up in jail?"

"This is just too unbelievable." I shook my head although she couldn't see it.

"Too what?" she yelled.

"Too unbelievable."

"Why is it unbelievable?" she asked. "I've been in jail before, Darlin'."

My belly, which was already been doing somersaults, did a triple full twist making it almost impossible for me to get in enough air to speak. "I didn't know anything about your criminal past," I said breathily. "But I'm sure knowing that fact wouldn't make me worry any less about you now."

"Don't worry, I'm fine. But I need you to come get me out," she said. "Me and the girls."

"The girls!" I wanted to squeal, but I let it out as calmly as I could. I glanced back at Rhett and moved further away from the two of them and stood in the doorway to the room. "Who is with you, Auntie?"

"The girls," she said. "I just told you. You have to stop making me repeat myself. We don't get but five minutes per phone call."

Oh lord...

"Are Mark and Leonard Winston with you?" I asked.

"Yes."

They were the most non-criminal people I knew. What had she done that she could drag innocent people into her mess?

"Who else?" I said, getting more concerned and exasperated by the minute. I was beginning to wonder how much this was going to cost me. I leaned into the doorframe, worried that my knees were going to buckle. "Delphine? Is she there?"

"Yes," she said. "And Nora and Avoyelles."

I could just picture the six of them in that big white boat of a car being pulled over by the police. I knew whatever had happened to get them tossed in jail had to have been instigated by my Auntie Zanne.

"Why are you there?"

"You have to speak up," she said. "It's noisy here."

Like I hadn't noticed.

"I said, why are you there?"

"I told you, we got arrested. My goodness, Romaine. I'm the one that shouldn't be able to hear."

"I mean what did they charge you with?"

"We were passing counterfeit money at the casino."

"Oh my God." I had to sit down. I put my shoulder against the wall and practically slid along it down the short hallway into the kitchen. With a shaky hand pulled out a chair from the table.

"What casino?" My voice cracking as I spoke.

"Naskila."

"You were gambling with fake money?"

"Didn't I just tell you that? Hold on..." Away from the phone's receiver, she yelled something to someone—I guess a *cellmate*, her words muffled before coming back to our conversation.

"What is going on there?"

"Nothing," she said. "Some people evidently weren't raised to know that you can't hear on the phone when they're screaming in the background." She said the last part loud enough for everyone in the whole jailhouse to hear.

"Are you okay?" I asked.

"Of course I am." I noticed the background noises had calmed. "I had to get some order in this place. They act like delinquents."

"Which they are," I mumbled, with a chortle. "Which *you* are."

"What did you say?" she said.

"I said, where did you get counterfeit money from?"

"I don't want to say too much," Auntie Zanne said, "they might be listening in on my conversation."

"Who might be listening?"

"Big Brother."

I rolled my eyes.

"But I'm sure it's okay to tell this part because it proves our innocence," she said. "We found it went we went through Eugenia's stuff."

"You took her money?"

"It isn't hers anymore, she's dead," Auntie said, her voice seemed annoyed. Like she was irritated with me. "And it's not money," she continued, "don't you know what counterfeit is?"

I rested my elbow on the table, holding up my head with my

hand, I closed my eyes. I couldn't think of any words to say.

"Are you still there?" she asked.

"Yes," I said, my voice starting to tremble. "You probably don't even have a bail set yet," I said, remembering the little law I'd learned working as an ME with the D.A.'s office back in Chicago.

Counterfeiting was a federal offense, although a state could enact its own laws, but I couldn't be sure if the feds were on their way to pick her up. One thing I was sure, she was going to have to see a judge before she got a bail.

"They were going to let me out on my own recognizance since I'm a justice of the peace," she was still talking, "and because I didn't have any of that funny money on me."

I let out a snort.

"But I didn't want to leave without the girls."

I was starting to feel faint.

"So you'll need enough money to bail everyone out."

"A bail has been set for them?" I asked, I sat up thinking perhaps I'd been wrong about the judge setting bail.

"No," she said. I slumped back down. "They said everyone else had to see a judge. But if you bring one of those high-limit credit cards you keep hanging on to without ever using, I'm sure we can talk somebody into letting us all go."

"That's called bribery, Auntie."

"That's called business, Romaine,"

"If that's the kind of business you conduct, no wonder you're in jail."

"You just let me worry about that. You just come get us. I'll do all the talking."

Lord give me strength...

Chapter Twenty-Eight

I was still sitting at the table holding my head with one hand, and the silent phone with the other when Rhett walked in. He stood in the doorway and didn't say a word. I could just feel him there.

After taking a moment, trying to compose myself, I held up my head and looked at him. "Auntie's in jail," I said. "She and her 'girls' were passing counterfeit money at a casino up on in Livingston."

He tried to hold back his chuckle, but it wasn't working. The rumble that started in his throat erupted, those eyes of his twinkled brighter than I'd ever seen them. He pulled out the chair across from me, offering full faced amusement. I didn't find anything funny, and that was the story my face told.

"Sorry," he said, still laughing. "But can't you just picture those little old ladies in the casino, pocketbooks stuffed full of fake money as they were being handcuffed and marched out."

"Oh my God," I let my head fall to the table with a thud. "I hadn't thought about the handcuffs. I think I'm going to throw up."

"It's okay," he said. He got up from the table and came around to the back of me. He laid a hand on my back. "They probably didn't put handcuffs on them. They're elderly women. I mean what are the chances they'd try to fight the police."

"We're talking about Suzanne Babet Derbinay here," I said. "A woman who thinks she could take on Muhammed Ali and win. If they did something she didn't like, she would've grabbed the first thing she saw and swung."

He started that chuckling again.

"Why do you think this is funny?" I turned around and stared up at him.

"I don't. Really, I don't," he said, his face still lit up with mirth. He swallowed a couple of times and seemed to swipe at a tear sown by laughter out of the corner of his eye. "Okay," he shrugged, "so what do we do?"

"I have to go get them, I just don't know how," I said. "I know I can't just call a lawyer like they do on TV." I shook my head. "I don't know what's wrong with her. Getting arrested at her age. They were going to let her out, but she wouldn't go. Not without her girls."

"How many 'girls' are there?" he asked, flexing two fingers on each hand gesturing air quotes.

"Five." I swallowed down my queasiness. "Six including her. Her little posse of late."

"One for all, all for one?"

"It appears that way." I let out a groan. "Said she wasn't going to leave without them. Although, I don't know how she would have left. I'm sure they all went in Avoyelles' car."

"So let's go get them," he said.

"I just said I don't see how we're going to do that. There's been no bail set for the other ones," I said. "Unless, Mr. If-You-Really-Are-FBI," I swung my head back and forth, "you know a judge that'll come in and set one at this hour." I checked my watch then flapped my arms, my voice starting to crack again.

"Or maybe," I continued, not giving him a chance to speak, "you know of an ATM that'll let me get out the thousands of dollars I'm sure I'll need." My shoulders drooped, I let my head roll back and I stared at the ceiling. "God, I hope they take American Express."

"Don't worry. I got this." He whipped his phone out of his pocket, punched in a number and put it up to his ear. While he waited for someone on the other end to pick up, he winked at me, those eyes behind his wire-rimmed glasses all aglow.

Twinkle. Twinkle.

* * *

Rhett walked out of the kitchen and down the hall to the living room while he spoke on the phone. I guessed it was a conversation I wasn't privy to hear.

Standing in the middle of a strange kitchen, I felt lost and alone. I wandered back into the room with Frankie. She sat on the bed still holding onto a picture. The edge of it barely sticking to her trembling fingertips

"Here let me take that for you," I said, and smiled.

"Where's Rhett?" she asked.

"He had to make a phone call," I said. I laid the picture on the nightstand. "I'm going to have to leave."

"Already?" she said. "You two just got here."

"Problem with my Auntie," I said. "She's...stuck. And I have to help her with something."

She nodded. "I understand. But you'll come back, right?"

"Of course, I will," I said. "Then you can show me those pictures of Rhett."

"These are the wrong albums," she said. "She placed her hand on top of them. I don't know what I did with that one with his trip to France in it." Her eyes scanned the room.

"We'll help you find it," I said. "Next time we come. I won't let Rhett get out of me seeing those pictures that easy.

"Good," she said. "Can you put this one back? It must have fell out." Her shaky hand reached for the photo I'd put on the nightstand.

"Let me," I said. I reached across her and got the picture. "Do you know which one it goes in?" I picked up the top album and started to open it.

"Not that one," she pointed to another one, "it's the one that looks like it's denim with the sunflowers on it."

"Okay," I said. I picked it up and started flipping through it to see if I could find an empty spot for the picture. That was when I saw his face. "Oh my lord." I pointed to the picture. "Do you know this man?"

"Sure, I do," she said. "That's Earle Wilder."

I felt a tear well up in my eye as soon as she spoke his name.

"And that's James Cochran and Ellery Perez on the drums." I heard her say the names of the two she mentioned after naming my dad, but after that I didn't hear anything else she said. It didn't take her long to notice. "Are you crying?" she gave me a nudge.

"Earle Wilder was my father," I said.

"Oh, sweetie." She lifted a feeble arm and put it around my shoulder. "You're Earle's little girl?"

I nodded.

"Is that what happened to him?" she said, thoughtfully. "I wondered why he stopped coming around. I figured he'd found his family. Moved off somewhere with them. He was so excited to get with them."

The tears were spilling out a faster than my brains could process her words. I sniffed back tears and realizing after a few moments what she was saying.

"What do you mean, he found his family?"

"He found out he'd been adopted, you know. Him and his sister. Now what was her name…" Frankie's eyes drifted off as she tried to remember.

"Julep?"

"Yep," she said and snapped her finger. "Julep Wilder. But I think then she'd gotten married."

"Her last name is Folsom."

"Sure is," she said nodding. "Is she still around?"

"Yep," I said. "She lives in Roble, too, but I don't understand about them being adopted. They weren't adopted."

"You didn't know?" she said.

"No. I don't know anything about that."

"Leave it to me to spill the beans. And I probably won't be around long enough to clean it up."

"Clean what up?" I said, sniffing back the tears.

"Did you know your father and aunt had more family around?"

"No, they don't," I said swiping away lingering tears. "There isn't...I don't have any other relatives. Just me, Auntie Zanne, Aunt Julep and Pogue."

She pursed her lips, gave a firm nod and didn't say anything else about my father. "You can give me that picture," she said instead, her head nodding toward the loose photograph I was still holding in my hand.

"I can put it away," I said. I didn't want her thinking she'd upset me.

"I don't remember where it goes," she gave me a smile that reached her eyes, "and it'll give me time to go over my pictures again."

"You still worrying about those pictures?" Rhett said. He had walked back into the room.

"No one's worrying over them," Frankie said. "Romaine said she had to leave." She looked at me. "But promised that she'd come back."

"That was nice of her," Rhett said and looked at me. "I'll be holding her to that."

"I'd be happy to come back," I said. "I enjoyed myself."

"Good," he said. "We'll hold her to it, won't we, Frankie?"

"You bet," she said.

Chapter Twenty-Nine

I planted a smile on my face as we said our goodbyes. I walked out with Rhett to the car, but underneath I was that shaky twelve-year-old child who had just lost her parents and had her entire life uprooted. It had gotten dark, which didn't add any levity to my mood.

"I got the address where they are," he said. "I'll put it into the GPS on my phone. You'll help me with the directions?"

"Mmm-hmmm," I said.

It was the only words I could muster up at the moment. I just didn't want to talk. No way did I feel like telling him about what Frankie had said.

It was hard having my past show up with a whole set of new facts just from an old photograph. I stared out of the dark window as Rhett started the car and backed out of the narrow alley. The landscape became a blur as I thought back on that picture.

What a small world. Frankie knew my father.

I remembered my father talking about playing in different clubs around Texas, and how he'd play those songs on his guitar and my mother would sing.

Who was this family my father was looking for? And why didn't anyone else know about it.

Or does my Aunt Julep know?

"Other than the call from your wayward auntie, did you enjoy yourself with me tonight?" Rhett broke into my thoughts. He glanced over at me before he put on his blinkers and took the on ramp to the freeway.

"Yes," I said and bowed my head. His words not only

interrupting my thoughts but broke into my heart. Trying not to blush, I added, "Not just with you, but with Frankie, too. I can see why she's your girl."

"She made me who I am," he said. "I owe her a lot."

"What's wrong with her?"

"Pancreatic cancer." His face didn't change and there was no hesitation in his voice when he told me.

"Oh Rhett," I said. "There's nothing I could do to help her."

"I know," he said. "I just wanted her to meet you before..." he glanced at me, "you know."

I nodded my understanding. I was feeling sad and confused about what I'd just heard, but that didn't compare to what she was going through. "Why isn't she in a hospital?" I asked.

"She doesn't wanna go. She's still able to get around and take care of herself. For now," he said. "And she says she's okay and there's no need to fight the inevitable," the one eye I could see misted up, "she said she's had a good life."

"How do you know her?"

"Frankie's the closest I have to a mother. She was there when my real mother wasn't."

I nodded, not wanting to say too much or pry. He never talked about his past. I didn't want to stop him if he felt like he wanted to share.

He stared out the windshield for a long time and concentrated only on driving. Eventually, he started talking.

"She's the one who taught me all about music." That memory brought a smile to his face. "Taught me how to play the guitar, the piano. The bass."

My highbrows hiked up. "You can play all those instruments?" I asked.

"Yeah," he chuckled. "If I wanted to hang out at the club, it was either play music or clean up the bathrooms. I got right on that saxophone."

"Oh wow, you play the saxophone, too?"

"No," he said firmly. "Me and that thing didn't get along too well. Too much blowing." He chuckled. "I like string instruments better."

All this time I thought he was fessing up to a love of music to get on my good side, and that he showed off speaking French just to impress me.

I drew in a breath and shivered. Was I that self-indulged that I would think he'd do those things just to get to me?

What kind of person was I? That type of pretense I'd seen in my "friends" in Chicago, was instilled in me. Those friends that I hadn't heard from. The ones that had shown me that out of sight was out of mind. They weren't the ones that cared for me.

Now I'm thinking that maybe that was me. That upset me to think that that was the kind of person I had aspired to be. The kind of person I couldn't wait to get back to Chicago to be.

Maybe that's why I didn't have any friends—at least according to Auntie Zanne.

But maybe I didn't want to be that person any more.

I looked at Rhett. Maybe doing that could start with a person like Rhett.

He turned toward me to check the side mirror before changing lanes. He caught my eye and held it. In the dim light in the car, I caught a glimpse of a smile.

He had been raised just like me. Music, language, and love from someone who'd taken on the role of a parent when we'd been left without one. Him having music inside him tugged at my heart strings.

"Frankie was from Houston?"

"No. I'm from Peterson," he said. "I just say I'm from Houston. Part of the life I wanted to create for myself."

"Like being an FBI agent," I said. I added a little sarcasm to my statement for old times' sake. I certainly didn't see him as cagey as I had before, although I still didn't know if he was part of the federal agency.

He glanced over at me. "That's something you find amusing?"

"No." I said. "I do find it amusing that you've convinced my auntie that you were this secret agent man who can come and whisk her right out of jail."

"I'm not a spy—"

"I know," I said. "You've told me that."

"I was going to say, if you'd let me finish, I'm not a spy, but I was...am in the FBI."

I tilted my head and stared at him. All the time I'd known him, he had let me tease him. Let my assumptions that he wasn't gel and become the truth for me.

"Why didn't you tell me that were in the FBI?" I asked. "And why did you let me tease you about it?"

"I didn't want to talk about it," he said. "So I didn't."

"Talk about it?"

"Right."

"So you just let Auntie talk about it for you?"

"It was a mistake to tell her." He blew out a breath. "Huh?"

"Yes. It was."

He chuckled. "But she was going to be my employer. She was giving me a job. I needed to let her know."

"Are you still one?"

"One what?"

"An FBI agent."

"Technically," he said.

"And what does that mean?"

"I lost my partner," he glanced at me. "My partner on the job." He wanted me to understand the distinction. "He was shot. In front of me. He died." His eyes were glazed, looking forward, I could see from the interior lights in the car that he wasn't blinking. "Nothing I could have done, but it made me rethink everything I was doing."

"The things you were doing?"

"Yep. The things I was doing in my life. The things I stood for. The things I wanted. Suddenly somethings just weren't as important."

"Like your job."

"Like my job. The status I felt I had as an agent for the United

States government. It all changed."

I knew exactly what he meant.

After that we both got lost in thought. It was cathartic—all the things I had been thinking about in my life, and how I wanted to change he'd verbalized. He and I were at the same place in the world, and as my auntie liked to say, the universe was settling in. Righting all the wrongs.

"Your destination is on the right."

The voice of the GPS broke our silence. Rhett pulled up into the parking lot of Polk County Jail in Livingston. He turned off the car and without saying a word, got out.

I watched him walk around the car and thought he was going to go in without me, so I scrambled to get the door handle, but before I could he had the door open. He reached out for my hand, taking it, he held it.

"I'm ready to get back to my life," he said looking into my eyes. Those gold flecks in his eyes twinkling. "Maybe not in the same way, but I don't want to hide out anymore. And all the things I want to do to get back to my life, I want to do with you."

"With me?" I asked. My heart started to pound in my chest and butterflies took flight in my stomach.

"Yes, with you."

"You barely know me."

He leaned in close to me, pushing me up against the car and lowered his voice. "I know everything about you."

"No, you don't," I said, my voice barely audible, not for effect, but because of how nervous this was making me.

"I know everything I *need* to know."

"You do?"

"I do."

Then he kissed me. Long and passionately.

In the parking lot of the sheriff's office.

And I let him.

They were probably going to throw me right into the same cell with Auntie.

Chapter Thirty

"There was a ruckus going on in the Polk County Jail lobby. I could hear it before we even got inside the double glass doors. And I knew, without a doubt my Auntie Zanne would somehow be in the middle of it.

And sure enough, her girls were crying and agitated, and she was fussing over and coddling each of them, moving from one to the other. Nola Landry walked out of the restroom as we walked in, her light skin bright red probably from scrubbing it with paper towels. She pulled out hand sanitizer from her purse and screwed off the cap instead of squeezing some out. She dropped a big plop—nearly half the bottle—into her hand.

Who I didn't expect to see was Hailey Aaron.

She looked prettier than the first time I met her, which had been months ago.

Why would she turn up now?

I looked at her and reached up to smooth my hair down and run a hand over my face.

Who looks like that to come to a jailhouse?

Younger than me she had thick brown hair that was smooth and shiny. Her dark eyelashes seemed to move at a slower rate than most people's, so it looked as if she was always batting then. Her FBI persona was evident in her jeans, suit jacket and boots attire. But the way those jeans and low-cut top fit, and the glow of her dewy, smooth, olive complexion made me think of a *Sports Illustrated* swimsuit model.

"What is Hailey doing here?" I asked when I saw the smile come over Rhett's face as we walked in. I knew it was for her. I'd noticed before how the two of them had a familiarity about them. I had suspected it was one that transcended a working relationship. If it did, after what happened in the parking lot, me seeing her would be quite awkward.

"She's our get out of jail free card," he said. "Hi Hailey," he said, raising his voice to be heard over the noise. He left my side and walked over to her. "You got here quickly." He gave her a quick hug.

"Would have been here sooner, but I was following the wrong suspect, took me a minute to realize."

"Who you calling a suspect?" Auntie Zanne said the temperature in her words hot.

"Auntie," I said, walking over to her. I wanted to calm her down. "I thought you were *inside* the jail?"

"I was," she said. "Hailey got us out."

I looked at her. "Hi Hailey," I said. "And thank you?" I said it as a question. I wasn't quite sure what she'd done or what she expected from me. Rhett had used the word "free," so I wasn't thinking I owed her money.

"You're welcome," she said. "I'd do it for my friend, anytime," she punched Rhett in the arm, "but this was work."

"Work?" I asked.

"How about we get these ladies out of here?" she said. "All of this has ruffled their feathers. Then we can talk."

"How about we go to Babet's?" Rhett said. "Maybe she could make us some tea and you can talk to them."

"Sounds good," Auntie Zanne said. Her cronies seemed to have calmed down, and the mention of tea always made my auntie cooperative.

I grabbed her hand. "You're riding back with us," I said.

"I am not!" she said and snatched her hand from mine. "I'm going back with Avoyelles. I may need to be the one that drives."

I looked at Avoyelles. She looked shaken which surprised me. Being such a large, sturdy woman I expected her to have more gumption.

"I'm okay to drive," Avoyelles said, her voice low, head hung down. "At least I think I am. I never want to be locked up again." She looked back toward the nondescript black door, presumably the one they'd come out of.

"Don't worry," Auntie Zanne said. "I'll be with you guys."

"We're going home," Mark and Leonard said at the same time. They had the reddest eyes of them all.

"Hailey," Rhett said, "you can follow us."

"Ten-four," she said and walked away. She turned, looked over her shoulder and give us—him—a smile and a wave.

"C'mon," he said, "we don't want to make her wait."

I probably should have protested, but I couldn't think of a single reason to say we shouldn't leave.

I would've thought that I needed to speak to someone, pay something, fill out necessary forms but there weren't any law enforcement officer nearby or standing inside of a bulletproof glass office waiting for me.

So I tagged along as he strode toward the door, not wanting to make Hailey wait too long. When he got to the door, though, he did stop and open it for me. Then he took my hand and walked me to my side of the car. He opened the door, waited until I got in and shut it.

"That was easy, huh?" he said as he got in and buckled his seatbelt.

"Thanks to Hailey," I said.

"Yep. Good thing I knew she was around," he said.

"How did she do it?" I asked. Not really caring so much about that than *why* she did it. Favor to Rhett? If so, then what did she want in return?

"Probably best if I let her tell you," he said. He grabbed my hand and gave it a squeeze. "She'll tell us at the house."

The first time I'd seen Hailey Aaron was at Bumper's funeral. Our last murder victim, the one that she or Rhett seemed too interested in solving. I remembered when I saw how Rhett looked at her, I got jealous. Didn't even know why at the time. In fact, I would've sworn if anyone asked, that I was singularly and deeply in love with Alex. I was quite rude to her that day. Later Auntie Zanne even fussed at me for walking away when Rhett tried to introduce me to her.

But after that kiss, need I worry about *her* anymore?

"You're telling us that Orville is a murderer *and* a counterfeiter!" Delphine said, she bawled up her fist and shook it in the air. "Eugenia should have been the one that killed him. And I would have been happy to help!"

"I don't know if he's a murderer," Hailey said, "but we've been suspicious of his counterfeiting activities for a while."

We'd arrived back at the house a full thirty minutes before Auntie and her girls arrived. When they got inside, we found that Nola Landry had been dropped off. She had said, according to Auntie Zanne, that she needed to schedule a skin peel. I didn't know what that was. She also told me that Mark and Leonard had gone home and gone to bed.

Auntie Zanne came in and went right to her cabinets, combing through them for the right ingredients for whatever concoction she wanted to brew. She had two teapots whistling on the stove. Avoyelles set at the table with a handful of tea steepers filling them with the dried plants Auntie passed to her. Next to her sat Delphine, the only other freed jailbird still standing.

"How did you know to come and see about us?" Auntie Zanne asked. She grabbed a few mugs from the cabinets, stuffing them in her arms, picked up the filled steepers and set one in front of each of us. I pushed mine to the side.

"I didn't know," Hailey said. She did a quick jerk of her head toward Rhett. "He called me and told me that y'all had gotten arrested for counterfeiting. He knew I was on the same kind of case. Initially, from what he told me, I thought it was unrelated to the counterfeiting case I was working on. But a call down to the sheriff's office told me it was the same one."

"How did you know that from a phone call?" Auntie Zanne asked.

"Serial numbers," Hailey said. "For some reason Mr. Elder used consecutive numbers, only he did a countdown of them."

"Countdown?" Delphine asked.

"His numbering always went down one from the last bill. We thought he was counting up at first until recently we got a bunch of them that proved he was doing it the other way."

"Clever," Avoyelles said.

Auntie went around and poured hot water from her teapot in each mug. When she got to me, she pushed the cup back in front of me and gave me the evil eye as she poured.

"That's apparently what he thought," Hailey said. "Thank you," she interrupted her explanation when Auntie poured her tea. "That's why I had him in my line of sight when the call came in about the six of you getting arrested with counterfeit bills." She put her cup to her mouth, steam coming from it.

"I'd probably ask what that is before I'd drink it," I said to Hailey. Unsuspecting people, I felt, needed to be warned about my auntie.

She lowered the cup and stared down into it, then over to Rhett who was lapping it up.

"Don't pay any attention to her," Auntie said. "It's mostly chamomile."

Hailey gave the brew an inconspicuous sniff then took a sip. "Mmmm. It's good," she said and looking up at Auntie, she smiled.

If I were her, I would've asked what was the part that wasn't "mostly chamomile." That was the part to worry about. But she'd been warned. I pushed my cup away and didn't say anything else about it.

"You were at the casino watching Orville?" Delphine asked.

"Sure was," she said.

"So were we," Delphine said. "Trying to see what he was up to and how it related to the murder. Figured he had used Eugenia's money." Delphine eyed me. "We didn't. Well, most of us didn't know then she hadn't left it to him."

"The murder?" I asked. "Auntie," I looked at her. "You're not supposed to be poking your nose in that investigation and now you've got other people doing it too."

"We weren't poking," she said. "We were just trying to keep up with him. He was at the casino, so we had to be at the casino. Who knew we had funny money?"

"And if I hadn't have gotten the intel that the serial numbers were consecutive numbers much higher than the ones we had but still in the same sequence, I wouldn't have left watching him."

"It was an older batch of bills?" Rhett asked, seemingly understanding her logic.

"Yeah, so that made me think that the higher up someone else we've been trying to track down was spending the money."

"The person making the bills?" Auntie Zanne asked.

"Exactly," Hailey said.

"And it turned out to be us," Avoyelles said.

"It did," Hailey said, "and it hit me, I knew exactly where you ladies got them from."

"From Miss Eugenia's trash," I said.

"It wasn't trash," Delphine squealed. "It was Eugenia's things. Her personal belongings. Her life." She hung her head and was easy to see that she was upset. "It wasn't trash."

"I'm sorry Delphine," I said. "You're right. It wasn't."

"That's right, Delphine, it wasn't," Auntie added. "And in those things we found that rose colored dress that Eugenia was so particular about."

"The one she wanted to be buried in," Delphine nodded as she spoke.

"And I'm going to get her ready first thing in the morning. Avoyelles is going to do her hair, and you come by if you want," Auntie said. "You can be here and make sure we get it right. Make sure everything's just like Eugenia would've liked it."

"I'll stop by the hotel and pick you up," Avoyelles said. "We'll all be together, just like we used to be, even if it is for the last time."

Chapter Thirty-One

I opened one eye and saw the first light of the day stream through my window. And there sat J.R. staring at me.

I knew I hadn't overslept. The sunlight was one clue, and the blaring red numbers on my digital clock confirmed it. It was six a.m.

I could already feel the sun bearing on me and knew the day would be a scorcher. I turned over, getting my face out of the sunlight and let out a groan thinking—wishing—I could go back to sleep.

Then I sat up. I touched my lips and smiled.

Rhett had kissed me.

All this time I'd been putting him off, thinking he was sneaky and up to something, and it turned out he was a man that I could like. No extra baggage. He loved music and French and maybe even me.

I let out another groan and took my fingers away from my lips. I thought about that picture.

My father and aunt, adopted?'

I couldn't believe it. I always planned my life. Everything in it. How I wanted to live. Where I wanted to live. What I wanted to do. And that's how I did it. Granted Auntie Zanne was always trying to disrupt it. And true, as of late I was feeling a lot different about how I wanted my life to be, still I didn't like surprises. And learning your family isn't what you thought it to be, was a big surprise to me—an unwelcomed one.

Am I not really a Wilder? How come my Aunt Julep never mentioned anything like that to me? And why doesn't she have anything to do with them?

I glanced at my cellphone sitting on the nightstand next to my bed.

Maybe I should call her...

I reached for the phone but changed my mind. What would I say? Do I have more family that you never told me about?

I shook my head. That just wasn't something that should be talked about over the phone.

I wasn't sure I wanted to talk about it at all.

I stood up and fell back on the bed. I felt hot, dizzy and agitated. I didn't know if it was the relentless Texas heat or the knowledge I'd gained from my visit with Frankie that had me reeling.

"Morning, Sunshine." It was Rhett standing at the door. I grabbed the sheet from the bottom of the bed and pulled it over me.

"What are you doing up here?" I asked. No longer feeling irritated with the things he did. This feeling was more akin to one that would cause me to blush.

"I've got a message from Babet," he said grinning.

"Where is she?" I pulled the sheet a little snugger around my thighs.

"Downstairs. In the kitchen."

"And she sent you up here with a message?"

"Yep. And this." He pulled a cup of coffee from behind his back.

Coffee. I let out a happy sigh. I scooted over and tugged at the sheet to get more coverage then held out my hand to take the cup. He took one giant leap in and extended his arm.

"You can bring it here," I said.

He walked over to me. "Actually, the coffee was my idea."

I took it from him, not taking my eyes off his. I blew in the cup and took a sip, looking at him over the rim. "Mmmm. This is good," I said smacking my lips. "You made this?"

"I did."

"How do you know how I like my coffee?"

"I've been watching you."

I took another sip. "Well, Mister FBI Man, you run a good surveillance operation, because this is perfect." I took another sip. "So," I said smacking my lips, "what's the message from Auntie Zanne?"

"Avoyelles and Delphine are downstairs. She told me to tell you that she knows that you and her are supposed to go see Nola today, to question her?" He ended his message with a question on his face.

"She told you that?"

"Yep. Do you know what she means?"

"I do," I said. After leaving The Grandview and speaking with Rayanne, we were supposed to get together and see Nola to find out what she'd done with "the bundle" as we'd taken to calling it. But with me spending the evening with Rhett all the way down in Peterson, and Auntie getting thrown in jail in Livingston, questioning Nola got put on the back burner.

"She told me no one is to know?" he said. The flecks of gold in his eyes sparked with mischief.

I laughed. "Then why did she tell you?"

"Because I'm in."

"In what?" I asked.

"In with the two of you."

"We don't need a third wheel."

"Is that what you think about me?" he said and came and sat next to me on the bed. I scooted over, away from him, licked my lips, and swallowed to try and get my heart to stop doing flip-flops. "I thought after last night."

"Last night was nice," I said and lowered my head. Thinking about last night made me smile, but him sitting so close made me tremble. I was having a hard time holding my coffee cup. "But now I have to get dressed to go on my secret mission with Auntie Zanne."

"You need any help?" he asked.

"No," I said firmly. "Thank you for the message, and," I held up the cup, hoping my hand was steady enough not to spill it, "thank you for the coffee."

"Okay," he said and stood up. "I'll see you downstairs."

"Okay," I said.

He walked to the door, but didn't go out of it. He turned around and looked at me.

"What?" I asked.

"Are you okay about last night?"

"I've been kissed before," I said. "It wasn't a big deal?"

"It wasn't?" he seemed taken aback.

"I mean...It was a big deal...It was...Nice. Very nice." I had to will my heart to be still. "But it didn't affect me. Well, you know it affected me..."

He walked back over and sat down again. No," he shook his head and looked into my eyes, "I already know how I affect you." I raised an eyebrow at that statement. "I mean about what Frankie said," he continued. "Didn't seem like you knew about that."

"You heard us? I thought you were in the other room on the phone."

"Didn't you just comment on my excellent surveillance techniques?" he asked.

"I never said you were 'excellent.'"

"You didn't?" He scooted closer to me. "Then I'll have to show you that I am."

J.R. gave out a bark, it scared me. I tried to hop up, but was tangled in the sheet I'd been using to cover myself and landed on the floor.

"Arghh!" I hit the floor with a thud.

Both J.R. and Rhett came to my rescue. J.R. had a more sympathetic look on his face than Rhett, but at least he extended a hand to help me up.

"I need to get dressed and see what Auntie wants."

"Okay," he said. "We'll finish this conversation later."

Yeah, later when I get a better handle on these emotions, I thought as he left. I went into the bathroom to shower. J.R. scampering in behind me.

"Why did you let him make me so nervous?" I looked at J.R. "Thought you were my protector." He let out a loud bark as if to say he wouldn't let anyone do anything to me. "Yeah, it's too late for that," I muttered as I stepped into the shower. "He's already stolen my heart."

Chapter Thirty-Two

Even with Auntie spending the evening before breaking the law and trying to break out of jail, she was up and at it already and she wanted me included.

The phones had been ringing off the hook since Eugenia died. Both the ones for the funeral homes and the ones to our house. That buzz just gave Auntie Zanne more momentum.

I threw on a skort and a sleeveless top. It was going to be hot, and I didn't know where else besides Nola Landry's Auntie was dragging me off to.

I grabbed the now empty coffee mug Rhett brought me and got J.R. to follow me downstairs. I walked into the kitchen, and as it had been for the past few days, it was full of people.

Avoyelles and Delphine looked like they had the night before. I wasn't sure if they'd ever gone home. The twins were nowhere in sight, I was sure they were still reeling from the previous night's escapades. And Flannery Poole was back.

"Good morning," I said. I stood at the doorway to the kitchen. I didn't know what they might be cooking up and I wanted to steer clear.

"You sure do sleep late," Flannery said. "I mean Babet gets up at the break of dawn. I'd think you'd have the same habits."

"She's got nothing to do," Auntie Zanne said. "No reason to wake up early."

"I definitely don't have any concoctions to brew up. Doesn't take me long to get my fix." I walked over to my Keurig. It was unplugged. Again. "I'll just pop my coffee flavor in and I'm good."

"Thought Rhett brought you coffee this morning," Auntie said.

"He did," I said and let my eyes wander around the room. "Thought I might need more than one cup." I didn't have to say it, Auntie knew that her herbalist cohorts were more than I could take. I wouldn't spend my morning hanging out with them, but I was curious on what they were doing. "You guys been up a while?"

"We didn't go to bed," Avoyelles' said.

"We embalmed Eugenia," Delphine said.

"All of you?" I asked. Auntie usually didn't let anyone that didn't work for her near her embalming stations. She claimed insurance reasons, but I knew she didn't want anyone else trying to tell her what to do.

"Not me," Flannery raised her hand like she was in school. "I only just arrived. Plus," she shrugged, "I really didn't know her that well to get *that* personal."

I chuckled as I rinsed my mug out in the sink, getting ready for my second cup.

"Well, I knew her that well and I knew I could count on Babet to do her right. She looks beautiful." Delphine face lit up, but then it turned to worry. She looked at Auntie Zanne. "Don't know how you're going to get paid though," she said. "I doubt Orville will pay for the things we picked for her."

"You don't know?" I asked. "You didn't tell her?" I looked at Auntie.

"Tell me what?" Delphine said.

"Auntie," I said scolding.

"Eugenia designated you as her beneficiary, Delphine," Auntie said. "She left you fifty thousand dollars."

Delphine Griffith didn't say a word. Her mouth dropped open and her arms went slack. I think if she hadn't been sitting down, she would have fell onto the floor.

"Now see what you've done?" Auntie Zanne yelled at me. She rushed over to Delphine like the woman had just had a stroke or something. Plus, I hadn't been the one to tell her, she had.

"I didn't do anything," I said protesting, my eyes getting big. "How are you blaming me?"

Then Delphine started crying. No not crying. Sobbing. Hysterically. She opened her mouth and let out a wail. Everyone leaned back, blown by her yowl. Then she became animated. She got up and ran, (her version of running) out the back door leaving us all flabbergasted.

Auntie Zanne glared at me.

"What?" I said, holding out my hands, I hunched my shoulders.

"You've got such a big mouth," she said. "It runs like diarrhea!"

I had told Auntie I was ready when she was, and that I'd wait in the car.

Actually it was the black van that she'd rented for me. We had it for another day, I figured we may as well use it. Plus, I wasn't a Cadillac kind of girl like my Auntie.

Auntie and Avoyelles had scrambled to catch Delphine even though a skunk could run faster. They got her buckled down into a kitchen chair and were feeding her a foul-smelling concoction. When I left, she was talking—babbling. She said that Eugenia had died for nothing. Orville had killed her for nothing. He thought he was going to get money when she died, and instead she got it.

I couldn't take all that wailing and misdirected blame any more. I left. I figured Auntie would come out eventually.

While I sat, I thought about the murder. This had been bad investigating on my part. There had been so much chaos that I hadn't had time to do much. We were on the trail of the server who had spilled the deadly drink. But she didn't have a motive so far we could tell. And getting her side of the story wasn't going to be easy because we didn't even know who she was.

Delphine was sure it was Orville Elder who had killed his wife. Certainly, he had motive, means and opportunity and I hadn't ruled him out.

Then again, I hadn't ruled out Delphine either. I had let Auntie get into my head, wanting to convince me it wasn't her tell. But that wasn't how an investigation should go. Maybe Delphine steered us toward Orville to keep us from investigating her.

"The vote is tomorrow," Auntie said, staring out the car window. I'd waited for thirty minutes before she came out, and for more than half the way to Nola's she hadn't said a word. I figured she was still mad at me for spilling the beans even though the words had come out of her mouth. "I think that I'm going to nominate Avoyelles."

"Is that how it goes?" I asked. I wanted to ease back into conversing with her. She could hold a grudge. "You nominate the person?"

"No, usually nominations are made by members. They send it in before our Boule. That's how Eugenia got elected. Now there's no time for the regular way of doing things."

"Can you do that?" I asked. I couldn't imagine it any other way. My auntie would never be the subordinate. She ran everything. Still I thought I would ask. "Tell everyone who you're picking, and they vote for that person?"

"I'm going to talk to Nola about that when we get to her house. She knows all about the bylaws and parliamentary procedure." She stopped looking out of the window and turned to me. "But Avoyelles deserves it."

"How do you decide who deserves it?" I asked. "Isn't everyone equally qualified?" I was thinking all they need to know how to do was keep a greenhouse and grind up the dried fruits of their labor to shove on some unsuspecting poor soul who was willing to pay for a little hope, even if it were a bogus fix.

"Remember how I told you that Vivienne Pennywell should have been the Most High?"

"Yeah." I nodded.

"Well, Avoyelles should have been elected the Lesser Mambo years ago. I don't know why she wasn't ever nominated."

"What's so good about Avoyelles?"

"She's left her signature all the way down the Mississippi."

"What does that mean?" I asked.

"She's lived in a lot of different places. Practicing as a Voodoo herbalist everywhere she went."

"Like a gypsy?" I asked.

"There's nothing wrong with gypsies," Auntie said. "I used to date this guy who was a Romani."

I pursed my lips and rolled my eyes. "I doubt if that's true."

"It is," she said and nodded. "Lots of things you don't know about me."

Like going to jail...

"Well, what about Delphine?" I asked, not wanting to hear any of the things she'd done. "She's helpful. She teaches all those people at her house about being natural medicine conscious. And she was the only one of 'the girls' that was able to extract ricin from the castor bean. Even Avoyelles wasn't able to do that. Delphine is a top-notch herbalist."

"That's true," Auntie said. "But she's never expressed interest in it before. Avoyelles has." Auntie sucked her tongue. "Anyway, I don't know if Delphine would be a good legacy for Eugenia's place as a Lessor Mambo. They had that rift. You remember the letter."

"Eugenia didn't even get crowned," I said.

"You don't get *crowned*," Auntie said.

"You know what I mean," I said. "And, even though we didn't see the first page of the letter, Avoyelles said Delphine and Eugenia made up."

"I just don't see how we'd give it to someone who Eugenia was angry at and had a falling out with."

"Oh my," I said. "Haven't you been listening? Miss Eugenia had a rift, as you call it, with everybody. Delphine. Orville. And whoever killed her."

"That was probably Orville," she said.

"Or maybe not. Maybe it was another person she'd had a falling out with," I said and gave an all-knowing nod. "She might have even had one with Avoyelles Kalty."

Auntie furrowed her brow. "I don't think so."

"Avoyelles said that Miss Eugenia had stopped coming to her to get her hair done. You remember that?"

"Yeah, but that doesn't mean anything."

"She said it was because Miss Eugenia had stopped driving. But she used to drive to our house all the time."

"Why are you advocating for Delphine Griffith? Did she offer you money?" Auntie asked.

I laughed. "No." I looked over at Auntie. I wanted to say it was because I felt bad. I still had Delphine on my list of suspects. I had added her and crossed her off a dozen times. But she was so distraught over the Miss Eugenia's death that I probably should have left her off the list a long time ago.

"Well, you got a reason?" Auntie asked.

"She, Delphine, is so sad about her friend that it seems right to make her the Lesser Mambo. Plus, I think she's a good herbalist. She didn't try to force me to drink some brew at her house and she helps others."

"Avoyelles helps others. She's sending her nephew to detail my cars tomorrow. Remember how nice her deuce and a quarter looks?"

"Yes, I remember," I said.

"Because I know her, I got a really good deal on it."

"Is that why you want her to be the Lesser Mambo? Because you get perks?"

"No," she said, pursing her lips, she squinted her eyes at me.

"So, then what? You're driving your fleet of cars up to Angelina County so what's his name can detail them?" I remembered that was where Avoyelles was from.

"No," she said still frowning. "He has a mobile detailing operation up in Angelina County. And his name is Pete, very nice young man."

"Do you know him?" I asked.

"No, but Avoyelles told me he's nice. He dotes on her. And he's coming all the way to Sabine County to clean my cars." She nodded and gave me a wink. "Now you can't beat that for service. That's a long way out of his service area. And if he's as good looking as Avoyelles says, maybe I can invite him in for tea?" She waggled her eyebrows.

"Please don't try and fix me up."

"I'm never going to get grandkids," she said shaking her head. "This family is just going to end with us."

I bit down on my bottom lip and chewed it. I debated whether to tell Auntie about the night before. Not the kiss. I knew better than to tell her that. But about the picture. About my father. His other family.

My family.

Could it be true? If it were, that would mean there was more to my history then I knew. More family to love.

"Hey," she snapped her fingers. "You listening to me?"

"I went to Peterson with Rhett last night," I said. I figured I may as well tell her. That way I didn't have to figure out what to do all by myself.

"I know," she said.

"What happened? You got started on me some grandkids?"

"Oh! No!" I looked at her as she said the words and almost ran over onto the median. "Why would you say that?"

"I was talking about grandkids and you started talking about last night. I just put two and two together."

"That's just bad math, Auntie."

"Is it?"

"We went to see a friend of his. Her name is Frankie." I glanced over at her. "He said she was like a mother to him. She's really sick."

"Did you do something to make her well?"

"Don't think there's anything anyone can do," I said. "She probably only has a little time."

Auntie sucked her tongue. "Why would you tell me such a sad story?" She shook her head. "Change the subject," she said, her voice practically ordering it.

"She had a picture of my daddy," I said.

"Earle Wilder?"

"That's the only father I have."

"What was she doing with his picture?"

"She ran a juke joint. That was the name of it at least."

"Oh," Auntie said smiling. She nodded her understanding. "He used to play at a lot of those. He was good. Always in demand."

"She said that he found out he and Aunt Julep had been adopted and he was going to look for his family."

Auntie turned and looked at me. She reached over and laid her hand on my arm. "I don't know what to say," she said.

"You? At a loss for words?" I tried not to let my voice crack. I could feel the tears welling up in my eyes. "You think it's true? That he—I have more family somewhere?"

"Could be true," she said. "Back then people helped each other out. We took in the needy and the hapless. Made them family."

"It's kind of scary to think about," I said. "It would change who I am. Who I always thought I was."

"It's not scary, Sugarplum," Auntie said and gave me a warm smile. "And it doesn't change a thing, it helps you to better understand who you are. It gives you even more people to love."

"But I don't know what to think about it." I felt a tear fall from my eye. "I don't know what to do about it."

"What do you want to do?"

"I don't know." The tears were falling faster. I was feeling like Delphine. Crying over nothing.

"Why don't you talk to Julep about it?" Auntie said. "She might know something."

"If she knew, wouldn't she have told me?"

"No necessarily, Darlin'. Everyone's got secrets. Some of them we hope to take to the grave."

"Oh," I said and sniffed back my tears. "That sounds ominous."

Auntie laughed. "How about when we leave Nola's, we go over and talk to Julep."

"No, I don't think I want to do that," I said shaking my head.

"Why?"

"I don't know." I hunched my shoulders. "I don't know if it's something I want to find out about. Something I want to know. I'm happy with the family I have."

"Oh, pshaw. You can ask her about what you learned in Peterson, and I can tell her about what happened in jail."

"I don't think she'd' want to hear about that," I said.

"Sure she does. Who do you think I went to jail with before?" Auntie said. "I just hope she doesn't feel left out..."

Chapter Thirty-Three

Picture 1950s Hollywood.

That was Nola Landry's home. It was a two-story mid-century modern. Inside the compound, marked by a brick wall the lawn was immaculately manicured, surrounded by topiary and beds of red roses everywhere. She had a white dogwood that, I soon found, matched the artificial one in the foyer of the inside of the house.

Auntie rang the bell next to the large double door. Waiting, I looked up and saw a surveillance camera sticking out of the corner of the house. I let my eyes drift over the entire area and saw more of them posted along the perimeter wall. I wondered what she had inside so valuable that she needed high-tech security. I didn't think the First National Bank of Roble, the only bank in town, had as much surveillance as she did. Heck, most people in Roble didn't even lock their doors.

We waited only a couple of moments, before a woman answered the door. It wasn't Nola. This woman looked like she belonged in this century. She smiled when she saw Auntie. "Mornin', Miss Babet," she said with a wide smile and stepped aside to let us in.

"Morning, Carrie," Auntie Zanne said, and matched her smile. "This is my niece, Romaine, "Auntie said as we walked through the door into the foyer.

The woman was petite. She was dark and wore her salt and pepper hair in a short afro. She had on a pair of jeans and a bright yellow blouse that reminded me of the pantsuit Miss Eugenia had worn to the Boule. On her feet she wore house slippers.

"Nice to meet you," Carrie said. "I've heard a lot about you."

I smiled and nodded my head. Up until the day of the Boule I hadn't known anything about Nola Landry. I didn't know who this woman was to her, but I could imagine what my auntie had said. It had to be about me moving back to Roble. That was her favorite conversation.

"Nice to meet you, too," I said.

"I let Miss Landry know you're here," she said and turned walking into the interior of the house.

I started to follow her in, but Auntie stopped me. "Take your shoes off," She instructed. "Put those on." She pointed to a basket that sat next in a corner. It was filled with footies, each rolled into a ball."

I did as asked, not questioning the reason I couldn't go the rest of the way with my shoes on. I slipped my feet out of my flats, lined them up against the wall and put a pair of the socks on. When I stepped out of the foyer, I saw why. The place was spotless.

The tile floor gleamed and the windows sparkled.

The inside was furnished in modern furniture upholstered in woven white material and brightened by orange velvet pillows there were matching rolled armchairs—all covered in clear plastic. She was going to make sure no dirt got on them.

The persimmon painted walls, dark oak tabletops, and corners were filled with surrealist wall art and contemporary sculptures. A baby grand set in the middle of the floor, the top down it was covered with pictures just as Frankie's front room had been. I didn't let my eyes linger. I'd have enough of pictures and the secrets they held.

I could see straight through the house to the back. The back wall was all glass augmenting the indoor with the outdoor living space. There was a large clear blue, kidney shaped pool. White wrought iron furniture with bright yellow and green floral cushions sat poolside.

I felt like I'd stepped back in time.

"Has Nola lived here a long time?" I asked.

"Looks like we walked straight into Ozzie and Harriet Nelson's home."

"Except it's not in black and white," I said.

"Nola used to be a movie star."

"A real movie star?" I asked. I didn't ask because I was in awe, but Auntie had a tendency to exaggerate. I probably should've asked her what her definition of one was. Even though Nola Landry's name sounded familiar to me and had been nagging at me since I first learned it, I was sure it wasn't because I associated her with Clark Gable or Gregory Peck.

"Yes, a real movie star," Auntie said. "Not a Greta Garbo or Ingrid Bergman. She's black, she couldn't have been that kind of star. But she was in a lot of movies. Would have been in a lot more if she'd been around today. She's good."

"Why thank you, Babet," Nola said, as she came floating down the stairs. She had on a white flowered kimono style robe that caught the air as she walked moving like a sail on a boat. It was worn open over a pair of white capri pants and a pale yellow shell.

"Hi Nola," Auntie Zanne said. "Hope you don't mind we stopped by without calling first."

"Always happy to see you," she said. "And who do you have with you?" She let her eyes drift over to me, locking them with mine.

I couldn't believe her. Was she playing a role with me? She'd just spent five hours with me the day before during the autopsy and I was the one who picked her up from jail. Granted she didn't say much other than asking how many of pairs of gloves could she put on, she did participate. And at the sheriff's jail in Polk County she was too busy getting clean to notice me.

But how could she feign not knowing that I was related to Auntie Zanne? I had called her that in front of Nola each time I'd seen her. Plus, how could Carrie know of me and Nola didn't? If Auntie Zanne had spoken to Carrie about me, I was sure she'd done the same with Nola.

This woman was such a phony.

"I'm Romaine," I said and stuck out my hand. "Babet's niece. I just saw you yesterday."

Nola looked at my hand, then at Auntie Zanne. She gave me a polite smile and turned away. "How about some tea," she said walking toward the living room. "I can have Carrie warm up the pot I made earlier."

"No, thank you," I said. Nola may have been a movie star in Auntie's eyes, but in mine she was a Voodoo herbalist. I wasn't drinking any tea made by their hands, especially something she'd previously made. What happened to brewing a fresh pot? I'd accepted coffee at Delphine's when I first met her, but it was out of a bag from a grocery store.

Auntie swung her hand behind her where I stood trying to hit me. "Tea would be nice, we'd enjoy that," she said, speaking for me too.

She could bring it, but I wasn't drinking a drop of it.

"So what brings you by?" Nola asked after summoning Carrie and asking her to bring out a tea service tray. She gestured for us to sit down on the plastic covered sofa.

It wasn't a good day for me to have worn something with my legs bare. I was afraid of sticking to the plastic. I sat and got stuck trying to scoot back. I had to lift up off the couch and move back before I dropped.

Auntie looked at me. I looked back. I knew she wasn't waiting for me to speak. She wouldn't ever think about me taking the lead on anything. So, I stayed quiet.

When I didn't say anything on my own, she made sure I spoke up. "Romaine has some questions for you."

"You do?" she said and tilted her head as if she was surprised that I would.

"If it's alright," I said, remembering my manners. Auntie Zanne told me that my elders would always be my elders, no matter how old I got. Show respect. But this woman seemed to think she was regal, someone from the Golden Age of Hollywood. But she wasn't. At her age which I estimated at around seventy, she wouldn't have been old enough to have done anything in that era unless she started as a child. I couldn't imagine her holding on to her arrogance if her exposure was early.

"Certainly, it's alright," she said. Carrie returned with the tea service. Nola waved toward the coffee table telling Carrie to put it down, then waved dismissing her. "Although I can't imagine what it is you'd want to ask me." She picked up the teapot and started pouring the dark steaming liquid into the cups.

"It's about Eugenia Elder," I said.

"Fascinating," she said, handing me a cup of tea. "The whole way you took her apart and was able to put her back together. Messy though. Very messy." She shook her head and reached over to the end table and picked up a bottle of sanitizer. I wondered if she had them stashed all over. "I believe after that and fishing through trash at her house," she continued, "I must've taken six baths."

So she did remember me.

I put my cup and saucer down on the table. "I wondered what you remembered about the server that spilled the liquid on Mrs. Elder." I waited for Nola to correct me on the generic term "liquid." I was sure Auntie had told her what it really was.

"Oh, I remember everything about her," she said and took a sip of her tea. "Uncouth. Clumsy. Very clumsy. I was appalled at her lack of competence."

Nola closed her eyes and shook her shoulders making her top half shudder as if just the thought sent waves of disgust through her core.

I waited until she stopped her dubious display of shivering expecting her to tell me what she knew, but she said nothing. Scene. Fade to black. Sip from tea cup.

"Did you find out her name?" I asked, wondering how I could get her to stop the theatrics and get to the answers. I wanted to know if she saw or knew anything I didn't.

"Of course not," she said. "I had no reason to get personal with her."

"I thought perhaps you had a conversation with her," I said.

"I did no such thing," she said, seemingly offended. "I just directed her on what to do and made sure she did it."

That part I did see.

"I saw that," I said. "You had her clean it up."

"Made a nice little bundle for her and had her discard it."

"In the dumpster?" I asked.

"Oh heaven's no," she said. "I despise landfills, so very nasty."

One thing she did like was the word "very."

"I had her take it to the incinerator," she said.

"The incinerator at the Grandview?" Auntie asked. "The one at the back of the building."

"The very same," she said and nodded. "Only one thing to do with messes like that. Burn them."

Chapter Thirty-Four

My heart dropped as Nola Landry said those words. Any evidence of finding the girl was probably gone. No DNA. No fingerprints. Nothing.

I was ready to go. I'd hoped that the tablecloth and the tumbler were in that dumpster. That would have been easy to weed through. "Very messy," in Nola's words but doable. Now? We were at a dead-end and I didn't feel like exhibiting any of the politeness I needed to show as company in someone else's house. My mind was already somewhere else. Trying to figure out my next move. *Our* next move. Where Pogue would get the next clue.

But in a far inner corner of my brain, still cognizant of where I was, I heard Auntie ask Nola to tell me all about her movie star days.

"I have pictures," she said and popped up out of seat. That brought the full attention of my senses back to the present. "And videos," she called back over her shoulder. In a flash, she floated away, gone to get her archive of pseudo-stardom.

Oh no, I silently prayed that I could get out of watching black and white videos of the Very-Phony-Ex-Movie-Star.

"Auntie," I leaned over and whispered. "I don't want to look at her pictures or her videos."

"Be nice," Auntie Zanne said. "It's polite to see them."

"I need to go."

"Go where?" she frowned.

"To Aunt Julep's. Didn't you say we were going to go to talk to her?"

"You didn't seem too keen on doing that before," she said. "You changed your mind?"

Knowing that I was going to have to look at Nola's pictures changed my mind. I didn't have the patience for it nor did I have the stomach. I'd had enough of reliving the past by looking at pictures. After last night I didn't want to see another picture of anyone's past.

"Wouldn't you rather go and get that bundle?" Auntie asked, breaking into my thoughts, not lowering her voice at all.

"What bundle?" I asked and frowned. I kept my voice lowered.

"The one Nola had that girl throw into the incinerator."

"We can't get that," I said. "It's toast," my whisper became strained as I tried to emphasize the words. "She threw it into the incinerator."

"Oh pshaw," she said and waved her hand. "That thing doesn't work. Hasn't worked in ages. Why do you think there's so much garbage in the dumpsters?"

That made me sit back and let out a "Hmmm..." That did make sense.

"It's still there?"

"I don't know," she said and shrugged. "Might have been other garbage pickers besides us. I don't know why I didn't think of it before, she's such a clean nut..." her voice trailed off, but she quickly focused back on the conversation. "Not too many people know that incinerator doesn't work."

"Like Nola?" I asked.

"Like Nola." She gave a firm nod.

"We need to get over there then," I said and scooted up to the edge of my seat. "We really can't take the time to look at pictures."

"Don't know that that would be such a good idea," Auntie Zanne said. "So be nice to her and we'll get out of here without her being suspicious."

"What do I care if she gets suspicious?" I asked. "But more importantly, why do you care?"

"It's obvious, and it's what you're thinking too, I'm sure," she said.

"What?"

"That it's strange that girl followed her orders without scoffing, even down to taking everything out to the incinerator. Nola wasn't in charge of anything. Why would she listen?"

"And according to Rayanne, she didn't hire that girl."

"Which is fishy, too," Auntie Zanne said.

"You're thinking that Rayanne is a suspect." That thought had crossed my mind. As soon as we'd left her office. I paused when I realized what she was saying. "And," I let the word out slowly, "you think that Nola is one too."

"She was the first to help and then made sure, or tried to make sure, that there wasn't any evidence."

"And if it was Rayanne," Auntie said, "she knew that Nola would get rid of it because—"

"Because she's a germaphobe."

"If that's what you want to call it," Auntie Zanne said. "Why you think she wouldn't shake your hand?"

"Oh, is that why?" I nodded.

Rayanne was nowhere in sight when the incident happened. Perfect alibi. But Nola was there, she wouldn't need that alibi if she made sure that there was no evidence of her crime.

Who burns a tablecloth because it's wet? A person that wants to hide evidence. That's who. And what about if it had been flammable? Just the thought gave me a shiver.

Then a thought struck me. Nola knew it wasn't flammable because she knew what it was. I felt like Logan—I wanted to whip out my cell phone and google it to see if it was.

My eyes settled on her bottle of hand sanitizer sitting on the table. I looked at Auntie, my thoughts running into each other in my head. Did she do it to cover up her deed, or, was she just a germaphobe?

Then what about the server? No one knew her. Not Rayanne, the person in charge of the whole shindig. Not Nola, the one who took the job of being her overseer.

"What if she really does know that girl? They're in cahoots?" I said to Auntie.

"Exactly. If we made her suspicious, she could call that girl and have her go over there to check and make sure there was nothing left before we could get there."

"She could be doing that now," I said and darted my eyes toward the archway that Nola had disappeared into to see if she was coming.

"Nothing we can do if she is," Auntie said. "We can't call Rayanne because we don't know if it was her."

"I've got it!" Nola came floating back in, Carrie on her heels carrying a box overflowing with photo albums and VHS tapes.

Oh lord, I thought. Is this worth not letting her become suspicious?

"I didn't bring my videos, maybe you can come another day Romaine and see those."

Thank the lord...

"We can do popcorn and everything. I have a viewing room," she spoke with excitement in her voice. "It'll be just like the personal screenings we used to do in Hollywood."

Nola instructed Carrie to set the box down on the floor and then she got down next to it. That surprised me. It's not I didn't think she could get on the floor, heck she could float she probably had some kind of magical powers. The floor just didn't seem like something she'd do, considering she and hand sanitizer had a close personal relationship. Then again, it did look clean enough to eat off.

"I brought instead," she beamed up at Auntie. "Our acting troupe's videos and screenplays!"

"Oh my," Auntie chuckled. "I plum forgot about those. Let me see." Nola dug into her box and pulled out a handful of them.

"Look," Nola said and handed me a plastic covered booklet. "Every time I came home from making a movie, they'd write one and we'd put on a performance."

"Yes we did," Auntie Zanne said. "Avoyelles would make the wildest stories. Car crashes, barroom fights, murder, all in three acts."

"They didn't know the first thing about moviemaking," Nola said, wide smile on her face.

"No, they didn't. Avoyelles—"

"And Eugenia," Nola added.

"Eugenia would add all kinds of twists into the story—"

"And stunts!" Nola shot her arm in the air, interjecting.

"And we'd try to act them out," Auntie Zanne said. "It was big fun. I swear Avoyelles should have been writing novels."

"Car crashes!" Nola leaned back and laughed. "You remember when we crashed my Rolls trying to teach Delphine to drive? We could go out to Hollywood to turn one of those," she pointed at the stack Auntie had, "into a film."

"That was part of the screenplay?" I asked.

"No one could have written that one," Nola said. "Fact stranger than fiction.

"No," Auntie said, directing her answer to me. "Delphine was afraid to fly. So she was going to drive up and meet us there."

"Eugenia was going to ride with her, keep her company, don't you remember?" Nola asked Auntie Zanne.

"I remember."

"But Delphine didn't know how to drive?" I asked.

"Right," Auntie Zanne. "And we weren't going to go without her."

"We never made that movie," Nola said, sounding disappointed. "Such a shame, I had a real director and a producer that had agreed to help us."

"But we did act it out several times," Auntie Zanne said.

"We acted them all out," Nola said, a big smile on her face. "Right here!" She turned her gaze to me. "I have a small theater in the basement."

I wasn't surprised.

"Yes we did," Auntie smiled at the memory.

"Where was I?" I asked. "I don't remember any of this."

"You weren't even a twinkle in your daddy's eyes," Nola said. "It was years before you came along."

"Did you know my father?" I asked her.

"Everyone knew your father," Nola said. "Handsome as anyone in Hollywood." She smiled at the thought of my father. Wasn't sure how I felt about that. "And speaking of Hollywood," she switched gears, "our little ensemble wasn't such a bad troupe."

"Not at all," Auntie Zanne said. "You and I were the glamorous actresses. Eugenia and Avoyelles were the blockbuster writers, and Delphine the costume designer outdoing even Edith Head. And," Auntie waved her hand in the air and bent over like she was gasping for air, "Orville was our leading man."

"Oh God!" Nola said. "What were we thinking? He was nobody's leading man."

"He was Eugenia's at the time," Auntie Zanne said. "Although sometimes I think you forgot about that."

Nola did one of Auntie's dismissive waves, her excitement tapped down a notch. "Oh, why'd you bring that up, Babet? I forgot all about it." She lowered her head and fingered something in the box. "You know, that was nothing. And Eugenia understood that."

"In the end," Auntie said. "I think she did."

Ah! Another person Miss Eugenia had a falling out with...

"What fun we had in those days," Nola said, letting her and Auntie's conversation roll over.

"Yes we did."

"I didn't know you could act, Auntie," I said, trying to help get past the awkward turn in the conversation.

"Oh my, yes," Nola said and placed a hand over her chest. "Your auntie was the spitting image of Lena Horne back in those days. Beautiful. The big screen would have loved her face. We all did."

"I love it too," I said and smiled at my still beautiful auntie. "So you guys were quite the group?"

"And you were the black Rita Hayworth," Auntie said swiping

a hand at her.

She still is...

"We were really something back then," Auntie continued.

"Yes we were. And all of us are still friends. Still together. We could do it all over again." She smiled. "Me, you, Avoyelles, Delphine, the Winston twins, Eugenia and all the others..."

She got quiet. May as well slapped a hand over her mouth as she realized, I guessed, that Eugenia wasn't there any longer. To me, her expression wasn't sad about that revelation. It looked more like she realized she'd made a mistake about everyone being all together and that embarrassed her.

"Wait! Romaine," she said and perked up just as quickly as she'd been deflated, "If we did do it again, you could take Eugenia's place!"

Chapter Thirty-Five

I waited outside for Auntie to finish up with her "just one more thing," with Nola. I didn't know why I thought me leaving out the door would push Auntie Zanne along with her goodbyes. It had never worked before.

She whispered that she wanted to give Nola a head's up on the next day's voting. I stood on the front stoop and waved at the cameras. Give Nola Landry something else to add to her video collection.

Auntie Zanne finally came out and we piled into the car. She was all smiles, rocking her head to some tune in her head nearly the entire way out to Yellowpine.

"That was a nice visit for you, huh?" I said. "Conjuring all those old memories."

"Those were young memories. Even when you get old, those are the ones that stay with you," Auntie Zanne said, a playful smile on her face.

"I didn't realize all of you were so close."

"Oh yes, we did everything together. Even became members of the Voodoo herbalist society together. That's why we always sit together at the Boule."

"You weren't sitting with them," I said.

"Of course not," she said, "I'm in charge."

"Which reminds me," I said, wanting to remind her that her "I'm in charge" mantra could only go so far in a police investigation. "You know if we find anything, we have to turn it over to Pogue."

"The heck we will," she said. "I promised Rayanne that no law enforcement would be coming out here if she cooperated, and I'm standing by my word."

"Your entire conversation with her was a lie," I said. "Now I know you didn't need Miss Vivee to coach you on what to do. You've been a big actress for quite a while."

"Whether I was lying or not, I'm going to keep my word."

"About the lie?"

"Yep. And what's the reason we can't get the evidence and take it to Pogue."

"Chain of custody."

"Chain of what?"

"Don't you remember Pogue said that when we were taking about the inhaler that killed Bumper?"

"No," she said.

"Yes you do," I said. "The inhaler that had the ricin went from Boone to Bumper to Chase to Alex back to Boone. He was worried it was going to get contaminated and he wouldn't be able to trace it back to Boone."

"Did Boone get convicted of killing Bumper?"

She knew the answer to that; don't know why she was asking me. "Yes, he did," I said.

"Then nothing bad happened from the inhaler being passed around."

I let out a puff of air. "You have to show a paper trail of how evidence was preserved from the time it was collected to the time it's presented in court," I said. "We were lucky with that case. You have to know whose custody evidence is in every step of the way."

"And so tell me why we need Pogue for that. Inhaler being passed around went off fine."

"You said that already about the inhaler, but there's a chance that it wouldn't have. Pogue needs to testify to its whereabouts at all times. He'll get, tag it and send it the crime lab. There'll be no issue about it being contaminated or tampered with."

"Funny you should say that," she said. "Didn't I catch you just yesterday ready to pull the whole kit and caboodle out of the dumpster?"

"I was not going to—"

"You had gloves and everything." She stopped me from finishing my sentence.

"I was just going to check to see if I saw it," I said. "I wasn't going to tamper with it." I took my eyes off the road long enough to give her a "gotcha" look. "I know how things go and how the lab needs evidence."

"He's going to send it to the crime lab?"

"Yes, that's what I said."

"Same crime lab you send your samples to from your autopsies?" she asked.

"Exactly," I said, happy that perhaps she was finally getting what I was saying. I know she'd heard me say a million times that I had to be careful about how my specimens went to the lab.

"Well if they trust you to send it to them any other time, why do we need to Pogue to send it this time?"

I huffed. Guess that was her "gotcha."

I didn't say anything the rest of the way to the Grandview. I was tempted to call Pogue and have him meet us over there to make sure he was the one collecting the evidence, I just wasn't sure our "little bundle" was going to be there when we arrived. I hated letting him know I was poking my nose in when he'd ask me not to.

But I just couldn't help myself.

We parked on the side of the building where Auntie remembered the incinerator was located. Of course it wasn't there. We had to walk around the building to look for it.

"Where are the two of you going now?" It was Rayanne. She was scurrying, trying to catch up with us, her heels clacking on the pavement, a wisp of hair falling into her face. She must've seen us out of her office window. "Your room for the vote won't be ready for three more hours." Rayanne pointed at her watch.

"I know I'm early for the vote. It's not why I'm here. We're going to check the incinerator," Auntie Zanne said.

"Good lord, whatever for?" she said, out of breath. She tugged on the jacket of her suit. "Babet, you know good and fool well that thing doesn't work."

"That's where Nola put the stuff cleared from the table," Auntie Zanne said.

"Nola Landry?" she asked.

"Yes," Auntie said.

"Oh," her face relaxed. "That makes sense, don't know why I didn't think of that. She wouldn't have put it in that dumpster."

Guess everyone knew of her proclivity for germ aversion. This from the woman who had told me earlier she "didn't really know the woman."

"This has just turned out to be the worst event I've ever had," Rayanne said. "I swear," she blew the strand of hair out of her face, "I should have known right from the start that something bad like this was going to happen. Flower mix up. Live pheasants being delivered instead of under glass, people wanting to change seating arrangements from the way it's been for years, errant servers appearing out of nowhere!"

She rambled off her series of mishaps just as we reached the incinerator. Once painted red, now it was red with rust. It was the size of a small window. I wasn't sure how we were going to fish anything out of there.

"And someone came and sorted through my dumpsters throwing everything overboard," Rayanne said.

"They did what?" Auntie asked.

"Yeah," she shook her head. "Had one witness who saw a black truck or van, they weren't sure," Rayanne said. "They said they thought it was the dump truck. But what garbage man turns the trash over?"

"That sounds crazy," Auntie said. "You'd better call them. You pay them good money, I'm sure."

"I sure do," Rayanne said. "But that's why I came out here when I saw you, you were the last ones out there, so I thought it was you."

"Wasn't us," Auntie said.

"You're in a black van," Rayanne countered.

"Wasn't us," Auntie repeated, raising an eyebrow.

"Well y'all the last people that I saw," Rayanne said. "Thought y'all had come back and tried to find that tumbler."

"Nope." Auntie shook her head. "Best bet is to check with your dumpster people." She knocked a couple of knuckles on the small metal door. "We just need to get into your incinerator."

"You have to go down the basement," Rayanne said. "That's where the shoot leads. You'll find the furnace for this thing there."

"Wait," I said. "A furnace? Is it on?"

"No," she said and shook her head, the strand of hair waggling in her face. "It's only for the incinerator. It's off."

"Well, I guess we'll have to go down there," Auntie said.

Rayanne pointed to the door. "I'll get the key for it, but you're on your own. It's nasty down there. I wouldn't want to be the one to trudge through it."

"Oh, I won't be," Auntie Zanne said, a big ole' grin on her face. "Romaine's got it covered. You know, chain of custody and all." She patted me on my back. "It's the law, right, kiddo?"

Chapter Thirty-Six

I had Pogue meet me out on Highway 87. I figured that way I wouldn't have held onto what I'd found in the dysfunctional furnace long enough for chain of custody to make a difference. And Auntie could keep her word to Rayanne about no law enforcement coming to her place. Not that Pogue would have initiated any kind of investigation just by looking at the expensive chandeliers hung everywhere.

He was going to take what we'd found straight to the lab, he said and stick around to see if they could pull any fingerprints. I don't know if that would make a difference. I had thought about everyone else being the suspect and not the girl even though I had witnessed her doing the deed.

But I had committed to following the clues and not jumping to conclusions like Auntie Zanne.

We'd see where these clues led to.

In passing the bundle over to Pogue, and him pondering about lifting fingerprints, I had to hope they wouldn't find any of Auntie's. I had to all but hold her down to keep her from going through the bag. I had only peeked in to make sure it was what we were looking for. It was amazing how much stuff was in the shoot to go to an incinerator that didn't work. Rayanne definitely needed to put a lock on it.

And I definitely needed a shower.

"Julep doesn't care what you smell like," Auntie Zanne protested all the way to our small detour to the house so I could freshen up. "Heck, she's smelled you worse than this."

Auntie Zanne had her nose scrunched and she kept it pointed toward the window.

"You can't even stand to smell me," I said.

"Just roll down all the windows," she said. "Let the breeze hit you."

"I am not," I said.

"I have a vote to get to."

"You've got plenty of time," I said. "Rayanne just told you the room won't be ready for three hours. And I hope when we get to Aunt Julep's you won't rush me."

"I'm not going to be hanging around with Julep all day. Just so you know." She looked at me and gave me a nod. "I never did get along well with her after more than five minutes, especially after she starts talking her Run Down Garden Funeral Parlor."

"Her funeral home is called Garden Grove, Auntie."

She waved a dismissive hand at me. She always gave Aunt Julep's establishment some made-up bad name.

"And," she kept talking. "I have to see to the caterers who are serving at tonight's voting. You can't get a bunch of women together and expect anything constructive to come out of it if you don't feed them."

"You get along fine with Aunt Julep, so don't give me that. And when did you have time to call a caterer?" I asked. I'd been with her all day. She hadn't made any plans.

"I had Rayanne call for me as soon as we worked out a room assignment yesterday." She glanced over at me. "Good thing I did," she said. "I wouldn't have been able to coordinate anything from jail."

I doubted if that was true...

I pulled into the driveway of the funeral parlor and put the car in park. "You know going to jail was not a good thing, right?"

"Of course I know," she said. "I'm not bragging about it, just stating a fact. Oh look, I forgot all about—" her voice trailed off as she got out of the car. Didn't take much to distract her.

There was a man in our driveway with a truck that was a moving billboard. The truck was midnight blue with large, bright lettering on the side that read, *Clean & Go. Mobile Car Wash and Detailing.*

"Auntie, what are you doing?" I asked. "I thought you were in a hurry." She was digging in her purse and talking to the man in the truck.

"I forgot all about telling Pete to come and do the cars."

"The funeral home cars?"

"Yes. They could use some sprucing up," she said. "This is Avoyelles' nephew."

"The one you've been talking about for the past two days?"

"Yep. One and the same."

"And that didn't remind you that he was coming today?"

"Plum skipped my mind," she said.

I shook my head. "You're going to have to start doing crossword puzzles or something. Make sure the hippocampus can keep doing its job."

"Using all your big words that nobody knows doesn't impress me," she said. "My memory is sharp as a tack." I smiled. I knew she knew what I was saying. "And I thought you were going to take a shower. You smell like Rayanne's dumpster turned over on you!"

Auntie kept sniffing me the entire ride over to Aunt Julep's.

"What?" I asked.

"I just wanted to make sure you smelled better. That smell lingered even after you left. I was embarrassed for you. Pete will probably never want to date you. He probably thinks you always smell like that."

"I'm not trying to date Pete," I said. "And I didn't smell that bad."

I turned up in the driveway to Aunt Julep's house and pulled all the way in. I'd always gone in the back door that led into the kitchen whenever I visited.

My Aunt Julep lived alone, and it showed on the outside of the house. It could stand for a few repairs, and I'd even mentioned it to Pogue. I'd have to bring it up to him again.

We knocked and it took a minute for Aunt Julep to open the door. As soon as she saw her, Auntie Zanne hugged her like she hadn't seen her in years. I knew that wasn't true, they were in the Red Hat Society together. That met once a month.

My Aunt Julep, in contrast to my Auntie Zanne, looked all of her eighty plus years. Her shoulders slumped, dark circles under her eyes made her look weary. She barely picked up her feet when she walked. Aunt Julep was dark, and her declining health from diabetes didn't help her complexion. Where her skin was once bright and shiny, now it was dull and ashen.

Still standing in the door, Auntie Zanne held Aunt Julep tight, rocking her back and forth, she kissed her on each cheek. I just shook my head, the way Auntie Zanne talked about my Aunt Julep anyone would think that she didn't like her, or anything about her. Especially her funeral home.

We stepped inside the door and stopped. The kitchen was as old and worn as Aunt Julep, but she kept it clean, even sitting in a kitchen chair to sweep and mop the maroon and white checkered linoleum floor. She called her refrigerator an icebox, and it looked like it had come from the century old retailer's catalogue when it was still called *Sears & Roebucks*.

"How's my Julep?" Auntie asked.

"Oh, fair to midland. Fair to midland," Aunt Julep said with a nod. "C'mon, now. Y'all come on in. Don't just stand here in the door." She stood back and waved us through.

"So good to see you, Sugarplum," Auntie Zanne said, calling her by a name she usually reserved for me. "I brought you some tea. Something to help you feel like a kid again." Auntie Zanne patted her purse.

She must've picked up some of her brew when I was taking a shower. She hadn't known for sure when we left going to Nola's that she'd be able to talk me into coming to Aunt Julep's.

"Oh thank you, Babet," Aunt Julep said. "I've been feeling kinda low these last couple of days. That's gonna really help me. Much appreciated."

"Oh don't think nothing of it, Auntie Zanne said. "You should have called me." She took Aunt Julep's by the hand and led her further into the kitchen. "Come on now, you sit down and I'm going to fix you some tea." Auntie guided her to a chair at the table.

"And how is my baby?" Aunt Julep, sitting in the chair, spread her arms out wide to embrace me in a hug.

"I'm good," I said. "You not feeling so good?"

"I'm okay. Don't you worry none about me," she said. No matter what was going on with her, nothing could beat that big wide grin she had whenever she saw me. "Don't nothing make me feel better than seeing you."

Auntie Zanne and Aunt Julip had this pseudo-rivalry when it came to me. Both wanted to raise me when my parents died. But Auntie Zanne had been the first to arrive in Beaumont. She got there almost as soon as the sheriff had gotten off the phone telling her about the accident. My mother wasn't the first sister she had had to bury, but she was her last. We were all that was left of the St. Romain's.

Likewise, my father, Earle Wilder was Aunt Julep's only sibling, leaving only her and Pogue as my relatives on that side. Neither one of them was a Wilder, I was the only person left with the name.

Now I wasn't so sure if that was true anymore.

Auntie started flitting around the kitchen, opening shelves and putting water on to boil. She was as familiar with this kitchen as she was with her own. She knew where everything was.

"We would've brought you something to eat," Auntie Zanne said, "but time just got away from us." She pulled open the refrigerator and poked her head in. "But I see you got something I can whip up for you to eat." She turned to Aunt Julep. "How about if I do that?"

"I ain't much hungry," she said. "Don't have much of an

appetite."

"Well," Auntie Zanne put her head back in the refrigerator, "you gotta eat." She stood back up. "It'll be done in a minute."

"Okay," Aunt Julep said and smiled. I think she just liked Auntie Zanne fussing over her.

"We came by because Romaine's got something she wants to talk to you about," Auntie Zanne said.

There she goes, I thought. She was making a racket pulling out pots and opening cans. But that didn't stop her from poking her nose into things. I knew why I was there, she should have just given me time to get to it.

"What you want to talk to me about, Baby?" Aunt Julep asked.

Auntie Zanne stopped what she was doing and came over to the table. She shook her head slowly and made her eyes all sad. "Something that's got her all worked up. We need to help her."

Auntie Zanne was like a chameleon. Wherever she was, whoever she was talking to, she'd adapt their manner of speaking and acting. She said it made others more comfortable. Her idea of Aunt Julep was the nurturing old grandmother, so that's how she acted.

"I can talk for myself," I said.

"Well, then go ahead and do it," her fake sad demeanor gone in a flash, she went back to the stove.

"Aunt Julep," I said, and sat across from her at the table. "I met this woman named Frankie."

"Frankie?" she said. That made me realize that I didn't know her last name.

"Yes," I said. "She's a friend to a friend of mine."

"Rhett Remmiere," Auntie Zanne interjected over her shoulder. "You know. The guy who works for me."

"Oh," Aunt Julep said and nodded her head. "And don't that beat all, another woman with a man's name. They don't name folks like they used to."

"She's older," I said. "And I think it may be short for something else."

"Uh-uh," Aunt Julep said, I guessed trying to be patient while I got to the point.

"She owns this juke joint—bar—down in Peterson."

"In Peterson?" She cocked her head to the side. "Wait. Hold on now. You talking about Frankie Averly?" Aunt Julep said, sitting up straight. "Oh my, I plum forgot about her. I know her. Sure didn't dawn on me who it was until you said she owned a juke joint." She nodded, her eyes lighting up with the memory. "That's the name of it ain't it?"

"Yeah," I said. "Lady Frankie's Juke Joint."

"*The*," she said correcting me. "It's The Lady Frankie's Juke Joint."

"Right," I said remembering the words on that neon saxophone out front.

"Your father used to play there."

"I know," I said. "She had a picture of him. Him and his guitar."

"He didn't go anywhere without it," Aunt Julep said, her eyes sparkling at the memory.

"She didn't know Daddy had died," I said, hedging around what I really wanted to say. "She thought he'd gone off to find some..." I took in a breath to finish, but she finished my sentence for me.

"Some family. Is that what she told you?"

I nodded.

"I remember that," Aunt Julep said. She folded her hands on the table and looked pensive. "He came back real excited about it. Saying he'd found out something about our family. You remember that Babet?"

"Vaguely," Auntie Zanne said. She didn't even turn around when she said it.

I gave her a look. She had never hinted to me that she'd heard about it. All she said was that I should ask Aunt Julep about it. But now it was obvious that she knew something.

"You knew?" I asked Auntie Zanne.

"Didn't you just hear my answer?" she said, answering my question with one of her own.

"Yeah. I remember," Aunt Julep said, not giving me a chance to continue my interrogation of Auntie Zanne. I'd have to talk to her later. "Came by here all excited. He had a name. What was that name?" She looked at Auntie.

"Can't say that I recall," Auntie Zanne said.

"Oh Babet, you remember what it was. Some uncommon name for black folks." I glanced at Auntie and waited for her to answer. Nothing. So Aunt Julep continued talking. "Well, I can't remember it, that's for sure. All I know is that he wanted me to go with him. Said they were right on the border of Sabine County."

"Did you go?" I asked.

"Oh no. Far as I was concerned my family was all dead and buried. If my Ma and Pa adopted me, I can tell you that I don't care one nary bit. They were all that mattered to me." She studied my face. "Are you telling me that you care?"

"Of course she does," Auntie Zanne said, this time she turned around. "Romaine has always tried to figure out who she is. That's why she ran off to Chicago. Trying to be somebody else."

"Did she now?" Aunt Julep said.

"You know it, Julep," Auntie Zanne said. "How many times did you ask me when you called to check on her, 'who is Romaine trying to be today?'"

"You said that Aunt Julep?" I asked.

"Now, I can't say that I recall..."

"Come on, Julep," Auntie Zanne said, a big grin on her face. "Tell the truth and shame the devil."

Aunt Julep hung her head and laughed. "She was always trying to be something." Admitting to it seemed to entertain her. "You remember that time she'd only speak French?"

"For a whole week!" Auntie Zanne said. "Teachers were calling, I had to go up to the school, sit in class just so I could translate what she said."

"Sure did," Aunt Julep said.

"I don't think—" I started.

"Everyone thought she'd lost her marbles," Auntie Zanne said, cutting in. "Only kid that put up with her was Catfish. I think he's still the only friend she's got."

"Catfish is not—"

"I sure did like that boy. Where is he now?"

"He's still around," Auntie Zanne said. "Still pining over our girl."

I couldn't get a word in edgewise. They had started talking about me as if I wasn't even in the room. I decided to just sit there and let them have at it.

"That's the one you should have married," Aunt Julep said, turning to me. I didn't say a word. "He's down to earth, he would've made you realize that all the stuff you need is right here at home."

"I've decided to stay—"

"Don't worry none about her," Auntie Zanne said interrupting me again. "I got something cooking that'll turn her right around." She nodded her head toward the teapot that sat on the stove.

"Some of your brew?" Aunt Julep asked.

"Mmm-hmmm," Auntie Zanne nodded. "Even threw a little love potion in it. Won't be long now, Julep."

"We gone have some young'uns running around here?"

Auntie Zanne put a big grin on her face and nodded. "A whole mess of 'em!"

Chapter Thirty-Seven

Saved by the bell.

My phone rang. It was Pogue. I was so happy for the interruption, I could've kissed him.

As soon as I said hello, I realized his call might not be to rescue me, but that he had information about "the bundle" I'd given him. I walked away from the aunts. I knew they had a tendency to listen in. I didn't mind that so much with Aunt Julep, but my Auntie Zanne was a whole different story.

"I've got an ID on the girl," Pogue said first thing.

"Wow. That was quick," I said, and looked at the aunts. They were still laughing and talking. I turned my back to them and lowered my voice. "So, there were fingerprints on the inside of the gloves?"

"There were. And all over that tray and tumbler."

"Who is she?"

"Nobody," he said. "No criminal record. Not even a parking ticket."

I frowned. "How did her prints come up if she doesn't have a record?"

"She worked for a bank at one time. They did it as part of a background check."

"Oh," I said.

"Her name is Carly Neely. She's twenty-seven," he offered. "She lives right outside of Roble."

"You going over to her house to talk to her?"

"No," he said. "I'm having her come over here."

I laughed. He sure didn't conduct his interrogations like Auntie and me. First thing we'd do is go where the suspect was. Now that I thought about it, that probably wasn't the safest thing to do.

"How did you reach her?" I asked.

"Called her."

"You had a number?"

"It was listed. She has a landline," he said. "I know, it's odd for young people nowadays, but I put her name in and got a phone number."

"How did she act?"

"Nice. Curious, but nice. I didn't tell her anything over the phone, so we'll see how she acts when she gets here."

"Okay," I said.

"That's one of the reasons I called you," he said. "I was thinking maybe you'd want to be here when I talk to her."

"I can do that," I said, surprised that he'd offered me an in. He was always warning Auntie and me about meddling, taking our help with information only if we hadn't actively obtained it. It usually never went that way.

I usually didn't *happen* on information, neither did Auntie Zanne. If I had some information, I'd either gotten from the autopsy, or, I had to admit, snooping. And then there were times I'd get it by trying to stop Auntie Zanne from leaping head first into some of her ludicrous schemes or hightail shenanigans before Pogue could find out or before she got us both landed in jail.

I wasn't all that good at stopping Auntie Zanne, but I could stomach her antics better than Pogue.

"Yeah," he was saying, "I figure that seeing you might lessen her propensity to lie since she knows you were a witness to the whole thing."

"It might help," I said.

"Plus," he said. "I don't have a female deputy here. I don't even have a male one. I don't want her accusing me of anything untoward. Best if another female is here." He paused. "You're the closest thing I have to another law enforcement officer. You could take the witness stand and testify if need be."

"That's probably a good idea," I said. "To have me there. And I'm happy to help."

I glanced into the living room, eyeing my two aunts and realized my circumstances might change his mind about me coming. "I'm at your mom's house," I said.

"Good. She's always asking about you."

"Yeah, so *we* were just finishing up here, and could be there in a few minutes." I emphasized "we" letting him know I wasn't alone.

"'We?'" he repeated the word.

I glanced and saw Auntie Zanne making a fuss over Aunt Julep, trying to feed her the food she'd prepared. Neither one was paying any attention to me. Still I didn't want to start Auntie Zanne's usual commentary about Pogue by letting her know who I was talking to, especially in front of his mother.

"Yep. Auntie Zanne and I came over together."

"So that means Babet would have to come, too?"

"That's what it means," I said it as cheerily as I could. I wanted to try to give the impression that I was talking to someone other than Pogue about something not related to Miss Eugenia's murder in case he didn't want Auntie Zanne to come. She wouldn't be the wiser about what we'd discussed.

He blew out a breath. I could just imagine how his mind was churning. It took a long time for him to answer.

"Okay," he huffed. "I guess that'll be okay." His words came out hesitantly.

"You sure?" I asked, because it really didn't sound like he was.

"Yes, I'm sure," he said. "And hurry, before I change my mind."

"I heard you talking in code," Auntie Zanne said.

We were in the car heading over to Pogue's office, me driving and Auntie directing me and everyone else who came across our paths that she thought couldn't drive either. She'd yell out the window and tell them exactly what they'd done wrong.

"What? When?" I glanced over at her, a small smile on my face. "I don't know what you mean," I said although I knew exactly what she was talking about. I still hadn't told Auntie Zanne the plan with Pogue, even though I had had her to hurry along.

We'd gotten Aunt Julep all squared away, I told her I was taking the job as M.E., which meant I was staying in Roble. She was elated, and it made it even harder to leave because then, as she put it, she had "a whole mess of questions for me."

"When you were talking to Pogue on the phone."

"You knew I was talking to Pogue?" I said and chuckled.

"Me and Julep both knew," she said. "You're not that opaque. Plus, you don't have any friends. We both know that. Not many people you could have been talking to."

"I don't know why you always say that. I have friends," I said.

"Who?" she asked.

"Catfish and..."

"And nobody," she said.

"Well, I'm going to change that," I said. "I'm going to get some friends. Maybe even a boyfriend."

"I could help you out," she said. "I know lots of people."

"No thanks," I said. "I'm going to have different kinds of friends than the ones you have."

"What's wrong with my friends?" she asked, it seemed with sincerity.

"Nothing," I said, moving my head back and forth. "Absolutely nothing."

"I was talking about a boyfriend, though," she said. "I could help you with that."

"I don't want any of your friends to be my boyfriend either."

"What happened with Alex?"

"I'm done with Alex."

"Good for you, Sugarplum," she said. "'Bout time."

"I'm glad you approve," I said.

"What about Rhett?" she said, an eyebrow arched.

"You've been feeding him enough of your tea," I said and looked at her out of the corner of my eye. "You think it worked?"

"Yeah, I know the tea I gave him worked," she said and gave a firm nod. "I just hope what I gave you did, too."

"You didn't give me anything," I said and gave her a firm nod. "I know better than to drink anything you brew."

"We'll see," she said. "Just remember, if you start getting any kind of hankering—"

"Hankering?" I repeated chuckling.

"Feelings," she said and drew the word out. "If you get any feelings for Rhett, don't count me out as having something to do with it."

That made my stomach lurch. "Because what did you do?" I asked, her words worrying me. I *was* having feelings for him—all of a sudden. I started racking my brains trying to think how she could have gotten some of anything into me.

"So what did Pogue want?" she asked, breaking into my thoughts.

"Uhm..." I shook my head to clear it. "He..."

Wow, I couldn't think. She had me rattled. I did everything I could not to drink anything she made.

Not that I believed she could control my emotions with one of her concoctions...

"He what?" she said, giving my arm a push. I'm sure she knew she had gotten to me.

I glanced at her. "He wanted us to come by while he talks to that girl."

"What girl?"

I took in a breath to help calm myself. "The server at the Boule." I took my eyes off the road momentarily and looked at her. "The one that spilled the drink on Miss Eugenia."

"The murderer?"

"Maybe so." I shrugged.

"And Pogue said he wanted me to come, too?" Auntie asked. Her face brightened at the idea.

"Yep. Said both of us could come." I nodded. "But you have to behave."

"Behave?" she said and scrunched up her nose. "Who is telling me to behave? You or Pogue?"

"Well..."

"I don't *mis*behave," she said, cutting in. "So I don't know what either one of you are talking about."

"I think you do, Auntie," I said, and gave her one of the all-knowing nods she always gave me. "You know how you're always getting in his way."

"I do not." That came out indignantly, her face turned up in a pout. I was sure she meant it to.

I wasn't going to get anywhere with her by taking Pogue's side or agreeing with anything he said. I changed tactics.

"He thought you and I could help with questioning her because we were there and we know what happened. You know, with you being Eagle-Eye Babet Derbinay, and all."

"He said that?" Auntie Zanne asked, a smile emerging from the pout.

"Practically," I lied.

Her face seemed to relax. "Well, I guess I oughta give him some credit for a little sense," she said. "He wouldn't have been able to handle it unless we were there."

Now that was going a little far. Thought I'd better help bring her back down.

"Don't take it like he needs us. He just thought we'd be helpful. But he'd do just fine by himself," I said. "And it's nice of him to include us. We have to show him we appreciate it."

"What is that supposed to mean?" she asked.

"You know what it means."

"I do appreciate that he's getting a little sense in that thick skull of his," she said. "I'm happy he's understanding that you and I can, and do, make a valuable contribution to solving these murders that have been going on around here. But I'm not throwing a party for him finally getting something he should have gotten years ago." She gave me a nod. "As big as his head was, you'd think it would've been filled with all sorts of smarts instead of—"

"Don't say it," I warned.

"Lead," she said it anyway.

"How about if we just change the subject..." I said and glanced over at her. "What do you think about me making some crawfish pies and inviting all the girls over to celebrate Avoyelles being voted in as the Lesser Mambo?"

She squinted her eyes at me. "We haven't voted yet," she said, her voice showing she knew what I was up to. She looked down at her watch. "And come to think of it, we don't have long. Rayanne gave us that room with short notice. We have to be mindful of the time she allotted."

Like there were people knocking down the door to have their events there.

"I know you haven't voted yet," I said. "But it's a sure thing, right?" I smiled getting her back on track. "I mean, if you say it's to be so. Then it is, right? I saw them the other night. They all look to you."

"We still have to vote," she said, a sly smile crawling across her face. "And while I'd never interfere..."

"Of course not," I said shaking my head.

"They all do look to me."

"Sooo?"

"Sooo," she said and swatted my arm. "I think you making crawfish pies would be nice."

We both laughed.

So shall Babet Derbinay will it, so shall it be done.

I pulled up and parked right behind Pogue's patrol car. I'd only visited Pogue there once or twice since I'd been back. The sheriff's office looked just like the one in Mayberry on the *Andy Griffith*

Show. Newly elected, he hadn't done much to make it his own.

It was small. There were two desks that sat opposite each other, but both faced the wall. An on-loan deputy who came to help when the need arose usually occupied one. The other was covered with papers and case files. From what I could see, Pogue was taking "public records" a little too far.

There was a stained coffeepot with remnants of coffee clinging to the bottom of it. Cups, sugar and creamer. A donut box sat with the lid partially opened. I was sure if any pastries were inside, they were stale.

Pogue's "office" was positioned behind a pony wall topped with glass. That was where he sat when we walked in.

"Glad you got here," he said. He come out and met us. "She should be here any minute." He glanced up at the clock on the wall.

"We're happy to come and help," Auntie said.

We followed Pogue into his office, went around his desk and sat down. Auntie sat in a chair to the right of his desk, and I took a seat in the lone chair in front of it.

"Don't need you to help like you're probably thinking," Pogue said in response to Auntie's remark. I could tell he was trying not to let her ruffle him.

"And how am I thinking?" Auntie asked, her voice going up an octave.

I had my fingers crossed that I hadn't made a mistake bringing her or trying to talk to her on the way over. Pogue was still the sheriff, no matter how much we interfered. I respected that, at least I hope that's how it appeared because I really did, but Auntie, I shook my head, when it came to Pogue, she seemed to forget the meaning of the word.

"I just need you two here for prosperity. I don't have any recording devices," he said and pointed to one of the empty corners where the wall and ceiling met. "I want to make sure nothing's thrown out because of a technicality or she comes up with a story of her own about what happens here today."

"You not expecting to get a full confession out of her today, are you?" she asked.

"I don't see why not," Pogue said, already getting defensive. "I've got her dead to rights. You are a witness to her act."

"You need more than that," Auntie said.

"More than your eyewitness account?" he asked.

"Yep," she said and nodded.

"I don't need more than that," he said. "The girl's guilty. It shouldn't take much to get it out of her. I've got her fingerprints all over everything."

"It doesn't mean she did it," Auntie said.

"I remember she said, 'It wasn't supposed to hurt,'" I said to Pogue interjecting. I'd remembered that before, but I didn't think I'd ever mentioned it to Pogue.

"Maybe someone got her to do it," Auntie said.

"She poured it into Eugenia Elder's lap, because of it, she died," Pogue said. "According to the law, Carly Neely is guilty."

"Well that's a stupid law," Auntie said.

"I can't change the law to suit you," he said.

"You shouldn't jump to conclusions," Auntie said, which surprised me because that was what she always did. "And the fact that it's a stupid law oughta change the way you talk to her."

I saw Pogue open his mouth to answer her, but she wasn't finished with her thought.

"Because if you talk to her the way you talked to Josephine Gail," she continued, "you'll never find anything out."

He shut his mouth.

Josephine Gail was Auntie's friend. Not one of her herbalist friends, but one she had a special affinity to because she suffered from depression.

Josephine Gail's mental health was in full view when she was the one who found a dead body at the funeral home. One that didn't belong there. It was the first murder we'd encountered the day I arrived from Chicago and Pogue was sure she had committed it.

Pogue had been hard on Josephine Gail because she'd been the only one there at the funeral home when the body turned up. I was pretty sure he had acquired better interrogation techniques by now. At least I hoped he had.

It was Auntie Zanne I was worried about.

Chapter Thirty-Eight

Carly Neely had smooth mocha-colored skin, and big brown eyes that were filled with determination as she entered the police station and looked around. She was breathing heavily as if she'd been in a hurry. Her ample chest moving up and down under her round-necked light blue knit top. Her jeans fitted snuggly around her shapely hips as she stuck her hands down into the front pockets.

I stepped out of Pogue's office on the other side of the pony wall.

"Hi," I said. "Are you Carly Neely?"

"Yes," she said, a polite smile on her face. "I'm here to see, um, a Sheriff Folsom?" She made her remark into a question.

"This way," I said, matching my smile to hers. I didn't want her to become intimidated or frightened and not give us any of the information we needed.

She stepped inside the office and let her eyes drift from Pogue to Auntie Zanne before she turned back and looked at me. Her eyes, lines fanning out at their corners, looking older than her years, showed recognition.

"Is this about the other night?" she asked. "The dinner at the Grandview Motor Lodge Motel out in Yellowpine?"

"Have a seat, Miss Neely," Pogue said. "Is it 'Miss?'"

"Yes, it is," she said. She sat in the chair I had occupied earlier, leaving me standing. I went and stood by Auntie. Carly turned and hung her purse on the rung of the chair.

"Look," she swallowed, turning to look at Auntie Zanne, "if this is about that lady's outfit, I can pay for the dry cleaning."

"Her name was Eugenia Elder," Auntie Zanne said.

"Okay," she said. "I can pay for Miss Elder's dry cleaning. No big deal." She shrugged and then reached around the chair to grab her purse.

"It's not about paying to have her outfit cleaned," Pogue said.

"Okay," she said. "What is it about?" She seemed to get defiant just that quickly, perhaps as a cover. It did seem to me that she had no idea that Miss Eugenia was dead. Carly crossed her arms over her chest and one leg atop the other. "I have to get back to my kids."

"You have children?" I asked. That worried me. I wasn't sure, but it seemed that Pogue was positive that this girl was the killer. And from his words earlier he wasn't planning on just letting her walk out when he finished questioning her.

"Yes. And a father. And a job." She tilted her head as she spoke. "I've already been sick for the last couple of days and haven't been able to go to work or take care of anyone. I can't miss another day."

"You have a job?" Pogue asked.

"Yes, I do," she said. "Why? You act surprised that I work."

"Because you were at that dinner the other night serving," he said. "I thought all those workers were from a temp agency."

"They were," Auntie Zanne said affirming.

"I do that on the side," she said. "To make extra money. I told you I have kids and a father to care for."

"You weren't hired for that job," Auntie Zanne said. "Why were you serving there?"

"Excuse me?" she said.

"Let me ask the questions, Babet," Pogue said.

"Well hurry up and get to them," she said.

"What is this about?" Carly asked. "I told you I'd pay for the clothes."

"And we told you that it's not about the clothes," Pogue said.

"Eugenia Elder is dead," Auntie Zanne said jumping the gun. "Murdered."

"Oh my," Carly said, taken aback. "I'm sorry to hear that."

"Babet!" Pogue said. "I'm asking the questions."

"That wasn't a question," Auntie Zanne said, indignantly. "It was a statement. If you don't know the difference, it's no wonder you can't ever solve anything."

"Romaine," Pogue said, his eyes tried not to show Auntie the pleading he wanted me to see. I knew he wanted me to do something with Auntie. I didn't know what he thought I could do.

"Auntie, let Pogue handle this," I said, knowing that wouldn't help.

"I am," she said. "I'm just helping. And *not* asking questions, just making *statements*."

"It's okay," Carly said. "I didn't know when I said that about her, you know, suit. It was heartless of me to worry about that." She looked around at us. "This is a murder investigation?" She nodded her understanding. "I don't know how I can help, but I can try." Her demeanor changing from combative to sympathetic.

"She died from what you poured on her," Auntie Zanne continued despite our warnings.

"No, she didn't," Carly said, a faint smile on her lips. She must have thought Auntie was kidding with her.

"Yes, she did," Auntie Zanne said.

"It was rosehips and acetone," Carly said, frowning up at Auntie like she didn't know what she was talking about. "No one dies from that. They only itch. That's why I wore the gloves."

"It was hydrofluoric acid," Auntie said.

Pogue sat quietly during the exchange. I think he'd decided to let Auntie talk. No need of looking bad in front of his suspect.

"Hydrochloric?" Carly repeated.

"*Fl*uoric," Auntie said. "Hydrofluoric."

Carly started shaking her head vigorously from side to side. "I smelled it, it smelled like roses."

"You inhaled some of it?" I asked, remembering that inhalation can cause a person to become ill, and in certain amounts kill.

"Yeah, when he gave it to me and told me what it was."

"Who gave it to you? Who is *he*?" Auntie asked then slapped a hand over her mouth. "Sorry about that, Pogue. I know you are supposed to ask the questions. That was two questions!"

Pogue shook his head, then looked up at me.

I shrugged. Who can stop the infamous Mrs. Babet Derbinay? Plus, my mind was on something else.

Auntie Zanne reached over and poked Pogue. "You going to ask the question or what?"

"Someone gave you the liquid that was spilled on Eugenia Elder?" Pogue asked without skipping a beat. It was a good question. One that Auntie and I had suspected, not one that Pogue considered relevant. In his eyes, Carly was guilty no matter what.

"Yes, I just said that," she said, using her hands as she explained. "He said he wanted me to pose as a server at the Grandview Motor Lodge Motel in Yellowpine. And he wanted to...well...it was a joke." She held her hands as she explained. "At least that's what he told me. A practical joke."

"If you don't mind, Pogue," I said, "I'd like to ask her a question."

He held out his hand, evidently figuring he wasn't going to get anywhere with the two of us here anyway.

"You said that you were sick the last few days," I said to Carly.

"Yeah," she shook her head dismissively. "Just the flu I guess."

"Chills, coughing, dizziness?" I asked.

She nodded. "And a slight fever, tightness in my chest."

"General weakness."

"The flu," she said, in a conclusory manner.

"Or hydrofluoric acid poisoning," I said.

"What?" she said, alarm written in her face. "Am I going to die, too?"

"No," I said. "I don't think so. Did you go to the doctor?"

"No," she said. "I thought it was the flu. And I don't have the money for doctor visits for everyday occurrences."

"Maybe you should let her get checked out," I said to Pogue.

"I'm still conducting an interview," he said. "Or at least trying to conduct one."

"Well ask some questions." Auntie Zanne waved a hand at him. "We're waiting." Then she looked at Carly, and before giving Pogue an opportunity to ask anything, she said. "I'm sorry you were sick. It probably was from you sniffing that stuff," she said. "You shouldn't ever put your nose in anything, didn't anyone ever teach you that?"

"Uh—" Carly started to speak.

"But I want to get back to this man," Auntie interrupted.

"What man?" Carly asked. Fear was written in her eyes. She had placed her hand over her chest, her face was contorted. She wasn't processing anything Auntie was saying.

"The man that gave you the stuff you poured on Eugenia," Auntie said.

Carly swallowed, then put her hand up to her throat as if it hurt. "What about him?" she said.

"What did he look like?"

"I don't know," she said, her voice shaky. "Short, balding. Dressed in suit and a hat."

Auntie popped up out of her seat. "Did he tell you his name?"

"Yes," she said. "But I don't remember it now. I mean, I could probably think about it." Her eyes darted around. "He said he wanted to play a trick on his wife. He said she'd just played one on him."

"His wife!" Auntie said and smacked Pogue on his back. "It was Orville."

"We don't know that," Pogue said.

"You may not know it..." Auntie said lifting an eyebrow.

"How did you meet this man?" Pogue finally got a question in.

"He was outside of the employment agency when I came out."

"What employment agency?" Pogue asked.

"Manpower," she said. "Over on Main Street."

"The one next to First National Bank?" I asked, to Pogue's chagrin. He gave me a look he usually reserved for my auntie.

"Yes," she said. "I had gone to the bank to cash my check then I stopped there to see about picking up a job for the weekend."

"And you didn't find one?" Pogue asked.

"Obviously," Auntie muttered.

Pogue ignored her and when Carly saw he wasn't saying anything else, she answered. "No. I didn't get a job, but when I came out, he was just standing there like he was waiting for me. I thought it was fate."

"What did he say?" Pogue pulled a yellow legal pad toward him and picked up a pen.

"I told you, he said that he could get me the job at the Grandview. Not as an actual server, just posing as one. Said he'd pay me a thousand dollars for twenty minutes of work."

"Didn't that seem too good to be true?" Pogue asked.

"Was it real money?" Auntie Zanne cut in.

"What?" Carly said and looked at Auntie. "Real money?" She shook her head. "I don't understand."

"Did he pay you with real money or was it counterfeit?" Auntie Zanne said.

I knew what she was thinking. In all of this time we'd only had come up with one male suspect.

Orville Elder. The counterfeiter.

"Let's get back to what happened," Pogue said, redirecting from Auntie's line of questioning. "Now," he looked down at his notepad and back up at Carly. "This man paid you to pour something on Eugenia Elder?"

"You're going backwards," Auntie mumbled.

"His wife," Carly answered. "He paid me to pour it on *his wife*. He didn't tell me her name, only what she'd have on. A canary yellow pantsuit and a hat the same color."

"And you poured it on her?"

"You already asked that question," Auntie Zanne said. "Move on."

Pogue didn't even glance Auntie's way. "Did he say why?" he asked.

"Asked and answered," Auntie Zanne said.

"See, Babet, this is exactly why I can't have you help me on any of this," Pogue said. I could tell he was trying to control his temper.

"What?" Auntie Zanne asked, as if she genuinely didn't know what she'd done.

"Romaine," Pogue said.

I shook my head. "C'mon, Auntie, maybe we should go."

"Why? Is he getting ready to go and arrest Orville?"

"No, I'm not," Pogue answered for me. "I have to corroborate her story."

"All you have to do is go and arrest Orville," Auntie said.

"I can't arrest him based on this information."

"You're going to arrest this girl with nothing," Auntie flung a finger toward Carly. "Now that it's obvious that Orville is the one responsible, you want to 'corroborate' information."

"Arrest me!" Carly hopped up out of her seat. She was visibly shaking all over. "For what?"

"Murder!" Auntie said, screeching. "You, but not Orville. How crazy is that!"

"I didn't murder anyone," Carly said. "Oh my God." She turned around and then stopped looking at me. "I think I'm going to be sick." She held onto her stomach and bent forward.

"You'd better get her a bag," Auntie said to Pogue.

"Babet, this is all because of you."

"What is because of me?"

"Are you really arresting me?" Carly said. "I have to be home to see about my kids. I have my father to take care of. He's old. He doesn't have anyone but me."

"Oh dear Lord," Auntie said. "Now look at what you've done!"

"I don't think I can let you go," Pogue said to Carly, switching from talking to Auntie.

"But I didn't do anything."

"That's what I've been trying to tell him," Auntie said. "And even with knowing the real killer he's still wants to lock you up."

"You admitted to pouring a liquid on Eugenia Elder," Pogue

was trying to speak over Carly's wailing and Auntie's jabbering. "That liquid killed her."

"I didn't know," Carly said. "Please," she pleaded, tears starting to roll down her cheeks.

"She didn't know," Auntie said, she went and stood by Carly.

Pogue looked defeated and deflated.

"The First National Bank has surveillance cameras," I said. I had thought about them earlier when I noticed the ones at Nola Landry's house.

"So?" Auntie asked, wrapping her arms around Carly.

"So, maybe Pogue can corroborate Carly's story. If the camera picked up what happened."

"Then you can let me go?" Carly asked. "Because it really happened. Just like I said. It should be there."

Pogue blew out a breath. "Do you think they'd have it?" Pogue directed his question at me.

"I don't see why not. If their cameras work. They probably can queue it up for you right now."

"I could see it now?" he asked.

"I'm sure you could," I said. "Usually tapes are erased and recorded over, but this quickly...I wouldn't think so.

"Then can I go?" Carly asked. "After you see the tape?"

"You're going to have to stay here," Pogue said, not saying the words, but I knew he meant he was arresting her.

"You go with him to see the video," Auntie Zanne said moving closer to Carly. "I'll stay with her."

"Don't you want to see who's in the video?" I asked.

"I already know who it is," Auntie Zanne said. "It's Orville."

Chapter Thirty-Nine

"That's not Orville."

Auntie stood up straight as she made her declaration. Like me, Pogue and the bank manager, we'd all bent forward to get a close up of the exchange between the man who claimed to be playing a practical joke on his wife and Carly Neely as caught on the bank's surveillance camera.

I had to admit it. Auntie was right. That wasn't Orville. He didn't walk the same. He wasn't as spiffy as the man I'd met on two different occasions. And he definitely wasn't driving the right car. Nothing shiny about it or the man.

"You're going to have to figure out who that is," Auntie said to Pogue. "But we have to go." She pointed a finger to herself then to me.

"Go where?" I said.

"Did you forget?" She turned and looked at me. "I have to vote for Avoyelles as the Lesser Mambo and now," she looked at Pogue and stomped a foot, "I have to go and see about Carly Neely's family. Feed them, make sure they do their homework, tend to their sick granddaddy. You talked me into coming here with you, and it's put me way behind."

"She didn't say her father was sick," I said. "She said he was old."

"Same difference," she said. "Still means I have to tend to him."

I had insisted that Auntie come with us to view the footage of

Carly and the man who hired her, but it wasn't with the intention of making her late for any of her activities. It was because I was afraid of what she'd do if we left her at the sheriff's office.

Pogue had locked up Carly. Put her behind bars. All the while Auntie protesting, loudly, to the cruelty of it all. I wasn't so sure that Auntie wouldn't have unlocked the cell after we left and turned Carly loose.

"Doesn't matter if she said he was sick or not," Auntie said. "I can't leave them to fend for themselves 'cause your cousin locked up their only breadwinner and caregiver."

"She killed a woman," Pogue said.

"She didn't mean to do it," Auntie Zanne said. "Didn't even know she was doing it. And if you were any kind of sheriff, you'd find out who that man is." She flung a finger toward the monitor.

"I plan on doing that." Pogue said. "But it's not that easy. All I got is a video of him." Pogue pointed to the computer screen.

"You got a license plate," Auntie said and tapped the image of the car on the screen. "Run it!" She grabbed my hand and pulled me out of the door.

Auntie was furious by the time we left the bank. She blamed Pogue for locking Carly up based on ludicrous laws and me for letting him. If she couldn't stop him, how was I going to do it?

And he was right. Being charged with murder could take as little as a defendant being a substantial factor in the death. That she was.

But after watching Auntie, and knowing her as well as I did, I wasn't sure anything Pogue charged Carly Neely with was going to stick. Auntie, I knew, had already decided to find her a lawyer.

The first place we stopped was at the Brookshire Brothers grocery store. I trotted behind her as she went in, not saying a word to me, she grabbed a cart and filled it up with food. The she walked up and down the pharmacy aisles. I didn't know what she was looking for, if it was medicine for Carly's father, she'd have a hard time picking any out, because Carly had never said her father was sick.

Finally, she decided on a box each of Tylenol, Advil, and Excedrin. She bought children's and adult cough syrup and some Band-Aids.

"You want me to pay for that?" I asked feeling bad.

"Carly doesn't need your help now," she said. "She needed you an hour ago."

That made me feel worse.

"C'mon," she said. "I'm going to be late for the vote if we don't hurry." She wheeled the cart out to the car. I opened the truck and started putting the bags in. "I sure do hope one of them kids is old enough to cook." She looked at me, then went and sat in the car.

Silence. Again. All the way to Carly's house. Auntie had made Pogue give her the address.

Carly Neely lived in a quaint little bungalow. It was neat and had flowers growing in the yard.

There was a little boy, probably no older than five, sitting on the front steps.

"Hi little fellow," Auntie said. We'd both gone up the walkway. She'd made me leave the groceries until we made our introductions.

"I can't talk to strangers when my mother's not home," he said.

"You shouldn't ever talk to strangers," she said. She looked up at the house. "Where's your grandfather?"

"How do you know my grandfather's here?" he asked.

"I know a lot of things," she said. "Can you get him for me?"

"Sure," he said and took off up the stairs and into the house.

An older man came out. Not the low sickly one that Auntie had concocted him to be. He was nice looking. He had dark skin and his low cut hair and lined moustache were gray.

"How are you ladies today?" he asked. "Can I help you with something?"

"Yes," Auntie said. She looked down at her watch. "I can't stay, but I'll be back."

"You're here now," he said. "Didn't you come for something?"

"I did," Auntie said and looked at me. I know it was hurting her to have to share the news. "I came to tell you that your daughter, Carly, got arrested and she won't be coming home today."

"Arrested?" He shook his head. "You must have the wrong house. The wrong Carly. My daughter wouldn't do anything to get arrested for."

"We bought you food for today," Auntie continued, she directed me to go to the car and get the food. "And enough for tomorrow. I'm going to get her a lawyer. A good one."

"What did they say she did?" he asked. Just then the young boy popped his head out of the door. "Go on back in the house." The grandfather palmed his head and turned the little boy's head around.

Auntie walked up to the bottom of the steps, hesitating before she ventured up. "I'm going to help," I heard her say as I brought the first bags to the porch.

"How much stuff you got in that car?" the man asked. "You want some help?"

"No," Auntie said, turning to look at me as I made my way back down the walkway to get more bags. "She's fine."

I didn't know what they said while I was gathering up bags, but as I turned to go back, they seemed friendlier. Auntie had moved in closer to him and had a smile much politer than the ones she reserved for her funeral home clients.

"My apologies," she said. "I didn't introduce myself." She stepped up on the porch and stuck out a hand. "I'm Babet Derbinay." She smiled. "I own the Ball Funeral Home and Crematorium in Roble."

"I know that place well," he said. "Fine establishment."

"Thank you," she said.

"I'm Rawley Morishita," he said and shook her hand.

Auntie stared at him for a moment, then looked back at me.

"You said Morishita?" she asked, letting go of his hand.

"Nice to meet you," I said. Auntie's anger with me made her forget her manners. "I'm Romaine Wilder."

"You have kinfolk down in Beaumont?" Auntie asked.

"Right outside of there," he said. "In Bevil Oaks." He said it at the same time as Auntie. His face brightened. "Oh you know the place?"

"I've heard about it," she said.

"Yeah, well I don't know too much of that branch of the family if you're aiming to ask me about them. We all got scattered and I ain't been too good on keeping up with them."

That seemed to make Auntie nervous. I wasn't surprised she knew of him, she knew everybody and if Bevil Oaks was close to Beaumont where she grew up, I didn't think it would be long before she helped him "unscatter" his family. Especially with her wanting to help Carly.

We got to the Grandview just in time, but according to Auntie we were late.

She'd been irritated ever since we left Carly Neely's house. I knew she wished she could have stayed—washed, cleaned and cooked for them—but she had to make her meeting.

I guessed that the Distinguished Ladies' Society of Voodoo Herbalists couldn't manage without a Lesser Mambo being elected.

Rayanne had given Auntie the banquet room again. But it wasn't as fancy. The table had plain white linen and there was a buffet set up along one wall. There were no servers on this go-round.

Auntie's dais table was up front. And as full as the room was, it appeared that everyone had stayed in town the extra days to get another Lesser Mambo voted in.

I glanced to the table that Miss Eugenia had occupied. It was there, but seemingly stood as a tribute. There was no tablecloth on it and no one sitting around it.

To the right, I saw the previous occupants of that table. I hadn't known it then, but it was Auntie's crew—her girls. She'd told me that they all sat together at every Boule. Today they were together again.

Mark and Leonard Wilson. Delphine Griffith. Nola Landry. Avoyelles Kalty.

Then it hit me.

I knew who had killed Eugenia Elder.

I couldn't pull out my phone quick enough. I had to get Pogue there before the vote and before everyone left town to go back home.

Chapter Forty

"Auntie!" I screeched. I ran up to her table just as she was trying to lift her headdress. I had stop her. Pogue was on his way. I'd told him to put on his sirens and drive like he was on the Autobahn.

"Help me with this," she said. "I can't get it off."

I blew the feathers away from my face and sputtered out a spit feeling like some of them had gotten into my mouth.

"Auntie," I said, "You can't vote yet."

"Why?" she asked. "We have to vote." She looked at me. "What's wrong with you?"

I hadn't realized what I was feeling was showing on my face. I tried to straighten it out.

"Because," I said and swallowed hard. I turned and looked out at the crowd of women all waiting patiently for their Most High Mambo to call for the vote. I lowered my voice. "I know who killed Miss Eugenia."

"You know—"

I didn't let her finish. I put my hand over her mouth. "Shhh!" I said. "You can't say anything. Pogue is on his way."

"Is the murderer here?" she asked in what I guessed she called a whisper.

"Yes," I said, making my eyes big, letting her know that should be obvious.

"Oh my," she said. "Who is it?"

"I'll tell you when Pogue gets here."

"You'll tell me now," she said, locking her hand around my

wrist and giving it a yank.

"I can't," I said.

"Why?"

"Because for one thing, you'll give it away."

"What's the other thing," she said as if she agreed with that.

"The other thing is that you need to keep everyone occupied and not let them get restless. We don't want anyone leaving or getting suspicious."

"Tell you what," she said and sidled up next to me. "You tell me what you know, and I'll tell you what I know."

"You know who the murderer is?" I asked surprised. She was not one to keep anything in, keeping secrets was not in her wheelhouse.

"No," she said. "That's what I want you to tell me. I'm saying I have something to trade for it."

"What?"

"You go first," she said.

"So you can trick me?" I asked.

"Okay," she huffed. "I do remember the name of the family your father found out he and Julep were part of."

"Auntie! You know? Why didn't you ever tell me?"

"I just remembered when Julep brought it up." She frowned at me. "I can't remember everything that's happened. I'm old. I've lived a long time. A lot of stuff has gone on in my life you know."

"Who is the family?" I asked.

"No. That's not how this trading of information works." She wiggled her finger back and forth at me. "I give a little. You give a little."

This time I huffed, then I whispered it in her ear.

"No!" she said. "I don't believe it!"

I nodded. "It's true. But you can't say a word until Pogue gets here."

She took the same finger she had just wiggled at me and used it to cross her heart. "Not one word," she said. "You have my word."

Auntie Zanne bumped me over with her hip and walked over

to the microphone. "Change of order," she said. "We're eating first. Then we vote."

Nary a complaint came from the crowd. They did whatever the Most High ordered.

This was the third time I had to wait for Pogue to come and pick up a murder suspect after I had figured it out. But this time he had a lot farther to come. It was a good thing that Auntie had decided to hire a caterer. The best way to keep people from becoming restless was to feed them.

"So you've done it again," Pogue said when he arrived. I had been waiting for him at the door. "You've figured out who the murderer was?"

"Yes, she has," Auntie said coming out to where we stood. She must've been standing behind me somewhere lurking in the shadows waiting for Pogue to pull up. I didn't know if Pogue had taken my suggestion and turned on his sirens on the way over, but when he arrived, the only noise I could hear was the clatter of silverware and glasses made by the Distinguished Ladies in the banquet room just off the hallway where I stood.

"I may as well just give you my badge," he said.

"No, that's not necessary," I said. "You're doing a good job. A great job." I gave his arm a squeeze. "We make a good team."

"So, let's go get her," he said. He looked around the lobby and pointed down the hall. "Is there somewhere we can talk to her?"

"Can't you do it in there?" Auntie pointed to the banquet room.

"No," he said. "Isn't there like a hundred people in there?" He looked toward the room.

"Fine," Auntie said. "I'll bring her out here." She marched back into the banquet room.

"Is there any way we can do this without *her*?" Pogue asked, head nodding toward Auntie.

"Sure," I said. "You can just tell *her* that she can't stay."

"Okay, so I guess she stays."

"I guess so," I said.

"Here she is," Auntie said walking back out.

It was Avoyelles Kalty she'd brought out. She was the murderer.

"Hi," Avoyelles said, a bright smile on her face. "Babet said you wanted to talk to me."

"It's more like he wants to arrest you," Auntie Zanne said.

"Auntie," I warned. "Don't start."

"Arrest me for what?" Avoyelles said, a look of fear on her face. "I had enough of jail the other night. I'll never go back there."

"Well you shouldn't have killed Eugenia," Auntie said. "And you wouldn't have to."

I hadn't told her what I based my determination on, still Auntie Zanne was taking the bull by the horns.

"I did not!" she said. "Kill Eugenia?" Her eyes went to each one of us. "How could you say that? She was one of my oldest friends."

"Tell her Romaine," Auntie said.

"There were only two people who knew Miss Eugenia thought Orville would kill her."

"You," Auntie pointed at Avoyelles and nodded, "and Delphine."

"So?" Pogue said. He had a look on his face saying he hoped we had more than that on her.

"No one else would have had someone play Orville," I said to him. "No one but a person who wanted people to think Eugenia's husband did it."

"Speaking of her husband or rather 'husband poser,'" Pogue said. "I ran those plates. They belonged to a Harvey Branston. He's an actor. And a con man. Got a record a mile long."

"Unlike Carly," Auntie added.

Pogue ignored her. "Mr. Branston lives up in Angelina County, so I contacted the sheriff up there. I was getting ready to head up that way when you called."

"Angelina County?" Auntie Zanne questioned and turned to stare at Avoyelles.

"I don't know what that has to do with anything. Or with me," Avoyelles said.

"She's from Angelina County, Pogue." Auntie jerked her thumb toward Avoyelles.

Pogue raised an eyebrow.

"You hired an actor to play Orville?" I said. I would have chuckled if it hadn't been serious business. "Nola and Auntie Zanne told me how you wrote those screenplays for them. With all your twists." I looked at Auntie. "This *was* one for Hollywood. Avoyelles hiring an Orville look-alike to carry out her murder plot." I turned my eyes on our suspect. "Then you had him hire that girl—"

"That poor girl," Auntie interjected.

"Yes," I nodded. "Carly. And had her pour hydrofluoric acid on Eugenia."

"I did no such thing," Avoyelles said. "How could I have done all of that?"

"That *is* convoluted," Pogue said. "Too convoluted for me. And probably for a prosecutor or a jury." He shook his head. "I hope there's more."

"It sounds just like one of her screenplays," Auntie said. "The ones she used to write. Convoluted. But I wouldn't worry about judge or jury, most people can pick things up quicker than you." Auntie rolled her eyes at Pogue then looked at me, squinting her eyes. "And convoluted is exactly the reason I should have seen through this whole thing."

"How could I have done that?" Avoyelles asked, sidetracking Auntie's revelation. "I was inside the banquet hall with Eugenia the whole time. I never talked to that girl. The server, whoever she was. I didn't even sit at the same table with Eugenia. There was no way I could have told her who Eugenia was. Or to pour something on her."

"You knew what she was going to wear to the Boule," I said. "You'd found out days before when you went to visit her then you told that to the actor you hired."

"And he told Carly," Auntie said. She looked at Pogue,

indicating again that he had wronged Carly. "And he never told Carly what it was for or what it would do."

"So you knew that was going to be the last time you saw her," Auntie said. "Coming into my kitchen with your fake tears."

"You pretended to be helping her, just so you could kill her?" It was Delphine. She came out of the banquet room shouting. A trail of women behind her

There was a collective gasp at her words. The women's eyes all went to Avoyelles

"Oh wow," Pogue said. He trotted around us and toward the hall where the women stood. "Please! Go back inside." He glanced back at us. "We need to close the door." He grabbed one of the double doors and tried to shut it. "Babet," he turned to her. "Can you help me?"

That's when Avoyelles headed out of the front door.

"She's getting away!" Delphine shrieked. And went after her.

Everyone followed behind her. I had to move out of the way of the stampede.

None of them could run very fast, but they could cause enough chaos that things could easily go the wrong way.

Pogue unable to keep anyone inside, came running out, somehow got ahead of the crowd and caught Avoyelles.

When Auntie and I got to them, he was trying to put handcuffs on Avoyelles. She was flushed and out of breath, twisting from side-to-side, she wouldn't hold still. I didn't understand how she thought she could get away.

"I didn't do anything. I didn't do anything!" she kept saying. "Let me go!"

"Did she do it...I can't believe this...He's got the wrong person," came the murmurings from the crowd.

"This is not good!" Pogue said. "We can't have all these people here."

"You all have to go back inside," Auntie said, being surprisingly cooperative. "Let the law handle this. We're not helping."

The women looked from Auntie to Avoyelles to Pogue and without a word, they turned and went back inside.

"You couldn't have done that earlier?" Pogue asked.

"Sorry," Auntie said then looked at me.

"Are you sure about this, Romie?" He looked at Avoyelles, he seemed unsure if I'd gotten this one right. "How did you figure this out?"

"Because Auntie told me that all of her girls sit at the same table. Every Boule. Every year. Together."

"We do," Auntie said, "except of course when I sit at the dais."

"Avoyelles wasn't at the table the night of the murder," I said.

Auntie squinted her eyes like she was trying to remember.

"And Rayanne," I went on, "said that people wanted to change their seats at the last minute. I bet if you checked with her, it wasn't 'people,' it was just one person who wanted to change their seat. Avoyelles Kalty. She wanted to sit somewhere else because she didn't want to be close to that acid when it was overturned."

"I sat where they put me," Avoyelles said defiantly.

"You always sit with the same people Avoyelles," Auntie Zanne said. "Always have."

"That wouldn't be my fault."

"And she was sick," I said.

"Sick?" Auntie said.

"From the acid," I said. "Just like Carly."

"Like Carly?" Auntie said and gave Avoyelles the evil eye.

"Yes," I said. "Remember the day of the autopsy when we went by the Elder's house to get Miss Eugenia's clothes?"

"Uh-huh," Auntie said not taking her eye off Avoyelles.

"Avoyelles was sitting in the car sweating. Out of breath."

"Those are symptoms of hydrofluoric acid poisoning," Auntie said, using her medical jargon.

"And," I continued, "Rayanne said someone spotted a black van that was seen when the dumpster was rambled through." I looked at Avoyelles. "I bet it wasn't black. I'm thinking it was midnight blue."

"Pete's van?" Auntie asked.

"That's who you were smelling when I went in the house to take a shower earlier, Auntie," I said. "He had been in the dumpster trying to get the evidence out for you." I pointed to Avoyelles.

"Because she was there when you told me you thought evidence might be in that dumpster," Auntie Zanne said, nodding her head, putting the clues together. "Is that why you've been so helpful?" She shook a finger at Avoyelles. "Trying to find out what we knew so you could cover up what you did?"

"I don't know what you mean," Avoyelles said.

"Ah!" Auntie sucked in a breath. "Hydrofluoric acid is used in rust removal for cars."

"Auntie, how did you know that?" I asked. I remembered reading about it, but I'd never told her that.

"Don't think you're the only who can do research." Auntie Zanne said. "I wanted to know about that stuff that killed my friend, too."

"She was your friend," Avoyelles said, a little venom creeping into her words. "And that was why she was your pick as the Lesser Mambo."

"What?" Auntie said. I saw a spark of anger. "I didn't pick her."

"You picked all of them, when you should have picked me."

"Don't. You. Tell. Me. You. Killed. Eugenia. Because. Of That!" Auntie enunciated each word and punctuated it with a finger in Avoyelles face. "Because you wanted to be the Lessor Mambo!"

"It should have been me," Avoyelles said.

"Let's stop this," Pogue said.

"Evidently," Auntie Zanne said, "we've just come up on the motive."

"Perhaps," Pogue said. "But I want to get back to the deed."

"The deed?" Auntie asked.

"How she did it," he said. "I need Romaine to tell me how she did it."

"I can tell you that," Auntie Zanne said. "It was her nephew. Pete." She turned to Avoyelles. "That's why your car looks new, isn't it? He did that. His little car detailing business?" Auntie got in Avoyelles' face, but she turned her head so not to look at Auntie. "Did you get hydrofluoric acid from him? Then used it to kill Eugenia?"

"That might be easy to find out, Pogue," I said.

"We'd compare the traces we found in the tumbler to..." his words trailing off.

"To whatever Pete has on that mobile car wash van of his that has hydrofluoric acid in it." I finished the sentence for him.

"And when it's not," Avoyelles said, "you won't have a thing on me."

"I think that I have enough, Miss Kalty, to arrest you," Pogue said. "And if Romie says you did it, I believe her." He smiled at me and winked.

Epilogue

Pogue failed to read Carly Neely her Miranda rights. He questioned her while in police custody about incriminating events, which triggered the recital of the warning. That technicality could get a case thrown out of court.

Sure, it wasn't Pogue's fault. He probably would have read them to her if Auntie Zanne hadn't kept interrupting him. But just the same, it never happened.

Of course, Auntie found and paid a lawyer for Carly who knew just how to exploit that technicality and she walked.

Free as a bird.

Then we had to stop Auntie from trying to adopt Carly, her father and all three of her children.

Morishita was an uncommon name for a black person in Texas. Or for that matter, anywhere. But that was the family my father believed we belonged to.

23andMe will tell me for sure.

Auntie had known all about my father finding out he and Aunt Julep were adopted, but she never mentioned it to me. Not even after I told her I knew. My Aunt Julep never really cared about it. She was happy with the family she had.

As to the murder—Avoyelles Kalty wanted to be the Lessor Mambo. She wanted it so much that she was willing to kill for it. But for some reason, after the conversation I had with Auntie Zanne in the car, or maybe because of all the mysticism that surrounds Auntie and her world of potions and spells, she had decided to "suggest" to the Society that Delphine Griffith be given the position instead of Avoyelles, even before she knew of Avoyelles deadly deeds. Delphine was voted in unanimously.

Avoyelles and her car-detailing nephew were both arrested. Come to find out, he'd been the one who suggested the hydrofluoric acid as the murder weapon. He had seen the same *MythBuster* show that Logan found on the internet and wanted to put it to the test for himself. It had been a bad choice. They'd both gotten more than they bargained for using it. It had made everyone that handled it sick. Avoyelles with what she thought were hot flashes. Carly's flu-like symptoms.

And then there was me. Middle-aged, highly educated, but still thoroughly confused me.

Coming back home turned out to be a good thing. It made me realize the things I was really running from were things that were all in my mind. I didn't need a big-time job or big-town life to make me happy. Happiness came from within. And it seemed, my happiness place was found within Roble, right where my family lived.

So, I made it official. I took all of my stuff out of storage in Chicago and converted the upstairs—all six bedrooms—to my suite. Auntie never came up there anyway.

I gave Alex the boot.

I was officially put in charge of the tri-county medical examiner's office. But folks around Roble called me for stomachaches, broken arms and stitches, too.

And I found that most days I could be seen wearing a smile.

And Rhett? Well, unlike the dead downstairs, he roamed the upstairs' halls quite often.

ABBY L. VANDIVER

Wall Street Journal Bestselling Author, Abby L. Vandiver, loves a good mystery. Born and raised in Cleveland, it's even a mystery to her why she has yet to move to a warmer place. Abby loves to travel and curl up with a good book or movie. A former lawyer and college professor, she has a bachelor's degree in Economics, a master's in Public Administration, and a Juris Doctor. Writer-in-Residence at her local library, Abby spends all of her time writing and enjoying her grandchildren.

**The Romaine Wilder Mystery Series
by Abby L. Vandiver**

SECRETS, LIES, & CRAWFISH PIES (#1)
LOVE, HOPES, & MARRIAGE TROPES (#2)
POTIONS, TELLS, & DEADLY SPELLS (#3)

Henery Press Mystery Books

And finally, before you go...
Here are a few other mysteries
you might enjoy:

BONES TO PICK
Linda Lovely

A Brie Hooker Mystery (#1)

Living on a farm with four hundred goats and a cantankerous carnivore isn't among vegan chef Brie Hooker's list of lifetime ambitions. But she can't walk away from her Aunt Eva, who needs help operating her dairy.

Once she calls her aunt's goat farm home, grisly discoveries offer ample inducements for Brie to employ her entire vocabulary of cheese-and-meat curses. The troubles begin when the farm's pot-bellied pig unearths the skull of Eva's missing husband. The sheriff, kin to the deceased, sets out to pin the murder on Eva. He doesn't reckon on Brie's resolve to prove her aunt's innocence. Death threats, ruinous pedicures, psychic shenanigans, and biker bar fisticuffs won't stop Brie from unmasking the killer, even when romantic befuddlement throws her a curve.

Available at booksellers nationwide and online

Visit www.henerypress.com for details

MURDER AT THE PALACE
Margaret Dumas

A Movie Palace Mystery (#1)

Welcome to the Palace movie theater! Now Showing: Philandering husbands, ghostly sidekicks, and a murder or two.

When Nora Paige's movie-star husband leaves her for his latest co-star, she flees Hollywood to take refuge in San Francisco at the Palace, a historic movie theater that shows the classic films she loves. There she finds a band of misfit film buffs who care about movies (almost) as much as she does.

She also finds some shady financial dealings and the body of a murdered stranger. Oh, and then there's Trixie, the lively ghost of a 1930's usherette who appears only to Nora and has a lot to catch up on. With the help of her new ghostly friend, can Nora catch the killer before there's another murder at the Palace?

Available at booksellers nationwide and online

Visit www.henerypress.com for details

STAGING IS MURDER

Grace Topping

A Laura Bishop Mystery (#1)

Laura Bishop just nabbed her first decorating commission—staging a 19th-century mansion that hasn't been updated for decades. But when a body falls from a laundry chute and lands at Laura's feet, replacing flowered wallpaper becomes the least of her duties.

To clear her assistant of the murder and save her fledgling business, Laura's determined to find the killer. Turns out it's not as easy as renovating a manor home, especially with two handsome men complicating her mission: the police detective on the case and the real estate agent trying to save the manse from foreclosure.

Worse still, the meddling of a horoscope-guided friend, a determined grandmother, and the local funeral director could get them all killed before Laura props the first pillow.

Available at booksellers nationwide and online

Visit www.henerypress.com for details

THE SEMESTER OF OUR DISCONTENT
Cynthia Kuhn

A Lila Maclean Academic Mystery (#1)

English professor Lila Maclean is thrilled about her new job at prestigious Stonedale University, until she finds one of her colleagues dead. She soon learns that everyone, from the chancellor to the detective working the case, believes Lila—or someone she is protecting—may be responsible for the horrific event, so she assigns herself the task of identifying the killer.

Putting her scholarly skills to the test, Lila gathers evidence, but her search is complicated by an unexpected nemesis, a suspicious investigator, and an ominous secret society. Rather than earning an "A" for effort, she receives a threat featuring the mysterious emblem and must act quickly to avoid failing her assignment...and becoming the next victim.

Available at booksellers nationwide and online

Visit www.henerypress.com for details

Made in the USA
Columbia, SC
01 December 2020